Through Better & Worse

A Montana Love Story

by D. L. Keur writing as C. J. "Country" James

Through Better & Worse, a Montana Love Story—Jake's bound to have her, but she won't see him for dust.

by D. L. Keur writing as E. J. Ruek

Old Hickory Lane—Raised white, half Native, a young veterinarian struggles to survive rural North Idaho amid poverty and prejudice.

To Inherit a Murderer, Book 1: The Ward—She suspects he's a murderer…and he is.

Space Fiction by Aeros
A Gathering of Rebels, prequel to Seeming Eidolon, a three book series

From Reading Country

comes

A *Country* James Novel (#1)

Through Better & Worse

A Montana Love Story

by D. L. Keur writing as C. J. "Country" James

Getting a boot in the door almost costs Jake Jarvis his life. It *does* cost him two good hats, some jail time, and a whole bunch of money.

But Dree won't see him for dust.

Guns, roses, and the flow of raw whiskey take them both *Through Better & Worse*.

Published by D. L. Keur, Sandpoint, ID 83864

C. J. "Country" James is a pen name of D. L. Keur.
www.CountryJames.com

For orders, inquiries, & correspondence please address:
D. L. Keur &/or F. W. Lineberry
P. O. Box 2419
Sandpoint, ID 83864

First Edition
Kindle Select Exclusive Release eBook ASIN: B013AUZTCK
Print: ISBN-13: 978-0692491751
Print: ISBN-10: 0692491759

Publisher D. L. Keur
Design by D. L. Keur, www.DLKeur.com
Cover art by D. L. Keur, www.zentao.com

Printed in the United States of America

DEDICATION

To the good folk,
the men and the women,
the ranchers, cowhands, and truckers
who keep this land, the life,
and the culture alive—
its traditions & values.

And to Laddie, my awesome Aussie.

ACKNOWLEDGEMENTS

Huge thanks to my hard-working editor Marva Dasef. Thanks also to all my beta readers and advisors, all of whom must remain unnamed due to new online rules of engagement.

Extra special thanks to a Colorado Sci-Fi/Fant author who, "Awww, yeahh…know[s] those guys." He's Nathan Lowell of nathanlowell.org, and he's super extra special.

Another person I can name is Patrick Tormey who bravely waded through this novel—not his cuppa—and helped with the land trust question.

Last, but never least, to my husband, Forrest W. Lineberry, the ultimate good guy—brave, kind, and, most of all, honorable to the highest degree. He exemplifies what's right and best.

AUTHOR'S PREFACE

This novel is purposely written in the vernacular of the area, both narrative and dialogue, so there are many odd contractions and odder grammatical (mis)constructs. You can also expect idiomatic phrases, along with dialog and narrative syntax that are not the norm. This is intentional. It's true to the culture; it's true to its people.

Through Better & Worse

A Montana Love Story

by C. J. "Country" James

1

Close Call

DREE DOWNSHIFTED FROM FIFTH to
fourth, but it wasn't enough. Her old pickup
just didn't have enough guts to pull the hills,
anymore. She dropped to third, losing momentum,
and the truck's speed stabilized at thirty-five. She put
on her hazard lights.

Behind her, several cars came up fast and, after
following for a minute, honked, then started weaving in
and out across the centerline, hoping for an
opportunity to pass. One of the Aussie dogs sitting on
the seat next to her whined and glanced back—Chip,
the more timid one. Laddie, the more aggressive but
smartest, got down on the floor. There wasn't a
turnout where she could pull over to let the cars by on
the narrow, two-lane highway, its asphalt crumbling at
the edges of a non-existent shoulder, remnant snow
berms still melting off over the steep drop-off into the
ditch.

A semi passed going the other way, its wash
buffeting the trailer enough that it swayed. White-
knuckled, Dree fought the urge to over correct. She
got to the crest and her pickup gained ground. She got

it up to forty-five, then kept it there as she started the descent.

The cars behind her were piling up. Traffic in the opposite lane was steady, though, and there was still no turnout. There wouldn't be until the bottom of the hill. Behind her, the line of cars was getting longer. And angrier, she guessed. Only half-a-mile to go to the bottom.

The oncoming traffic finally cleared.

In the rearview, she saw a fancy, black, RAM crew cab dive out to pass from three cars back. Ahead, a car came around a curve. Then two more, another semi behind them. "Omigod. You *fool!*"

The pickup roared past her.

Panicked, she jerked the wheel just in time to avoid collision with the black truck's rear-end as its driver dove for safety, nearly clipping her. Her passenger side tires caught the pavement edge and gravel. The trailer yawed, pulling her pickup's back-end sideways. She hit the trailer brakes and prayed, her grip ferocious, painful, on the wheel. They were going over. Chip joined Laddie on the floor.

But they didn't go over. They steadied. She swore. Fought hysteria, red-darkness rising. And she cursed the black pickup for his stupidity. "*Jack*ass!"

Finally making the bottom, she saw a pullout and, signaling, pulled in…braked. A state patrol car, lights flashing, made her jump as he screamed by. She put her forehead on the steering wheel and closed her eyes, waiting for the sound of traffic to thin out. She was shaking all over. *Dree, you're being a wimp*, she told herself, and, forcing herself to, she opened her eyes and tried to take a deep breath.

...Only the deep breath wouldn't happen. It was as if her chest was locked. So she took shallow ones, instead, and opened the door to let in the cool, late March air...sat a moment longer before getting out to check Cougar.

"You okay?" Her voice was breathy, barely a whispered croak.

The silver-dun mule swiveled an ear. As usual, he was unconcerned.

She leaned her forehead against the trailer. The ringing in her ears was deafening, muting the sounds around her. A spot in her left field of vision was pulsing. Again, she shut her eyes and attempted to will herself calm. But the pulsing seemed to intensify. So did the ringing. Then the roaring started, and she fought vertigo. She fought a sound of screaming and the flood of red-darkness still rising, intensifying, under her lids, chaotic voices shouting at her, pulling at her from somewhere outside herself, from underneath a crushing weight that smothered her. She was drowning in red. The vision of Adrian's bloody, faceless body rose.

Desperate, she opened her eyes, the sunlight bright enough to shock the vision gone. The red-darkness receded, and, finally able to draw a deep breath, she bent over, hands on her knees.

The gravel crunched as a car pulled behind the trailer. She heard a couple of doors shut. ...Footsteps. "You okay, honey?" came a woman's voice.

Unable to speak, yet. Dree nodded.

A hand touched her shoulder. "You need us to call someone?"

Grabbing hold of herself, Dree straightened. A woman with a weathered face, bright red hair, and startling blue eyes looked at her, worry lines crinkling her forehead and around her eyes. "I just almost got clipped by someone," Dree said. "I'm just trying to catch my nerve back."

"You're sure you're going to be okay? We can drive you somewhere, and Denny here will drive your rig for you."

Dree shook her head as a man's voice agreed. She looked over at him—elderly, with kind, brown eyes— like her grandfather's. "I'll be fine. I just need to gather my wits."

It was true. She felt better, either because her body and brain had finally calmed down or because of the strangers' kindness. Maybe both.

"Okay. If you're sure. We're not in any hurry, if you're just trying to spare us the trouble."

"No." Dree smiled, albeit a shaky attempt. "I'll be fine. I'm almost to the four-lane. From there, it's easy."

"Okay."

They followed her, though, keeping their car behind her, their hazard lights on. Dree blessed them. Wished she'd gotten their names.

Two miles down the road, the state patrol car and a sheriff's rig had the black pickup pulled over. She couldn't help herself, her anger at the driver boiling up. "Good!" The logo on the side of the black pickup burned its way into her memory—a figure eight in a circle with a line running through it, all copper-colored, the top part of it filled in with gold-on-white, the bottom part silver-on-black. *I'll remember you, and I won't forgive and forget.*

QUICK-THINKING AND SLOW TALKING got him down from reckless driving to improper passing. "There was nobody coming when I committed to pass, Officer, and it *was* a passing zone. Too late to do anything but punch it when the traffic showed up. Just bad luck and worse timing."

"You were in a hurry."

"Actually, not. Just thought I had plenty of time to get around 'em. I misjudged."

Ultimately, he got off, Marty and his Uncle Rick hazing him once the cops let him go with only a warning. Waiting till traffic cleared, Jake pulled out nice and easy. Behind him, the cops pulled out, too, going the same way. He kept it just at the speed limit.

Twenty miles up the road, the state patrol still shadowing him a couple cars back, Jake came over the rise to find the pesky, old, white beater chugging along in front of him, again, a car with its hazard lights on following close behind. And there was nothing at all he could do to get around them—no alternative roads, and the whole stretch all a no-passing zone. He had to suck black, stinking exhaust from the beater all the way to the four-lane.

Finally free to get by when they got to the north-south highway, he resisted the urge to blow by the nuisance. The state cop still had him in sight.

Easing by at the speed limit gave him plenty of time to see that what he'd thought was some old codger driving was actually a plain-faced girl with wavy, shoulder-length, mousy hair. There was a mule in the trailer.

He touched the button that rolled down the passenger window. "Get some horsepower," he yelled.

Next to him, Marty rolled his eyes and put the window back up using the controls on his side. "Ya just blew my eardrum out, Jake," the man said. "Ain't no way she heard ya."

Jake grinned. "Yeah. But *I* feel better."

"You're just damned lucky you talked 'em out of that ticket. Franklin would have your truck and your ass, both, if you hadn't."

"Not if he didn't find out."

"He'd find out," his Uncle Rick said from the back seat.

Jake glanced around, still grinning. "Not if you don't tell him."

The man raised his hands. "Not me. Nope. Franklin tends to flog the messenger along with the guilty party."

"That's the truth," Marty agreed. "Claims if you know it, then you should'a done somethin' to stop it."

Jake knew that only too well—*way* too well.

C. J. "Country" James

2

The Test

FORTY-FIVE MINUTES LATE, Dree called Larry Carter once she had cell phone signal. As usual, he sounded nice about it, even though she knew he was ticked. "We'll see you when you get here."

Ten minutes later, she pulled into the truck stop and, rolling the windows down for the dogs, got out and walked over to the café. There, a brand new rig with the Montana Department of Agriculture shield on it was parked near the door. So Larry Carter had finally gotten the new truck he'd been bucking for since he'd taken over the fieldwork from retiring Glen DeWalt. Dree preferred the old one. Heck, she preferred Glen, for all that, Larry was her first cousin from her mother's side of the family. This truck looked smaller and less like a truck with its shorter bed and fancy sculpted lines. Dree went inside and, spotting Larry's sandy head and Mike's shaggier brown one, went over, but didn't sit down. "Sorry. Had trouble pulling the hills and almost got clipped."

Larry, looking more white-faced than ever without his summer tan, waved a hand at her. "We had a chance to eat some lunch. Are you hungry?"

She was, but shook her head. She'd already put them far enough behind schedule.

"All right. Let's hit the road," he said, getting up. "I called Jarvis. He knows we're coming in an hour behind when I said we'd be there. Seems his dad has made us a little test. Wouldn't say what." He grinned. "Forewarned is forearmed."

Dree stifled a groan. She hated her cousin's false positives.

◆

TWO MEN CAME OUT to meet them as they drove in. The eldest looked like a caricature out of a movie with his jean-clad, bandy legs, his beat-up hat, and his plaid, flannel shirt. The other was a weathered fifty-something, broad-shouldered and tall, with hard, gold-brown eyes, a scar running down the right side of his face. He wore a very expensive Stetson, a clean shirt and jeans, and nice boots. And he immediately intimidated her. He was set-jawed with a dead-reckoning eye and no-nonsense look to him. *Not good for Larry*, was Dree's thought.

The old man motioned at her, pointing backwards. She put it in gear and backed up.

Larry Carter introduced her after she parked her pickup and trailer where the elderly man indicated, his stained, battered hat pushed back on his head as he made her maneuver back and forth until he was finally satisfied. "That should do you," he said, opening the passenger-side door to poke his head in. His sharp blue eyes sparkled with good-natured humor.

The dogs wagged—unusual—and popped up to beg strokes. The man obliged, rubbing fingers over happy ears, and got licks on the mouth and face from both Chip and Laddie for his troubles. He laughed and wiped his mouth with his sleeve, a broad grin showing slightly yellowed, slightly crooked teeth. But he still seemed to have them all, despite his age.

Joining the men over at Larry's pickup, Dree was very aware of the gold-eyed man named Franklin Jarvis eyeing her, then her beat-up old pickup, as his father, who *was* actually called 'Old Man', quizzed Larry, his blue eyes now suspicious. "We've always been cut men, here. Never had no problems. What's so durned good about *your* way?"

Dree glanced toward Mike who seemed to be trying to hide under his hat, head down, eyes on his boots. She wished she was wearing *her* hat. Instead, she looked around, noticed the barns, corrals, a round pen, and a big, double-story bunk house, men standing around talking, some of them smoking, on the long building's porch, as Larry listed off the usual pros: less stressful on the animal, little chance of contamination or problems with flies, and approved by the animal welfare people. Of *course*, he didn't mention the potential hazards. Sliding a quick glance toward the man named Franklin, Dree thought that stupid.

Franklin Jarvis's eyes caught her looking and locked on. She quivered a smile and dropped her head away just as, at the mention of animal welfare groups, the old man spit a stream of tobacco juice out of his mouth, the brown slurry splatting real near the toe of Larry's boot. Then he muttered something Dree couldn't quite hear and nodded to Franklin Jarvis.

She heard Franklin reference the weather and something about last year, and the old man grunted, then looked back to Larry. "Well, I'll see you do it, first." Then, he set off down the main tractor lane, his stride quick and ground-covering despite his bowed legs, crooked back, and a slight limp.

Larry glanced her way. "Mike, Dree, get your tools," he said, grabbing a bag from the bed of his pickup.

Getting her castrators—all three of them—Dree toyed with the idea of the spray bottle, decided no, then grabbed it anyway. Her dogs wagged, begging out, but she told them to stay.

"Let 'em come," said a voice behind her.

She turned to see the younger of the two Jarvises standing, waiting for her. She looked back at the dogs. "Mount out. He says it's okay."

♦

FRANKLIN JARVIS SAID NOTHING as he walked along beside her, keeping well to the side of the trailing dogs. From the corner of her eye, she caught him raise a hand toward the bunkhouse and point a jabbing finger. The men disappeared.

Inside a log barn that had to be one of the original homestead's, a dozen young bull calves stood bunched up in a corner. Their mothers lowed from the other side of a divider made of use-burnished rails stacked between pairs of stout, log uprights.

Franklin Jarvis, moving slow, climbed over the rails and maneuvered the first calf into a wooden squeeze.

"Where are the calf tables I had shipped to you?" Larry asked.

Mike Guthrie ducked his head, fingers toying with one of the straps on his chaps like it needed adjustment.

"They necessary?"—Franklin.

Dree watched Larry's face freeze into a tight-lipped, very forced smile. "No," he said, his ears getting red with what Dree knew was his formidable temper. "Just makes things easier."

She stepped back.

Larry Carter came from a family of sheep ranchers. While college probably had prepared him for handling everything from Alpacas to maybe even Zorses, the academic environment wasn't ever like the real deal. Dree felt a measure of pity for Larry, but, at the same time, thought he needed to wake-up to real life. Working on a wiggling, standing calf that struggled and bawled for its momma, that momma calling back as she worried the fence, was a lot different than lazily working at one's leisure on a pinned animal laid on its side in a crush. Larry managed, but not before getting a load of sloppy, runny manure on his person in the process when the bull calf defecated practically right in his face. Thankfully, nobody laughed. They wouldn't, though. The bull calf was stressed pretty bad by the time Larry got the job done.

"It takes that *long*?" Franklin demanded, his face, stern before, now downright stormy.

"Not usually," Larry replied, his voice tight and face whiter. "Dree, you want to handle the next one while I clean myself up?"

Why pick on me? she thought, but didn't—wouldn't—argue. Not with Larry. She did eye the squeeze, then chanced a glance to the old man. "Could I borrow a rope and piggin' string?"

Her request seemed to catch him by surprise.

"...Or, if they're not handy, I can run to my truck."

He pointed toward the front of the barn.

Following his point, she spied what she'd asked for and went to grab them.

"What do you need?" Franklin Jarvis asked her, stepping up to the fence as she trotted back.

"I want to do him on the ground."

"Okay." He took the rope and leather strap from her and lazily threw a loop over one of the calves, sitting back on the rope as it fought. He let it get itself cornered, the other calves breaking to the other side of the small pen. Then, he walked himself up the rope and easily flipped the calf on its side with a quick trick with the bight, kneeling on the neck and folding the upper foreleg with one hand while he grabbed a hind leg with the other to anchor it between the two front ones. Dree climbed over the fence as he wrapped a quick-release hitch, decided to use the numbing spray, then did her job, nodding to the man to let the calf loose as she finished the last pinch.

"Your turn," Old Man Jarvis said to Mike. "Let's see you beat that. She was under two minutes flat from the time she went over the fence." He actually held an antique stopwatch. It was worn, burnished gold.

Dree saw Larry glare her way and felt her face flush. Moving away, she chose a piece of fence farthest from them to get herself out of the pen. Daylight beckoned, but she resisted the urge to turn tail and run.

◆

EACH OF THEM HAD TO DO FOUR, and Dree was careful not to work any quicker than Larry or Mike after that. She went ahead and used her spray, simply because it kept the calf quieter. At the end of it, once the calves were returned to their mothers, Larry was back to his easy self, even when Old Man Jarvis announced, "Well, we'll see how they fare come mornin'."

Dree went back to her truck to stow her tools, happy to be clear of the 'man politics' Larry seemed to thrive on. She put the dogs in the cab and told them, "Stay."

"What's that spray?" Franklin Jarvis asked her, startling her as he came up to stand just out of reaching distance.

"A quick-acting topical anesthetic I get from my vet. It helps when I have to do the job alone—" She stopped, knowing she shouldn't have said it, and, again, felt herself go red in the face.

His face stayed deadpan. "That happen often?"

She shook her head. "No."

He watched her and his eyes changed, got browner. …Didn't say a word. Then, after what was for Dree a long, tense moment, he turned on his heel and walked off.

3

Trapped

ROUNDING THE LAST BEND in the long drive up to the ranch house brought Jake up short. His tires ground gravel, the ass of his truck slewing sideways as he hit the brakes too hard. It was the *nuisance*—the ugly, white, beater truck and trailer—parked right where, normally, visitors pulled in. Only the rig was parked sideways, across the breadth of the parking area. "What the hell!" What was *she* doing here? How did she know where he lived? How had she found him? His license plate? Did she have that good a connection with state law enforcement? He bet her dad or her uncle or someone was a cop. That would make sense of it.

'She' walked around the front of her truck, just then—a walking four-by-four. Well, not really. Not yet. She was just wearing a shirt five sizes too big, the shirttails left to flap in the wind. The signs were all there, though, that she would be, and in a very short time—squat, stocky, square-bodied.

Putting the truck in low, he stared as he rolled by her—couldn't help himself. She stared back, her face emotionless. She had slate gray eyes. Jake's heart thundered. Franklin didn't brook "jackassery", as he called it, and there was nothing Jake could or would say to defend himself—not to Franklin. He'd been reckless—in a hurry—and he had almost run her off the road...almost killed her, maybe all of them, truth be known. That he hadn't was pure Jarvis luck. That luck had just run out. "Shit." He might as well write off both his spring and summer, right now.

He hit the garage door opener, slipped into his bay, and shut down, listening to the big diesel's whirring and ticking sounds as it tied up all its various processes, the engine cooling down. He laid his head back, unbuckled his seatbelt, then just sat for a long minute more, dreading what he knew was coming next—facing Franklin's wrath.

D REE STOOD FROZEN, deer-in-the-headlights, watching the black pickup roll up the drive, then slow as it passed her, the driver turning his face to keep his dark brown eyes locked on hers. It was the pickup that had almost clipped her, almost caused her to wreck, the symbol, despite its colors, not a logo like she'd originally thought, but a brand—the Jarvis ranch brand. She knew that when he pulled in front of the very last bay of the ranch house's huge six-car garage, the door sliding up automatically for him to disappear inside. That told her all she needed to know. The man in the black truck was blood relative to the Jarvises. He lived here. Anger climbed her back, her scalp prickling.

Larry came down the steps from the front door of the house. "Dree?" he called. "Franklin says we'll be staying here in the main house…to put your mule in the barn. The second stall on the left is open."

He walked over to his pickup, got a suitcase from the back seat, then disappeared back inside before she could summon a diplomatic way to tell him that she wasn't staying, that she was backing out.

She went after him, trotting across the turn-around and up the short flight of broad stone steps, the sandpaper treads catching at the soles of her boots. Franklin Jarvis opened the door, stopped, then stepped out and stood when she stopped, too, hesitating to step on the ranch brand inlaid into a huge piece of stone. It was inlaid with what looked like real gold or bronze, silver, and copper. "Thought I'd help you get your mule settled," he said, walking across it. He paused, held his arm out to the side, inviting her to turn around.

Dree didn't know how to say no, how to politely extract herself from a situation she found uncomfortable. She knew how to make others comfortable—that was easy. What she couldn't come to make herself do was blurt out the prickly truth, so she always wound up stuck doing things she didn't want. Obediently, she turned to head back to her truck.

Her boot caught on the friction tape.

A hand caught her arm, steadying her. "Easy. I hate those treads. It's why I always use the sides of these stairs."

"Thanks," she mumbled. "I'll take the advice. I can be pretty clumsy sometimes."

"The back ones don't have this. It's all for insurance, anyway, but they only stipulated doing these and the one's out the great room onto the deck, not the ones out the kitchen."

Dree realized he was giving her permission to use the back way. It was a nice thing, and it made her feel better.

"How's your mule around horses?"

Dree shot him a glance. "Fine. Why?"

"I don't think we've had a mule on the place in years. Not sure how some of the younger horses will act. Just so you know."

Dree smiled…couldn't help herself. "I'm used to that. So is Cougar. He's a real gentleman and just backs off. Doesn't retaliate."

"Good. Then, let's get him and you settled-in before dinner. We've got a few minutes, yet."

CLEANING THE SOLES OF HIS BOOTS, Jake jerked his hat off and hung it on its peg in the hall by the back door. Then, bracing himself, he went through to the kitchen where Marguerite and Olivia were filling the serving dishes.

He gave Marguerite a peck on the cheek, then grinned at Olivia who flashed a smile at him. Only fifteen, the girl was already a looker. "Smells great, Marguerite!"

"You're going to make dinner late," she scolded.

"Be right out. Just let me go get washed up."

After sloshing water on his face and scrubbing his hands with a brush to get the day's ground-in dirt out of the creases, he headed into the dining room, prepared to face Franklin's worst. *Why'd it have to be a girl?* With a guy, Franklin would have gone easier. Straightening his shoulders, he stepped through to the dining room.

"Here he is," Franklin said. "This is my grandson Jake...Jarvis, of course. Jake, that's Ms. Dree Blake from the Blake Ranch down south, Larry Carter, who you met last month over at the sale yards, and Mike Guthrie, a hand from over by Billings."

Franklin nodded to him. "You're late, young man. And what held you up?"

Here it comes. Jake braced himself. Despite Franklin's friendly tone, he wasn't fooled. The 'and' was the give-away. "Marty and Uncle Rick needed a ride. Their rig broke down. I think the injectors are clogged, again."

Heads shook, and Jake steeled himself for what was coming next, pulled out his chair, and sat down in his usual place next to Franklin.

"You mean 'carburetor'," Old Man Jarvis said.

Jake dodged a glance at his great-granddad. "I don't think they even make carburetors for cars anymore, sir."

"EPA probably banned them," Franklin said with a chuckle. "Now, it's a couple of computers feeding the fuel straight into the engine."

Eyes on his granddad, Jake wondered what the hell was up. It wasn't like Franklin to hold off, even in company. Still, best play along. "At least it's still under warranty."

"Yeah." Franklin turned a half-raised brow to him. "And the last time it broke down, it took 'em two months to get it back." He pointedly looked around the table. "We used to call those 'lemons'. Now it's just called 'regular maintenance'.

Laughter from around the table, Franklin grinning at his own quip. He was in a good mood. Confused, but grateful, Jake relaxed a bit.

Marguerite and Olivia rolled in the serving carts, and Franklin got up, introduced them, then helped them distribute the serving bowls and platters along the table length, like always. Jake rose, too, lending a hand like he always did—like he was expected to.

The women sat down, and Franklin said a quick prayer, Marguerite crossing herself on the "Amen."

"Dig in," Franklin told them, snatching up the basket of rolls with a smirk just as Jake reached for them. He took one, then passed them out of reach over to Old Man who passed them on down the other side of the table. Jake's eyes followed them, then stopped when they came to the frumpy girl. So, maybe she *hadn't* said anything.

"Jake." Franklin held the bowl of mashed potatoes out to him.

He grabbed it, took a gob, then passed them on. Caught the pass of the vegetable bowl, then the meat platter, got himself a portion of each, then passed those on as the gravy boat came around. "Can I get a roll?"

Wil Strakes tossed him one from down-table. He caught it one-handed on the fly, Franklin frowning at Wil, then Jake. Jake grinned. So did Lane, Tom, Shawn, and the guy named Mike Guthrie.

24

Down near the end of the table, Jake saw the girl hide a smile under her napkin. So she had a sense of humor. And knew how to use a napkin, to boot. Maybe not quite so country trash as he'd thought. And she *hadn't* said anything. She couldn't have for Franklin to be in this good a mood. Jake couldn't believe his good fortune. He might have a spring and summer left, after all.

4

The Rodrigo Connection

"SO, MS. BLAKE, how'd you get wrangled into helping Larry Carter, here, with this edja-ma-cation project?" Franklin asked.

Jake saw the girl look up, her eyes startled. She put the bowl of veggies down, pulled her hands into her lap, her eyes on them as she shook her head. "I'm not sure."

"I brought her along because Glen DeWalt said she's been doing it right since she was a little kid," Larry Carter broke in. "He told me there's never been a busted penis or a steer gone staggy in the Blake herd, and that's *her* doing."

The table went quiet. Jean-clad legs rustled.

Getting over his discomfort, Jake said what he knew the older men wouldn't, "Busted penis?"

"Catching the urethra."

"Any other potential hazards with this…er, method?"

The man stared at him, the eyes going what Jake could only think of as 'snotty'. Then they went squinty as he grinned. "Well, not getting a good crush, or even missing completely."

Old Man Jarvis frowned. "And this is better than *cutting*?" He turned to Franklin.

Franklin fended him off with a wave. "Ms. Blake, who taught you, and how old were you when you started doing this job?"

A quiet answer Jake couldn't hear.

Franklin cupped his ear. "Say again?"

"Since I was ten. R–Rodrigo taught me." Jake heard a catch in her voice as she said it. He saw her face go oddly white just before she dropped it away.

"Rodrigo?" Franklin asked.

She raised her head, but didn't look toward them...just stared straight ahead. "H–He was our foreman for a little while."

"You mean Rodrigo Sanchez?" Old Man Jarvis boomed out.

Jake saw the girl hesitate, then nod. Around the table, Wil Strakes, Lane, Tom, Shawn, and, even Franklin nodded and went suddenly easy.

"Okay. That's good enough for me, then," his great-grandfather said, chuckling.

Who the hell, Jake wondered, *was Rodrigo Sanchez*? He whispered the question to Franklin.

Franklin grinned, then nodded toward his old man. "Ask *him*."

"Great-grandpa? Who's Rodrigo Sanchez?"

The old man started to chuckle, again. "Jes' the best durn vaquero north of the Rio Grandé. You know old Cassie?"

You bet Jake knew Cassie. Who on the ranch didn't? Hell, who in Montana reining horses didn't? "Yeah. That's my Coal's dam."

"Rodrigo Sanchez trained her."

Jake frowned. "What does that have to do with castrating calves?"

"Nothin', son."

"A vaquero," Marguerite put in, "is an all-round stock man, Jake. Rodrigo was well respected by all, what you call a top hand. If Rodrigo taught Ms. Blake, you can know she is...what word?" She shrugged. "Good."

"What happened to this Rodrigo? Why isn't he here?" It wasn't like the Jarvises to let a good hand loose.

Down table, Wil looked elsewhere. The Jarvis seniors, both Franklin and his great-granddad, were steadily focused on their forks. Finally, Marguerite said, "He died," then crossed herself, ducked her head, and went back to eating.

Jake took the hint and went to working butter into his roll.

UNCOMFORTABLE, Dree couldn't wait till dinner was over. When finally the men around her sat back and the two Latino women rose and started clearing the dishes, Dree got up and helped, ignoring the 'you don't have to do that's from the two older Jarvis men.

Trailing into the kitchen, she tried to help there, too, but the two ladies—well, lady and girl—shooed her gone.

Finding the back door midway down a connecting hallway, she stepped out on the stoop and tried to get her eyes to quit burning, kept blinking until the evening cool finally eased the sting. Larry came out, the glazed-in screen door banging. "Sorry about bringing up Rodrigo. I didn't know there was a connection between him and the Jarvises."

Dree forced a smile. "It's fine. It was a long time ago. I'm going to take my walk."

"One question."

Dree stopped and waited.

"I know Rodrigo died on your dad's ranch, but what from? Do you know what happened?"

Dree shrugged. "I was a little kid."

"You were what, eleven, right? Don't you remember?"

Dree looked out across the lit back lawn, her eyes lifting to take in the snowy mountain bathed in moonlight beyond. "I remember explosions and lots of screaming and blood."

◆

GETTING THE DOGS from the truck, Dree struck out down the drive, the cold evening air clearing the cramped feeling from her chest, the burn from her aching eyes. Clear and fine, the air was brisk and invigorating after the big meal and uncomfortable table talk. Dree walked longer than she'd planned, well into darkness, her eyes drawn to the sparkling ceiling of stars appearing overhead. The stars always made her feel the magic, again. They were the only thing, except maybe the morning rays of first sun. And the full moon.

By the time she turned around, she realized that she must have walked a couple of miles. A glance to her all but useless cell phone showed her it was nearly 9:30.

Reluctantly, she turned around, the dogs bounding ahead of her to lead the way. They stopped suddenly, Chip alert and upright, Laddie crouching down, his hackles rising. She stopped dead as she heard them both growl. The sound of gravel crunching reached her ears, then the swish and snap of brush as something in the darkness ahead moved off the road into the woods.

She waited, heart pounding, breath pent. When she heard nothing more, when the dogs finally relaxed, she moved to the other side of the road and went on. Probably a coyote or maybe a moose, she reasoned. When she finally climbed the final curve to see the lights of the Jarvis ranch house, she relaxed. Her leg with its artificial knee joint was beginning to ache. She'd walked too far.

Getting a flashlight, she put the dogs in the trailer, fed them, then waited till they were done. Letting them back out to relieve themselves, she followed, picking up their dung and sealing it in a plastic bag. She filled their water bowl from a tap in the barn, then re-trailered them and stuck the bag of poo into a garbage sack in the truck box.

The back door was locked when she tried it, so she walked back around to the front, took the sides of the stairway, then scooted around the inlaid brand purposely illuminated by an overhead spotlight and the lights of twin electric sconces that were mounted to each side of the massive front door. Trying the latch, she found it was open and stepped inside, again avoiding the brand inlaid here in the entry floor.

Franklin Jarvis was sitting in a chair in the great room. He looked up when she walked in. "Thought I was going to have to send out a posse," he said.

Staring at the huge stone hearth, the Jarvis brand also inlaid into its face, again, in colored metals, it took her a moment to answer. The thing must have cost a fortune! The whole house had cost a fortune. "Ah, I walked longer than I meant to. Sorry. The stars carried me off."

"Yeah. They'll do that. Where are your dogs?"

"I've got them locked in the trailer."

He got up. "Bring 'em in. I want them with you in your room. Too many men in the house."

She smiled and thanked him. "I'll be fine. The guest room I'm in has a lock."

"Bring 'em in."

It was a brook-no-argument command. "Okay."

Doing as bid, Dree went out and got the two Aussies, the dogs skulking in behind her as Franklin held the door. "Breakfast is at 5:30," he told her as he led the way up to her room. Unlike Larry and Mike, she'd been given a room upstairs, and the room had its own bathroom. It even had a shower and a Jacuzzi tub—a big one—man-sized. "Lock the door," he commanded.

When she had, she heard him whistle. Something thumped down on the floor outside, and her dogs growled. She waited until she heard the clip of Franklin Jarvis's boots fade on the hardwood floor, then, unlocking the door, she peeked out.

A big, black, lion-headed, bearish-looking dog, maybe some sort of Great Pyrenees crossed with Rottweiler, but huge, stopped chewing on what looked like a cow's thighbone. He watched her—silent, still. A chill ran down her neck. She closed the door and twisted the dead bolt home.

5

Jarvis Bulls

U P AT FOUR, DREE UNLOCKED the door and peeked out, her dogs pushing their noses into the crack. Laddie shoved, his nose pulling long sniffs, then tried to leverage it wider with both nose and paw. "Quit."

The guard animal was gone. So was the bone. She heard faint sounds of activity. Slipping out, her dogs at her knee, she cautiously made her way along the open balcony to the nearest arm of the double staircase leading down to the great room. Then, when there was no sign of man or the big beast, she went through to the kitchen.

The two Latino women were there, one grinding meat, the other mixing up a batter. "Anything I can help with?" she asked.

The woman called Marguerite smiled, but shook her head. The girl just flashed her a curious look.

Dree let herself out the back door and, after the dogs did their duty and she cleaned up after them, she stuffed some hay into Cougar's feedbag from the bale in the truck bed and got some grain from the box. Then, grabbing her grooming kit, she headed to the barn to feed him.

His 'brinny', the mule equivalent of a whinny, greeted her, and, when she opened the stall door, Cougar stuck his nose on her shoulder and nuzzled his greeting. She kissed him on the soft spot between and below his nostrils, and he stuck his lip up and grunted. She poured his ration into the corner feeder, then clipped up the hay bag and began brushing him down. Somebody had already topped off his water bucket, the water fresh and ice cold.

Done, she cleaned his feet, picked up his droppings from the stall, then, just to be ready, went and got his saddle. It was twenty-to-five when she was done saddling him, and she still had plenty of time for her morning walk. This time, though, instead of just heading off, she set her cell phone alarm.

Whistling the dogs, she set off down the drive, again. When she came to what looked like a tractor lane angling off through the trees, snow berms still melting to either side, she followed it.

A half mile later, the trees ended, and the snow berms were down to small humps as she found herself walking along a formidable stock fence, its heavy duty, tube-steel panels attached to six-inch steel posts buried in concrete.

Dree recognized a bull fence when she saw one, albeit a very expensive bull fence, not like her Dad's post and rail one. An inner strand of heavy gauge electric wire running through enamel, rather than plastic, insulators audibly pulsing with life reinforced her conviction. The pasture seemed empty, though, but, since the fence was on, there had to be bulls in there somewhere. She wished she could see them.

Another half-mile or so down the tractor lane that edged fields and loafing sheds, her cell phone alarm went off. She turned around and headed back. This time when she got to the bull fence, a small herd of purebred Herefords stood watching her, or, more accurately, watching her dogs.

Stopping, she stood looking at them—big, solid, well-developed yearling bulls. They carried the ranch brand on their left hips and what looked like freshly laid freeze brands on their necks. These were prime stock. No wonder the Jarvis Ranch had such a good reputation.

Back at the ranch house, she went to her room and washed up, then headed to the dining room. She was the first one there, and, uncomfortable, she went to the kitchen.

Again, she tried to pitch in, but the women were having none of it. So she sat down on a stool and simply watched, feeling out-of-place and out-of-sorts. If she wasn't 'doing', she wasn't comfortable.

Jake Jarvis walked in, got himself a mug of coffee, turned, stopped, then just stared at her. Then, when she just stared back, he stalked out. Marguerite pushed by with a serving cart, the girl, Olivia, behind her with another. "Breakfast?" Marguerite said, giving a lift to her chin.

Dree got up and, when the women just stood waiting, went through to the dining room ahead of them. The men were already seated, talking.

"There you are," Larry said. He got up and held a chair out for her.

"Thanks."

◆

THERE WEREN'T ANY PANCAKES, and there wasn't any ground sausage for breakfast. That must have been for the hired hands, Dree realized. It was biscuits, gravy, bacon, hash browns, and omelets— enough to feed almost twice the number at the table. Thankfully, there was also orange juice, a gallon pitcher of it set near her. She poured herself a glass, offered Larry some, then, when he declined, put the pitcher back on the table.

The biscuits came her way, and she passed them on. Same with the gravy. When the bacon came by, she took two slices.

The omelets were huge and filled with peppers, onions, mushrooms, and bits of ham. She sliced a section off of one with her knife and the serving fork, then sent the plate of them on.

"You're not eating much," Larry commented when she passed on the hash browns without taking any. "Still trying to diet?"

Dree ignored his jibe. "You know I'm a two eggs, two bacon, and orange juice girl," she told him, looking at his laden plate. "I wouldn't be able to move if I ate all that."

"You want some toast or something?" Dree heard Franklin Jarvis say to someone.

Nobody answered.

Dree looked up to find him watching her. "Are you talking to me?"

"Yes."

"Ah, no. Thank you. This is...plenty."

"You're sure."

"Yes. I'm sure. Thank you."

The man eyed her, looked at her plate, then got up. "We've got a long day ahead of us."

"I'll be fine."

"At least have some hash browns."

He picked up the dish of fried onion and potato mixture and came around the table. "Here. Let me," he said, scraping a small pile onto her plate. He looked up the table. "Pass me the bacon," and, when somebody did, he dropped a couple more pieces on top of those already there, snagged the omelet plate and slid the rest of the one she'd cut a piece from onto her plate, too. "Eat up. We've got some four-hundred-plus calves to work through today. I don't want you passing out on us."

Beside her, Larry was smothering a grin and chuckles. Down the table, so was Jake Jarvis. Even Old Man Jarvis up at the head was grinning. Dree wished she could crawl under the table.

JAKE COULD BARELY STOP HIMSELF from busting out laughing. He'd suffered that treatment from Franklin a lot, and the look on Ms. Dree Blake's face said it all. *There goes her diet.* But he'd felt just that way when, from the time he was six on, he was faced with having to eat through what Franklin considered a meal. When he'd managed his way through the pile, Franklin keeping a dead eye on him while he did, he'd always felt like a foundering horse. He didn't envy her Franklin's attention. "You learn to eat big here," he said, trying to catch her eye, but she didn't react, just kept her head tucked.

She might not be a looker—too short, too stout, too plain-faced, and way too much mousy, blowsy hair, but he still felt sorry for her. He had a small warm spot for her, very grateful that she hadn't told Franklin about the incident on the highway. He'd have been stuck mending fences up on the northwest sections with no help for days, maybe weeks.

Getting a refill of coffee for himself from the pump pot, he quizzed Wil about assignments.

"Franklin, you, me, Lane, Shawn, and Tom are learning to castrate. Six men will vaccinate and run the irons. A couple or three, if we need, will handle the dehorning spoons. The rest will run the calves up the chutes and in and out of those calf tables."

Jake looked at Franklin for confirmation, and the man nodded. "I'm going to cut?"

"No. *We're* going to learn this newfangled crushing method."

"It's only new here on the Jarvis spread," Larry said with a laugh. Then he looked at Jake. "And it's not hard. Just tricky."

Jake blew breath. Castrating made him feel sick at his stomach, and Franklin knew that.

"You're going to run this ranch some day, Jake. You gotta be ready."

Jake flinched as, across the table, Wil buried his face in his coffee mug. There were hard feelings about Franklin's decision to pass the ranch onto him, and Wil was strong in his sentiments that Jake wasn't right for the job. In private, Jake was "Little Jerk" to Wil, even though Jake now stood a good six inches taller and five inches wider in the shoulder than the rangy ranch foreman and horse wrangler. To Wil, Jake fell from the wrong branch of the tree, a good-for-nothing bad apple, a cull, and Jake knew he'd probably never outlive the man's bad opinion of him, especially for what had happened with Lea, no matter how hard Jake tried to make it up to him…and her.

6

Jackassery

REE WAS TRYING TO FIGURE OUT how to get rid of all the food Franklin had piled on her plate. There was no way she could eat it, no matter how much he wanted her to. And he kept watching her.

She managed the hash browns. Luckily, he'd gone light. But the rest of the omelet and extra bacon were just too much. She should have kept the dogs with her, but hadn't. She'd locked them back in the trailer.

As the discussion centered itself near the head of the table, she surreptitiously scooted chunks of egg onto the paper napkin on her lap. Finally down to just the bacon, she waited till she was sure everybody was watching Franklin and Jake, then dropped those into the napkin, too, rolled it up, then wondered what next. The napkin paper was warm and getting soggy.

It was Old Man Jarvis who came to her rescue. His sharp blue eyes on hers, he tipped his head toward her, then, looking down at his feet, did something with his hand.

Moments later, from under the table, Dree felt a big, black-furred head and wet nose stick itself between her legs. Then, it just waited. Carefully, Dree unfolded the napkin, and the muzzle—a huge muzzle—opened, the teeth gargantuan, but delicate as they took first one, then another of the pieces of bacon, then the omelet, painstakingly selecting just one piece at a time.

It took forever, but, by the time Franklin stood up to tell them to "mount out," him glancing down toward her, then nodding when he saw her cleaned plate, the great hound had finished and, just as silently as he'd come, vanished.

Wadding up the napkin, she quickly helped clear dishes, dumping the soggy lump of paper into the plastic-lined pail Olivia was using for the paper trash. Then she fled to her room's bathroom to wash her hands and face.

Everybody was gone except Old Man Jarvis and the women in the kitchen by the time she came out, even though it had been just minutes. "Thank you," she said to the old man.

"Anytime. You best get to hoofin' it, girl."

Dree took his meaning and bolted for the door, glad she'd saddled Cougar before breakfast. Strapping on her chaps, she grabbed her saddlebags and hat from the trailer, the dogs bounding out. At the barn, Jake Jarvis stood in the alleyway next to a big, black Quarter Horse stud.

The animal was blocking her way. She waited, but the Jarvis boy ignored her. Finally, she just squeezed under the black's neck, her saddlebags dragging the cement, and got to Coug's stall.

Checking the girth, she threw the saddlebags on and buckled them home, then waited for Jake Jarvis to lead his horse out. But he didn't. He just kept standing there—leaning, actually—his back to her, blocking the stall door. "Could you move?"

He turned around, a smirk playing his mouth, dark brown eyes full of 'dare me'. "Why, su-uure." He moved, all right, but only to get on the other side of his horse to shift the black over so it completely blocked the opening.

"Is this payback?"

The young man looked over the saddle, grinned, then shook his head. "Nope."

"Would you please let us out."

"What's a little thing like you doing riding a great big, ugly, ornery mule?"

"None of your business. And he's not ugly. Or ornery. But *you* are."

"Whooo. A missy with a mouth."

"Please let us out."

He shrugged, then, untying his horse, mounted up right there in the aisle. But he didn't move. Instead he shifted his horse with a clatter of shod hooves until its barrel and hip were pinned up against the doorway.

Getting ticked, Dree looked at Cougar, looked back at the black's big body filling the stall door, then grabbed Cougar's water bucket and flung, the cold water hitting the stallion under the flank. The horse grunted and squealed, and, shod hooves clattering, swung away.

Dree had her foot in the stirrup, hissing to Cougar. The mule launched himself, ears pinned, toward the now cleared doorway, his momentum swinging her up just in time to miss getting smashed by the uprights. It was a dangerous thing to do, but Dree was mad.

She dug her heels in, and they were out the barn, driving hell bent for sunrise toward where she saw the men riding out ahead, her dogs running full out, trying to catch her.

Heads turned, the men frowning as she galloped toward them. She reined up as she neared and heard pounding hooves behind her. Again, heads swiveled, and, with a glance back, Dree saw Jake pull up, his stallion's ears pinned flat, the horse's tail wringing in temper. She maneuvered Cougar in between Mike and Larry's borrowed horses, and settled there, but Jake Jarvis moved in close by, riding just off to the side and behind.

"Where'd you disappear to?" Larry asked, frowning.

"I had to use the bathroom."

"Looked like more than that to me," he muttered, and Dree felt her face flush.

A LL HE'D WANTED TO DO WAS APOLOGIZE and thank her for not telling on him. Why he'd baited her, he didn't know, maybe to try to break the ice. He wasn't used to approaching women. They always initiated. And he'd thought she had a sense of humor. Obviously not, though. Sour bitch was more like it. And now Coal was pissed at him, too, the horse tossing his head, and popping his tail. The day was not starting out well.

Behind him, a horn honked twice. He sidepassed Coal, the riders ahead of him splitting to let the rig through. Before they closed ranks, he urged Coal through to catch up to Franklin and Wil.

"Who put the burr under your saddle?" Franklin observed. "Coal looks like he's ready to eat somebody. And why's he all wet?"

"I sprayed some dirt and manure off his sheath."

"You should have used warm water. You know he's touchy about his privates. Fran's told you again and again."

"Cuz he's too much in a hurry to wait for it," Wil snapped, putting his horse into a lope to catch up to the truck hauling Carter's calf tables and the extra panels to make run-in chutes.

"He's right, you know," Franklin said with a nod. "You gotta find more savvy and slow, Jake. Cattle or horses, neither one, like hurry-up. It's gonna be your undoing."

Stung, Jake touched just a finger to his hat and nodded. "Yes, sir."

"Don't 'yessir' me. Just *do* it."

7

Change Up

FIFTEEN MINUTES OF RIDING, and, suddenly, the men beside her pushed ahead, catching up with those in front. Then, with whoops and hollers, all of them took off at a mad gallop to disappear over the crest of the hill, Mike Guthrie right with them. Cougar bounced once in surprise, then, one ear swiveling back toward her, pulled at his bit. "Walk," she told him, and, heaving a rib-spreading sigh and a blow of snot in protest, he dropped his head and went back to long-walking, albeit a little faster.

She pulled up in surprise at the top of the hill and stared. There, scattered over what had to be a fenced quarter section was a gather of mother cows and their calves more than twice the size of her father's whole herd. "We're doing all these *today*?!" she asked Larry as he circled around to pull up beside her, his horse jigging and tossing its head as it fought the bit.

"That's the plan. And tomorrow and the three days after that, too, we'll do that many and more."

"How many mother cows do the Jarvises run?"

"Around sixteen-hundred, I think. Maybe eighteen, now. Nobody's really told me. I know they keep expanding."

"Wow."

Larry laughed. "There are a lot bigger herds than that in this state, Dree."

Dree knew that. She also knew about the huge herds throughout the western states all the way down to Texas. Still, though, considering the work she did daily at home with just over two-hundred cow-calf pairs, she couldn't even imagine trying to manage this many. "We're branding, vaccinating, tagging, and dehorning, too, right?"

"Well, *they* are. We're here to train."

She looked again at the size of the herd. Shook her head. "We're not going to be able to get through this bunch all in one day unless *we* do the castrating."

"Oh ye of little faith."

But Dree was proved right. It was clear from the start that the job wasn't going to run smooth unless they worked *with* the teams, rather than holding up the works trying to teach the men to use the emasculators.

And the calf tables—brand new—were sticking, their pretty paint jobs making them bind.

Franklin was the one who called a halt after the first hour. They'd gotten a whopping twenty-four calves done. "This is stressing the calves too much," he snapped. "It won't work. We're going back to the old way." With a sharp, piercing whistle that hurt Dree's ears, he raised his hand.

Dree stepped up. "Mr. Jarvis?"

He turned to her, but Dree sensed his anger. He didn't like it that his calves were stuck so long on the calf tables and suffering for it. "Let us do the castrating. We can do it on the ground without the tables. Your men will pick up on it as we go. That's how I learned—by watching. Then, when Rodrigo saw I was ready, he guided me through my first few, and it was easy from there."

Franklin Jarvis muttered something, then turned and walked away.

Dree shook her head, scolding herself. Men didn't like it when women got involved. She knew that. Her dad was bad that way—real bad. Men put up with you helping—silently—as long as you did the job well, but they didn't take kindly to being told anything.

She went back to her assigned team and got her gear.

She was halfway to where Cougar was grazing when an out-of-breath Larry ran up beside her. "Where you going, Dree? Get back to your team. Jarvis went for it. But we're stuck working in the corral. He's dead set against using the calf tables, so it's going to take me a bit of work to get him sold on those. The Jarvises are stubborn." He touched her back, then, just like he did at family picnics, and, just like she always did, she ducked away. A flash of hurt, then anger crossed his face. Just like usual. "Anyway, thanks. At least we can convince them about the castration. The calf tables will come after that."

Turning around, she watched Larry trot back to the huddle of men. She hated the calf tables, and she bet the Jarvises had had their fill of them, too, so she doubted Larry could convince them of anything. Maybe Glen would have, but not Larry, and Glen didn't like the new contraptions, either. Larry was full of himself, though. *And if this doesn't work out, you'll blame me or Mike, or both of us. Thanks.*

Bridling her thoughts, she headed back to the melee. Whatever the outcome, she'd do her part and take her pay.

HELPING TO BREAK DOWN THE CHUTES and move the calf-squeeze contraptions that had proved nothing but trouble, Jake quizzed Mike Guthrie about them. The slow-talking thirty-something mostly just shrugged. When Jake pressed, the man said, "We don't use 'em. I've never used 'em before now."

"Has *she?*" Jake asked, tipping his head toward where the Blake girl was trailing back from where Carter had caught up with her heading toward her mule.

"Don't know. Probably not."

"That makes no sense," Jake said. "Why bring along help that doesn't know the program?"

"What program?"

Frowning, Jake did a double take, then realized Mike wasn't party to the deal Carter had presented to Franklin—a package of three calf tables and a dozen emasculators tied to the field school for eighteen grand. He wondered if the Blake girl was, but, by the storms crossing her face as she approached, he guessed not. She looked ready to use her emasculators on anybody who got close. "What do you think she's mad about?"

Guthrie glanced over at the girl. "My guess would be she don't much like Carter putting us on the spot to take the heat. She's good crew, Dree is. I worked with her last year when Glen was still running the field schools." Then, "Miss that. Think this will be my last go-round with Carter taking over."

THINGS WENT A LOT SMOOTHER the second hour. Franklin had them widen the holding pen, then set up three stations, two men at each as wrestlers, the rest handling the branding, any dehorning required, and vaccinating. Larry, Mike and she would do all the castrating. Dree was surprised at only two wrestlers. Usually it was four. It worked, though. The men were used to this method, but, despite their skill and speed—and they were all top hands—Dree had little to no problem getting done by the time they were ready to let the calf up.

While the wrestlers held, one man dehorned the calves that required it, another vaccinated, tagged and recorded, while a third hit the calf with the branding iron. By that time, Dree working from the back, between the hind legs, had to be done…and the job had to be done right.

The calves were down less than two minutes, three max if the dehorning proved troublesome. Despite the speed they worked, Dree only got caught twice by the branding iron, and then only glancing sears.

Franklin Jarvis caught wind of it, though, and, ordering the man to go help with the roping, took over. She didn't get burned again with Franklin working the iron. Plus she learned something. He only left the iron on for three seconds, maybe. The calf barely seemed to notice. "Only have to have enough heat and burn to make the hair grow in crooked and the brand show up under the clippers nice and clear if we aren't sure if it's our brand or one like it," he said, when she commented. "Don't need to sear the hide deep like I see some do. Just a quick burn with a hot, black iron, nice and easy."

◆

THEY BROKE FOR LUNCH AT NOON, a truck coming in over the rise. It was Marguerite driving a fancy, modern chuck wagon. "It looks like one of those trucks you see that sells hot dogs in New York," Dree told Larry.

He laughed. "When were you in New York?"

"No. In the movies. You see them in the movies," she tried to explain.

"Yeah. The movies," he laughed. "Well, I don't think this is hot dogs."

At his scoff, she felt frustrated and stupid for saying anything. But he was right. When Marguerite opened the sides, it definitely wasn't hot dogs.

Dree's mouth started watering. The smell was delicious—charcoal barbequed something. She went to get in line.

It was pulled pork in barbeque sauce, baked beans, and potato salad, with pickles on the side. When she got to the top of the line, Franklin stepped up and, grabbing the edge of her plate, spooned up what he thought were the right portions. Dree tried to object, but he just growled at her. Then he followed her and sat down right next to her with his own plate.

"You're going to watch me eat?"

"Yep."

"You know I can't eat all this."

"I know you can, and I know you will."

"Mr. Jarvis—"

"Franklin."

"Franklin. Seriously. I never eat more than a half a sandwich for lunch."

"Well, consider this dinner, then."

"I had to give breakfast to your big dog."

"I saw you. But you ate the hash browns, and don't tell me that they didn't stand you well. You worked as hard as any of my men out there, and I saw your face when the chuck wagon rolled in. There was hungry written all over you."

"Your cook is—"

"Bull. You're hungry. I saw it. Now, eat."

♦

Mike and Larry came to join them on their hump of high ground upwind from the smell of cow, Larry sliding in too close next to her on the other side—way too close. She scooted back, and Franklin scooted back, too.

Mike got up and moved himself in next to her, Larry dodging them a hurt look. Then, his ears got red. He got up and left…went over to the chuck wagon and began talking to Marguerite.

Wil, Jake, and a couple of the other men came over, and, in a short time, the whole crew, except Larry, sat around. All of them just ate, though, never speaking.

Dree worked around the edge of her plate taking a bite of this, a bite of that, keeping quiet and to herself, her eyes on her plate. After awhile, things loosened up and the men started talking—low at first, then more and more naturally as they forgot about her. By the time she'd managed the potato salad, half of the beans, and about a quarter of the pork, they were bantering back and forth like normal.

Behind her, a nose nudged her back. Cougar blew a soft grunt.

"What's he want?" Franklin asked her.

"My pickle. He loves them."

"Nooo."

She picked it up from her plate and held it up. The mule brought his teeth down and bit it neatly in half, chewing.

Franklin laughed. "Well, I'll be."

She gave Cougar the rest, then shooed him off.

"How are you and your mule for roping?" Franklin asked.

Dree looked at him. "We do okay."

"We've separated the heifers out, and I want to work through them next so we can cut 'em loose to their mas. I thought you might like to trade up and have a little fun."

When she nodded, he got up, saying, "You'll be with me. But, first, young lady, you finish your plate."

Thank God for dogs. "Laddie? Chip?"

8

Galled

SURPRISED THE GIRL HAD BEEN asked in to rope, Jake watched Franklin herding Dree and grinned. His granddad didn't trust women around stock, afraid they'd either get hurt or, more the usual, get somebody else hurt. His granddad never much hired women as hands, not that some didn't apply. Two ton of one-hundred-twenty pound square bales tossed up onto a semi's flatbed usually culled them easy, though. It was one of Franklin's standard tests. No woman but two, and both those man-built, had ever lasted through even the first ton before they walked off, got in their rigs, and drove away. To be fair, most of the men drove away, too. Nobody could say that Franklin wasn't an equal opportunity discourager.

Trading jobs was standard after lunch—all the hands knew it, those who had spent the morning sorting, roping, and dragging putting up their horses, and trading out ropes for irons, vaccinating guns, and dehorning spoons. Jake hadn't learned a whole lot as he'd worked with Mike. He hadn't watched all that much, being too busy laying brands. So much for Dree Blake's idea that watching was learning. There just wasn't the luxury to stand around gawking, not with calves bawling to get back to their mothers.

"You just going to sit there grinning or are you going to get to work?" Wil said, riding by. Jake grinned even wider. That was Wil's way of teaming up.

Nudging Coal, Jake moved toward the calves and shook out a loop. Coal picked, positioning himself so all Jake had to do was drop the loop over and dally. The young heifer fought, then ran, Coal spinning to keep her from looping around behind them, the horse angling off toward the branding pots once the rope tightened. This calf stayed on her feet, and Jake let Coal pull her along easy until they got closer to the propane-fueled furnace. The hum of it wasn't something Coal much liked, and Jake had to fight him pretty hard as Wil closed in for the heels to stretch the calf out for the wrestlers to pin down—pin down real easy, else Franklin would bark at them.

The work went quick, and Jake barely had time to snap his rope clear before the next team moved in. The next team was the Blake girl and Franklin, Franklin on the heels.

Coal pinned ears and snapped teeth at the mule. Jake reined him away. "Sorry."

They got through the heifers, then finished up the remaining bull calves. It was nearing three by the time they were done, and they still had to bring up another herd. Dinner was going to be late tonight. They'd be lucky to get in by dark.

But Franklin shifted the plan. Instead of moving the cow-calf pairs, he had the men move the portable panels to *them*.

Setting up went fast. They were done and home just after four…had the horses put away by four-thirty. Everybody hit the showers, Jake included. Then he went to find himself a well-earned whiskey before dinner.

DREE WAS WAY TOO TIRED for her therapy walk by the time she got Cougar settled in for the night, then fed and watered the dogs. She was filthy, and her knee hurt from a hit she'd taken when, castrating one of the last of the bull calves, the animal had slipped a leg from the wrestler's grab. What she desperately wanted was a long soak in a hot bath, but a shower would have to do. Getting out, she wrapped a towel around herself, then, with a glance at the time, gave herself permission to lay out on the bed for ten minutes.

Ten minutes turned into almost ten hours, and, sometime in the night, somebody slipped her dogs into her room and turned out the overhead light. She sat bolt upright at four, realized she'd slept right through and got up to fight a brush through her now tangled, curly mop. It took ten excruciating minutes to get her hair unsnarled.

She didn't bother to even ask Marguerite or Olivia if they wanted her help this morning, just smiled and said, "Hi," and went out the back door, her dogs eager for freedom. At the barn, she took care of Cougar and then took the tractor lane past the bulls, again. Her leg was stiff and bruised, but it soon loosened up with the walking.

The bulls were at the fence, grazing, but gave her just a glance as she came up on them. Instead of going on, she studied them.

They were broader, deeper, and fuller, carrying more densely packed muscle on good, solid bone. They were a lot better than her father's bulls, and the cows she'd seen yesterday were, too. There was something more to these animals, though what that was she couldn't quite figure—a smoothness, maybe. "They're...rich." Then, she laughed at herself, but that was her sense of them—richness...like the difference between cheap chocolate and the imported, very expensive stuff made in England that her Gram Blake served up with brandy.

Backtracking to the barn, she brought Cougar out to the trailer and saddled him there, loading him up once she was done. She wasn't going to be trapped in the stall by Jake Jarvis, again. "Fool me once," she muttered, then went to the house.

Today, instead of being last, she decided to be early. Only Old Man Jarvis beat her to the table. Franklin came in right after, the big, black, lion-bear dog padding silently beside him.

"May I ask what breed or mix your dog is?" Dree asked.

"Tibetan Mastiff," Franklin said. "Good against wolves. You sleep well?"

Dree swallowed, wondering if he was the one who'd let her dogs in and turned out the lights. She decided she didn't want to know. "Yes, thank you."

"Good. We've got another big day."

"The bulls in the pasture to the north," Dree said. "They're yearlings?"

"That's right."

"Are you selling them?"

"They're already sold. Just waiting for their new owners to come get them."

Dree nodded. "What does a bull like that go for?"

"Around five thousand."

Dree sucked a breath. It would take four such bulls to cover their two-hundred head, and five would be better.

"You looking to improve the Blake Ranch stock?"

"That would be up to Dad. I just saw them and…well, they're very impressive." She smiled, then. "We could never afford even one, right now, though."

Franklin nodded. "Well, they're probably not what you need. We breed to increase marbling. My—" He looked over at his father. "Our animals produce better than prime, with heavy marbling and large ribeye EPDs, not the leaner grades. We feed them out, both grain and grass-fed, over on another spread managed by Wil's cousin, and process them ourselves."

"You feed them out yourself?"

The man nodded, "And butcher them," he added, then sucked down some coffee from his mug.

"Can I ask why?"

Old Man Jarvis grinned and nodded to her.

Franklin glanced back her way, turned in his chair, angling himself to face her, then leaned back and threw a leg over the chair arm, settling in. "We sell to an exclusive clientele—high-end restaurants and butcher shops in the big cities, mostly. Built up our private sales when America went lean, and we were facing bankruptcy. I won't sell to the big four." He leveled a curious look at her, then said, "I believed in our beef, then, as I do now, so I found a way to make it work."

And had the land and money to do it, Dree thought as, in her head, she worked through just how much it would take to finish out even a thousand head.

He sat watching her, then added, "If you're selling to the usual buyers, shipping off to the feedlots, you don't want our bloodlines. We're old-school, here."

Dree laughed. "Well, the usual buyers, as you put it, aren't keeping us in clover, and you seem to do plenty well. I need to take lessons." She didn't mention that their net was in the red, not black. Their cows were losing them money, while, too obviously, his were making him lots.

The man rubbed his thumb up and down the side of his mug, then asked, "You're university educated, right?"

Dree nodded. "Agricultural Economics. But I only have a bachelor's. It's enough to know that the future isn't looking good for a ranch as small as ours."

"You're running how many mother cows?"

"Half of what Dad used to run—two-hundred, give or take."

He nodded, and she silently thanked him for not laughing.

"You farm, too, right?"

"A little hay. Not much."

"Irrigation?"

"Yes. But just—" Larry and Mike came in. Dree didn't want to talk specifics with Larry present. It would wind up coming back to bite her, as usual, via her dad who was still tight with the Carter clan.

Franklin tipped a nod to her, then, dropping his leg down, straightened up and turned away to say something to his father.

STANDING JUST OUT OF SIGHT in the doorway leading to the kitchen, Jake sipped his coffee. On one hand, he was proud that the girl recognized the superiority of Jarvis stock. On the other, it galled him that she would dare quiz his granddad for an asking price. She couldn't even afford more than an old beater pickup and a rusty, second-hand stock trailer. Even her saddle looked like it came from early last century.

He shook his head. It wasn't her fault about her dad's ranch. It probably wasn't even her dad's fault they were failing. Success was a matter of smarts, good management, *and* luck. The Jarvises had luck. Franklin had turned disadvantage into advantage by smarts, but it was luck that he'd approached the right people just when the right people were desperate for what he was selling—top quality, high-marbled beef. What *was* pure arrogance was for Dree Blake to think herself qualified to even look at Jarvis bulls with an eye for buying...to even think she had some right to meddle in her dad's business. "Ours," she had said. "A ranch as small as *ours*." Like she had some stake in it. That set badly with Jake, and it angered him that his granddad was pandering to her just because she was a guest in his house. No, he decided. It was because she was female. Franklin didn't pander to guests. But he did to women and girls...unless they were bitches.

"Jake?"

He jerked, coffee spilling down the front of his shirt. "Oops. Sorry, Marguerite." He got out of her way, then followed her and Olivia into the dining room, an eyeful of Olivia's lovely, jean-clad backside a good start to the morning.

Franklin caught him looking and leveled a warning glare. Jake grinned and shrugged. What did Franklin expect? The girl was a looker—a *real* good looker. It wasn't like he was going take advantage of her, for cripe's sake. He knew she was only fifteen, and, besides, she was family. And, suddenly, he wondered how old Dree Blake was. Obviously older than doe-eyed. She'd said she'd graduated college already. ...And that was another thing. Why the hell would a woman need a degree in Ag Economics, anyway? Just about anything else, okay. But Ag Economics smacked of meddling in affairs that weren't hers to mess with. He bet she was still a virgin, too. Nobody'd bed that, or wouldn't admit it if they had.

C. J. "Country" James

9

The Push

AFTER SUFFERING HER WAY THROUGH yet another Franklin Jarvis dish-up of breakfast, this time, even though Franklin was watching, Dree put her plate down on the floor once she'd choked down one of two sausage patties, some scrambled eggs, and half a pancake. The man shook his head at her, but grinned doing it. Moments after, the big, exotic dog appeared, padding down the space between the chairs and the line of buffets and cabinets that lined the wall. She studied the animal, finally getting a close look as it chewed its way slowly and delicately through, first, sausage, then pancakes, then, finally, the scramble.

The dog gleamed 'clean', and he actually did look a lot like a cross between a lion and a black bear. That was because somebody had clipped him that way, clipping the hair on his head to about an inch long, clipping the rest of his body to about four inches long, leaving only a thick mane of very long hair ringing his shoulders and neck all the way up to in front of his ears.

"I'd be real careful," Larry said. "Chows are absolutely untrustworthy and extremely vicious." Dree didn't correct him on what she'd been told was the dog's breed.

The "mount out" order was given, and Dree didn't help clean table, just ran to the bathroom, washed up, and went out to get Cougar out of the trailer. She was just about to put her foot in the stirrup when Jake Jarvis walked up. "Sorry about yesterday. I don't know why I baited you. I'm not good at approaching strangers, but I only wanted to tell you sorry for almost clipping you and thank you for not telling Franklin."

Drop-jawed, before she could come up with a reply, he touched his hat and walked off. She stared down at her dogs. "Fat lot of warning you gave me!" They sat doggy-grinning up at her, undocked tails brushing dirt.

THERE. HE'D DONE IT. Now he could get her off his conscience.

Stalking in to grab Coal, Jake burned with anger…and he didn't know why. The horse sensed it and put his ears back. "Easy, Coal. It's not you. It's that *girl*."

The horse blew, sprinkling a moist mist over his face and shirt. And, suddenly, surprising himself, he started laughing…couldn't quit.

Wil poked his head in, then just stood. "You okay?" he finally asked, a worried frown crowding his eyebrows.

Jake waved him off, trying to stop, trying to catch his breath as, bent over, hands on knees, paroxysms shook his whole body.

Now Franklin joined Wil in the doorway. "Jake?"

Unable to breathe, unable to stop, Jake finally gave over to it and sank into the shavings, Coal nickering and pushing his nose into his face. "Quit, you black devil," Jake gasped.

Franklin stepped in and, with a wave, sent Wil on his way. Then he did something uncharacteristic. He closed the sliding stall door and squatted down, careful like, so his spurs didn't jab him. "You in love or something?"

Somehow, that made Jake laugh all the harder. Ultimately, Jake confessed about almost clipping Dree Blake's truck, then being terrified she'd told on him. "I couldn't believe it when I drove in and saw her old beater here. Thought I was a goner. When I figured out she hadn't told you what a stupid ass I'd been, I wanted to thank her and apologize. Then I got even more stupid! Pissed her off even more. ...With good reason," he gasped, still unable to stop chuckling.

Telling Franklin about it made him feel better. What surprised him was that Franklin laughed, too. "I figured something happened when she came flying around the corner of the barn on that mule yesterday, you right after her," Franklin said. "Never rile a woman, Jake. They can really, really hurt you if you get 'em mad enough, and ain't nothing I know that can stop 'em at that point."

His granddad pushed up from where he'd been sprawled, back to the wall, long legs stretched out, feet crossed at the ankles. "Okay. We'd best get a move on. We're holding up the works."

The men were long gone by the time he and Franklin mounted up, Franklin riding his Monty, today, the small, sorrel Quarter Horse stallion stretching out his neck and long walking so fast that Jake's taller Coal had to jog every few steps to stay even. "He'll get it in time," Franklin said. "He's still growing into himself," then, with a glance, added, "So are you."

DREE SAW THEM when they came over the hill, the two Jarvises looking like something out of an old Western. There was something special to it, maybe the way the morning sun hit them, and, on a whim, she snapped off a couple of shots with her phone as they rode in—the seasoned cowboy and the young protégé.

Immediately, Franklin Jarvis went over to the ranch foreman and settled his horse in beside his. She watched the men confer, then the foreman gave a whistle and galloped over to the man sitting in the gear truck that, today, was hauling extra panels.

Franklin Jarvis trotted over to Larry, Mike and her where they stood near Larry's truck. That Larry had chosen to drive out today instead of ride didn't surprise Dree. Larry couldn't rope, a fact that came evident yesterday afternoon. There was no reason for him to ride.

"We're going to do what we did yesterday afternoon, only on the fly and all day," Franklin said, looking down on them. "You'll be on the teams doing the bull calves, while we set up another couple of branding pots to run the heifers through. You think you can keep up?" Franklin glanced toward her as he said it, and, pulling her eyes from his golden-sorrel with its big dark eyes and gentle demeanor, Dree nodded.

His eyes shifted from her to Mike, and Mike shrugged with that specific nonchalance men use that means "no problem."

Larry's face set. "This isn't teaching your men how to—"

Franklin cut him off. "Can you keep up? Because, if you can't, we'll go back to cutting, right now."

Larry's ears turned red—just his ears. "Yes, we can keep up."

"Good. We'll worry about the learning later. The weather service is predicting heavy thunderstorms with possible hail by Friday, and I've got to get these animals into the hills before that happens." He wheeled his horse and loped off.

To Dree, that meant they were going to try to do the rest of the herd today and tomorrow, then the men would spend Thursday moving cattle. The problem as she saw it was that Franklin didn't have enough crew to run five teams.

Larry turned to Mike, saying something she couldn't hear. Mike nodded, but, as soon as Larry turned to Dree, Mike gave an odd glance toward Larry. Then he trotted off—Mike who never moved faster than a slow walk unless he was horseback.

Dree waited for Larry to say whatever was on his mind. Her cousin frowned at her for a long moment. "Dree, would you try to help me, not take the Jarvises' side on everything? You're pissing me off."

Shocked by the accusation, she just stared, uncomprehending, as he walked around the front of his truck, got in, and drove it over near where the calf tables had been stacked out of the way.

JAKE HADN'T HAD A BREAK in over four hours. Coal was all sweat, his neck foamy where the reins rubbed, and Jake felt like his arm was going to fall off. Amazing to him was that his granddad who was working with one of the men less skilled with a rope looked as fresh as when he'd started. So did Monty

who was sweating, sure, but just kept his head down to
business, Franklin mostly never even having to touch a
heel or rein to him. There was something to say about
using a small horse like Monty. They were quicker.

Dragging the next calf into a branding team that was
coming open, Jake saw Dree Blake laugh at something
Wil said as they waited for wrestlers to get the calf
down. Calf laid over, they stopped talking suddenly
and went to work, Wil laying the Jarvis brand as the
Blake girl squatted down to begin working on her part
of the business—the part that made Jake sick in the
gut.

Jake booted Coal back out to catch the next one.
They were barely keeping up.

Franklin rode over. "Jake. Give Coal a break.
Grab the bay Tom rode."

"Yes, sir." Jake gave Coal a pat as Franklin wheeled
Monty to drop a loop over a calf that sprang by. Coal,
just four, needed the rest, but Jake was proud of him.
He'd really held his own, despite it being his first year
at the *real* hard work.

Hobbling Coal and getting the bay, Jake adjusted the
stirrups, then, arm aching, gritted up and went back to
it.

DREE FOUND THE PACE QUICK, but the job
easy with the men there to wrangle the calves

and handle the bulk of the work. She just crimped, held for ten seconds twice going each side, then got out of the way until the next calf was pulled in. She felt positively guilty for not being more useful. The good thing was that they were maybe two-thirds done with this herd when the lunch wagon showed up. Maybe, just maybe, if things kept going this smoothly, they *could* get the whole Jarvis herd done by tomorrow afternoon late. It would be a hard push for the men and for the horses, but, one thing she knew, she wasn't holding up the works, and that had been her big concern, mainly because crushing the spermatic cords just right was so critical.

"How you holding out, Missy," Franklin said, as he dragged another calf in.

"Good."

"This is your last. We're breaking for lunch," he said, glancing around at the men as they went to work, Dree getting to her job. "Wil, I need to talk. See me at the chuck wagon."

Dree glanced toward the foreman and wondered if it was about her, especially with Franklin's comment about this calf being her last...that maybe Franklin thought she was slowing things up. She didn't think she was, but the men she was working with may think differently. Maybe somebody had complained. Maybe Franklin himself was blaming her or the castrating procedure in general. She knew a good team was said to be able to process a hundred calves an hour, and, from the look of the number of calves still penned, they weren't near to coming even close to that—maybe fifty. "Not my fault," she muttered.

"What's not your fault?" Wil asked.

She shook her head. "Sorry. Nothing." If she was told pack up and go home, she would, no tears, no argument. She'd still get paid for her work, and even half of the money she'd been promised would be that much more off her debt to Gram Blake.

WHEN THEY FINALLY QUIT FOR LUNCH, Jake was about done. He could barely lift his arm, his shoulder screamed so bad. It was that way for the whole crew. They looked whipped.

Getting a plate after loosening the saddle on the bay, Jake sat down next to where Franklin was laid out on the ground talking to Wil. "…One for every two-to-three," he heard Wil say.

"Nothing much I can do about it," Franklin answered.

Jake waited for more to try to make heads or tails of it, but nothing else was forthcoming.

"How's your arm holding out, Jake?" Franklin asked.

"A little tired. I'll make 'er."

"I want you to take over branding for Wil. You think your arm is up for that?"

"I'll do what you need me to do," Jake said, but a relief spread through him. He honestly didn't know how much longer he could keep throwing a loop.

"Good. You'll work on Team One."

Jake eyed his grandfather and saw the man smirking at him. Team One was where Dree Blake was doing the castrating. "Whatever you say."

"Just watch yourself," Wil told him. "That girl's fast as lightning with those nippers. Don't get your crotch too near."

"And no puttin' the Jarvis brand on her, neither," Franklin said with a faked heavy drawl, a grin, and a laugh.

Jake knew he was being teased, and he forced himself to grin back. "Wouldn't dream of it, sir. The bulls would come gunning for me."

10

Old Timers

J AKE DROPPED THE IRON into the pot and grabbed the next one. They had four wrestlers, now, him and the rest of the crew doing double duty to keep up. The heat and the dirt made his eyes burn. Sweat soaked his shirt. He wanted to strip down, but couldn't stop even that long, not and keep up with the Blake girl. Damn her. She was fast, just as Wil said. And Franklin had the ropers pulling bull calves in as fast as she and Mike Guthrie could do them, both of them outworking Carter two and three to one. Jake counted. Now he understood what Wil had been telling Franklin over lunch.

Jake didn't have time to get queasy, even though he was close enough to get an eyeful of the emasculating. Somehow, having to focus on doing his job fast, but doing it right made him numb to everything else going on, and he was glad for it. He hadn't run to go puke somewhere private, not even once. He hadn't had to go find the port-a-potty because he got the runs, either—first year ever. Maybe this year, he wouldn't be the butt of the crew's jokes at parties because of his touchy gut. And, honestly, he liked this method of castrating. It was less...raw—no white-sheathed, slippery oblongs pushed out, one after the other, their cords split and severed. It seemed less severe, though he didn't know if that was true or not. The calves sometimes jerked, but not the way they did when the knife cut their ball-sack. And they didn't tense up. Neither did he.

"Tom, Dree, Jake! The rest of you. Ease up."

He looked up to see Wil standing there, a rare grin on his face.

"Take a break. We're down to the last for the day, and Franklin's called the chuck wagon back. They're bringing wash water along with ice tea and some sort of snacks."

Around him, the crew put their tools down, rubbed the sweat running off their faces, then sank into the dirt, some of them laying out flat.

"Once the truck gets here, we'll take thirty minutes, then finish up. Hoping to be done by four." Then, "Good work, men. ...And Dree." He touched the brim of his hat, then mounted his sweaty, blowing horse.

Jake glanced at his watch. It was two-forty-five. He glanced at the number of calves in the pen and frowned. There were half as many as there'd been when they started at one. And there were still two more gathers to process by tomorrow afternoon. What the hell was Franklin thinking? They didn't have time to stop, not if they were going to beat the incoming storms.

Spotting his grandfather, he walked over. "We're not going to make it, are we?"

Franklin, who'd kept on roping and was filthy with dirt-streaked sweat, looked down at him. "What do you mean?"

"We've still got nearly a hundred head to run through with this gather. That means we're not going to finish till Thursday, earliest."

Franklin started to chuckle. Then, at Jake's frown, said, "This is the Milton Creek herd, Jake. We've only got about five hundred calves to finish after this bunch. We should be done by around noon tomorrow."

"You moved them?"

"We brought 'em up, yes. A few at a time, nice and slow."

"*When?* When did you have *time?*" Jake hadn't seen any of the roping crew take off to do what Franklin said they had.

"Didn't need time. Just men." Franklin pointed. There, beyond the holding pens, sat his great-grandfather on Cassie, a bunch of grizzled old-timers and their cattle dogs with him.

D REE HAD THE TIME OF HER LIFE listening to the aged cowboys talk about "the old days" over a dinner of melt-in-your-mouth steak grilled over a pit built into a giant rock deck off the back of the great room. The brand was inlaid into the stone here, too. It shimmered in the fire light. She stayed, forgoing her walk, drinking rich, dark, chocolate-laced coffee, as they all sat around sipping whiskey and beer once the food was eaten.

She listened far past bedtime, rapt in their stories of times when cattle were still run to the railheads, the herds moving through the main streets of towns along the way, something that only happened, now, in parades, if then.

Some of their stories were crude, some cruel, some ribald, but, mostly, there was respect in their tales— respect for favorite horses and for wily maverick cows that made them "work real hard." There was a whole lot of laughter in them, mostly directed at themselves. These were the last of their kind—real cowboys she'd grown up dreaming about as a child when her granddad would sit her on his knee and speak about being a boy down in Texas.

That night, locked in her room with her dogs, the mastiff on duty outside, Dree slept and dreamed her old childhood dream for the first time since she'd been a small girl, her riding side-by-side with her cowboy, driving their cattle up into the Montana mountains, there to camp by the light of a full moon under a canopy of sparkling stars to await the coming sunrise.

C. J. "Country" James

11

Personal Questions

THE OLD COWBOYS STAYED ON. They would stay until the Jarvis herds were off the flats and safely run through the foothills into the treed mountains and draws where there was protection from the incoming storms.

Dree was thrilled. Breakfast brought out more stories, mostly about bad cooks and spoiled food, but some, prompted by the threatening thunderheads, about turning stampeding herds and the sight of St. Elmo's Fire dancing on cattle horns—"Them cows glowed."

"Ghost cows," another man said.

Dree caught Franklin watching her, and, realizing she had her elbows up on the table, her chin on her hands, she winced, shrugged him her 'sorry smile', then got back to minding her manners.

◆

TODAY, EVERYBODY PITCHED IN to move the big, heavy corral panels. The crews went to start at it the previous afternoon, but Franklin had called a halt after the last calf was released, claiming he was too worn from a marathon day. They'd done over a twelve-hundred calves, Dree found out.

On the ride over, Wil asked her to pull the drop pins, which meant she had to pull the big, short metal rods from the hinge couplers, then wire them down so, when the panels were loaded into one of two waiting trucks, the pins and their attachment chains didn't tangle with another panel.

She had to move quickly to keep ahead of the two-man carry teams, shoving and twisting the heavy tubular steel spans when the pins were bound up. She pinched fingers over and over, and she was glad she was wearing her gloves.

Then they had to set them up again in a pasture that ran right down to the river. This pasture had an irrigation unit tucked up against a fence, aligned to the prevailing wind. She hadn't known the Jarvises irrigated their hay.

"So all their flat land is hay ground?" she asked Larry as they waited for the cows .

He shrugged. He was suspiciously clean, unlike she and Mike, and Dree guessed he'd made himself scarce during the brawny work of loading panels, but, then, he was here to convince the Jarvises to switch to bloodless castration, not as manpower.

A whistle, and Dree saw Wil loping towards them. "Set up at the north end," he yelled, then turned back to disappear down over the rise. Dree got her burdizzos, grabbed a propane tank and dragged it with her over where she thought Wil would want them. Mike followed, hauling two of the big canisters. They went back to the gear truck for the pots, then again for the dehorners, vaccinating guns, and branding irons. Dree couldn't find the record books, so she left that to Larry who was working on something on the passenger seat of his truck cab.

Mike had to help her attach the propane tank to the pot, and wound up doing the whole job himself. She couldn't get the couplers on the rubber tubing to stop leaking. They distributed the tools, three irons, a dehorner, and two pre-loaded vaccinating guns per station. "Where're the record books, Dree?" Mike asked.

"I couldn't find them."

"I'll take a look," and he trotted off back to the gear truck. The cows were moving into sight when he came back. "Nope. Couldn't find 'em, either. Maybe they keep 'em locked up somewhere."

"Maybe."

Mike shuffled, then cleared his throat.

She cast him a sideways glance. "What?"

"Can I ask you a personal question?"

She shrugged. "Sure."

"Are you…are you…."

"Spit it out, Mike."

He sucked a breath. "Are you screwing Larry?"

She felt her mouth drop open, quickly shut it. Horrified by the suggestion, she could only just shake her head until she finally found her tongue, again. "No."

"I didn't think so."

"What gave you that idea, Mike?" she asked, and heard the icy cold in her voice.

"He said it. Yesterday morning."

So that was the reason Mike had given her that odd look, then run off. "The son-of-a-bitch," Dree whispered.

Larry walked up a few minutes later as the cow-calf pairs started filing in. "You forgot these." He handed each of them a ledger, keeping one—the record books. He looked up. "Here we go. Last day of this nightmare."

Dree glanced at Mike. Mike shook his head, a grim look in his eye. "Yeah."

SEPARATING A MOTHER COW from her calf wasn't hard. What was hard was keeping the calf from slipping through, too. Coal wasn't quick enough, so Jake had taken one of the seasoned geldings this morning, a sorrel that was a natural at cutting—one of Monty's first get.

Again, Franklin told them to separate the heifers into one group, the bulls into another. "We'll do the bulls first."

Once they got them sorted, Wil made the assignments. Jake was assigned to work branding on the team with Larry Carter. He got to see firsthand just how slow the man was, and chafed when he wound up standing around waiting. Meanwhile, Franklin, working the irons on the team with the Blake girl, and Wil with Mike Guthrie, were running them through lickety-split.

"So, how can I learn to do this," Jake asked as, finished branding the calf, he watched Larry Carter repeatedly feel for what he guessed was the spermatic cord in the stretched hide above the scrotum. The man looked up at him. "In these conditions, you can't," he snarled.

Jake stepped back. "You mean normal ranch conditions?" He hadn't liked this guy from the first time he'd been introduced. Now, he really didn't like him "Odd thing is that Ms. Blake and Mike Guthrie are doing fine in these conditions, as you call them," Jake said, and watched the man stiffen. "I guess you're just maybe not as practiced, huh? That, and you use gloves to keep your hands from getting dirty?"

Finally finished with the calf, the man stood up, his ears bright red. He wiped sweat off his face with his filthy, long-sleeved shirt. "You'll pay for that someday, kid. Maybe real soon. Now, get out of my face."

Jake couldn't help himself. He grinned and touched his hat with a middle finger salute. "Why, yes, sir."

◆

THEY WERE ALL DONE with the bulls by ten-thirty, Jake's team letting the last calf loose to find its mother. He saw Franklin walk off with Dree Blake toward where the horses were hobbled to graze. Wil came over, wiping sweat off from where his hat snugged his forehead. "Mike's a damn good hand," he said. "You okay to rope or you want to keep branding?"

"I'll rope," Jake said.

"Shoulder's okay?"

"Yep."

"Okay. You're with me."

Jake wished they'd stop babying him because of his college rodeo injury. He was fine.

Finding the sorrel, Jake was glad for the change. Roping was fun, especially since they didn't have to run quite so hard today. Yesterday's sprint marathon had paid off. They'd probably be done right after lunch like

Franklin figured. Jake took the heels of their first calf after Wil made the catch. Lane and Tom came right in behind them, Franklin and the Blake girl last.

It went on that way, smooth as greased lightning until the team after his had a rodeo as one of the calves got behind Lane's horse, the rope burning under the young gelding's tail. Dree had position, but Jake doubted she knew what to do. He was wrong, though. She moved in and laid a loop around the calf's hind legs pretty as anything. Then her mule backed up fast and hard, angling to drag the calf backward so the rope came free. It was a canny piece of work, and it was clear the mule was savvy. The animal practically flew backwards while squatting hard on its haunches as Larry got the horse to come around and drag the calf to the branding station. Jake saw the man who was his mentor and best friend turn to Dree and touch his hat. That meant something. Lane was a top hand. And, grudgingly, Jake had to agree that she deserved that tribute. So did the mule.

They got through the heifers, stalling lunch forty-five minutes. When the last calf went loose, the men let out whoops and hollers. "Good job well done," Franklin told them. Then, with a hiss, a lean, and a lift of his hand, he let Monty loose, the small stallion bolting from an ear-lazy, cocked hind leg stop into a dead run, ears flat, tail popping.

Jake and everybody else took the cue, and it was a race to the chuck wagon...for everybody but Larry

Carter, Mike Guthrie and Dree Blake, that is. Larry Carter had somehow beaten them all. He already had a plate by the time Jake got there. Mike and Dree walked in on foot, having ditched their mounts somewhere.

"WE'LL MOVE THEM TOMORROW," Franklin said over lunch, him sitting next to her like he'd done Monday. "Do you want to ride along, or would you rather head out for home?"

"I'd love to help," Dree said, happy to have been asked. "What's happening after lunch?"

"We've got to break down the holding pens."

"If you need, I can help with that, too, if I won't be in the way."

"You're welcome to pitch in," he said.

"Can I ask you something?"

"Shoot."

"Your brand? I expected it to be a 'J' something."

The man laughed. "It's based on kind of a vow made by my dad's dad when he came to this land."

Dree waited, and, when he didn't elaborate, asked, "The figure eight?"

"Ah, well. Not a figure eight. The sun and the moon.

She tipped her head, and, sliding his eyes to hers to pause there a moment, finally said, "The top is day and the sun, the bottom, night and the moon, the bar being the land."

"And the circle?"

He shrugged, then said, "Life, I guess you'd call it."

"What's the vow?"

He shook his head. "Not important."

In other words, private.

Movement caught her eye, and, standing up, Dree scrambled to dig her cell phone out, hitting the video icon. There, coming over the hill to the northwest, were the old cowboys framed against the wide-open sky, their dogs running out in front as, in a line side-by-side, they slowly came toward them, their horses long-walking, heads down, reins slack. It was like a scene from a movie with the hills and mountains behind. It was a forever moment, and she fervently hoped her phone battery held. She filmed them all the way in until they disappeared behind one of the gear trucks.

"You're a *romantic*," Franklin said when she sat down, again.

Dree frowned. "Ah. I don't know. Nobody's ever accused me of that. Maybe the opposite. It just struck me... *they* struck me. How come they're here?"

"They're going to run this herd up to a pasture nearer Fernie Creek for me." Then, the man chuckled, shook his head, and went back to eating.

Dree didn't see the humor. Maybe the old timers? *Maybe me.*

12

Battered & Beat

"**J**AKE, I WANT YOU TO KEEP TABS on the Carter fellow after dinner," Franklin said, pulling in beside him as they rode home.

"What for?"

"Just do it. If he takes off to follow the Blake girl, you tail him a-horseback and make sure he knows you're there."

Jake frowned, then dodged a quick glance at the girl on the mule. "Ah.... Is this any of our business?"

Franklin glared at him. "He's followed her out every night when she's gone out to feed her dogs or go walking."

"Grandpa, this is the 21st century. Girls are loose and easy—"

"Jake, don't give me lip. Do as I say. Wil's gotta drive over and back to the Heron spread tonight, so I'm asking you to do it this once."

Jake touched his hat. "Will do."

Sure as anything, Jake wound up chasing out to the barn to mount out on Coal bareback after Carter suddenly got up from where he was watching TV in the great room to head out the front door. Jake didn't even have time to throw on a saddle.

Catching sight of the man around the second curve, Jake eased Coal to a walk. He saw the man glance back and frown. The Blake girl wasn't anywhere to be seen, though. Carter was probably just out for his own walk, Jake guessed. Still, his was to do as told, not question Franklin's orders.

As they came out onto the straightaway, far ahead he saw a figure, two dogs beside—the Blake girl. So Franklin was right. Carter was following her. Did they have an 'arrangement'? Larry Carter wore a ring on his left hand, but that meant nothing to some girls.

Jake needed to piss. Stopping Coal, he slid off and, using the horse as a shield, relieved himself. When he flung himself back aboard, though, Larry Carter had vanished.

Putting Coal in a jog, Jake got to the rise in the road before the final curve that descended to the old highway. Still nobody in sight. "Shit." He squeezed Coal into a lope, rounding the curve. There, marching toward him was the Blake girl. He stopped. *Now what?* She'd seen him.

She didn't even pause.

"Evenin'," he said, touching his hat as she walked past, her dogs beside her.

"Evening."

He went on down toward the highway, not turning Coal back till she was a good couple hundred yards distant. Then he let Coal mosey along. He'd lost Carter, so he'd just keep his eye on her till she was safely back to the ranch house.

NERVOUS, DREE WALKED FAST, her dogs trotting to stay up with her. They kept glancing toward the woods, then back behind, growling under their breaths, hugging her knee. She kicked herself for walking so far. She'd been daydreaming, full of calculations, exploring half-formed ideas about her father's ranch. It would be dark before she reached the house.

She wanted to run—didn't dare, not on the gravel, not with her knee. Behind her, a yell, and, daring to, she glanced back. She saw Jake jump down off of Coal and jump across the ditch.

THEY WERE HALFWAY HOME when Coal snorted and jumped, spooked by something in the woods to their right—something wearing a hat, a particular hat—Larry Carter. "Hey!" he barked, and slid off Coal. "What the hell do you think you're doing?"

He wasn't expecting it. He wasn't anticipating it, at all—something coming at him from aside and above.

It hit him hard to the side of the head, and he felt his knees buckle.

His sight went dim and foggy. Far away, he felt something hitting him again and again. Then it stopped, and the smell of whiskey breath rolled by real near his face. ...It went away.

HORRIFIED, DREE SAW A SHADOW leap out from the woods by the side of the road—a man—and hit Jake Jarvis with a club. Then, the man began to kick Jake, even as Jake rolled and crawled away from him.

The black horse raced toward her. The man kicked again and again. She sent the dogs—"Get 'im."—as he bent down over Jake Jarvis, then began kicking him all over again.

The black swerved, his headlong run broken by the dogs racing past.

Holding an arm out toward the big animal as, confused, it slowed, then stopped, she kept saying, "Whoa, easy, whoa," half her attention on the horror still playing out down the road.

The horse turned toward her...lowered his head some...stretched out his nose, then suddenly raised it, again, at a yell. Dree's dogs had reached Jake and the man assaulting him.

Dree grabbed the broken reins. "Easy. They're okay. You're okay. Come here."

The man fled back into the woods, her dogs giving chase. She heard one yelp...another yell.

"Omigod. LADDIE! CHIPPER! *COME!*" she screamed.

She stroked the stallion's neck as he shifted and shuffled at her yell. "It's okay," she said, softening her voice.

He jumped as her dogs came out of the woods, but settled, again, when she just kept stroking. Her dogs stayed put, though—didn't come—which meant the threat was still there. They were agitated, circling and barking, their hackles up.

She walked toward them and the still body lying on the road. She was terrified the attacker would come out of the woods, again. She was terrified that Jake Jarvis was dead.

As if reading her thoughts, the stallion snorted, jigging, his eyes showing whites. "Easy. Walk."

Dogs were barking...growling. He heard hooves on gravel. Again, someone came up beside him, and he jerked, expecting another blow.

"It's okay. Easy. Are you okay?"—the Blake girl's voice.

Jake tried to sit up...had to catch himself with an arm to stay there. The world wouldn't hold still. "Yeah."

"You don't look all right," she said, the glare of a small, bright light blinding him. "I don't want to leave you, but I've got no reception."

"I'm fine," he snarled.

"No. Actually, you're not. Your eyes are dilated."

"Yeah. It's *dark*."

He heard her mutter something he couldn't quite catch. Then, "Let me try to get you on your horse."

He wanted her to go away, but, as he finally managed to get himself standing, her supporting him with her shoulder, he realized, no, he wasn't all right. Not at all.

When he told her it was dark, Dree knew there was something wrong, for sure. It wasn't dark, just mid-twilight. And his speech was slurred.

Tall and slim-looking, Jake Jarvis was heavier than she expected—at least a hundred-eighty pounds of rock hard muscle. What Dree had thought would be an easy thing wound up leaving her breathless as, maneuvering his horse into the ditch on the side of the road, she was finally able to get him aboard.

She led the horse with the reins in her outside hand so she could keep a hand on Jake Jarvis's leg in case he began to slip off. He was bent oddly over the stallion's neck, his hands wrapped into the animal's mane in a white-knuckled grip.

He didn't talk, he didn't argue, just stayed quiet. That terrified her. Silence from a man meant they were either really angry or they were really, really bad off.

She took it slow, the animal next to her walking quietly. By the time she finally saw the ranch lights, she knew Jake was in a whole lot of trouble. *"HELP!"* she hollered. *"HE-ELP!"*

Nobody heard her. The TV was blaring loud in the bunkhouse. She led the stallion right up to the front door. *"FRANKLIN! HELP!"*

The front door crashed open. Both Franklin and Old Man Jarvis, along with Mike and a couple of old timers rushed out, crowding around. They took hold of the horse and pulled Jake down. He was limp.

"What happened?!" Franklin demanded.

Scared of the 'hard' in his voice, the harder look in his eyes, Dree stumbled for words until, finally, grabbing a hold of herself, she managed, "Somebody. Down the road. They hurt him." Then, the rest all came out in a flood. "I don't know who. I was too far away. He hit him with…a club, maybe, then started kicking him. My dogs got a piece of him, but he ran back into the woods."

"Where? How far?"

"Ah, halfway…a mile, maybe."

Men were coming out of the bunkhouse, some of them running over. Franklin barked orders for them to take horses, dogs, ATVs, trucks, and start checking the woods, beating the brush, and running the drive and the road. Then, gripping her shoulder, he steered her up the stairs and into the house, slamming the door.

"I think he's got a concussion. His eyes…."

Franklin Jarvis didn't answer. He just marched her, dogs and all, through the kitchen, grabbed his hat from one of the pegs on a wall in the hallway, then marched her on into the garage. "In the car," he ordered, pointing to a big, fancy car, the usual black, but without the ranch brand painted on its side.

"I–my dogs—"

"You and your dogs, in front in the car," he said, again, opening the garage door with a flick of something on his key ring.

Men came through the opening garage door carrying Jake whose eyes were half-open and dead-staring. They put him in the back seat, Marguerite in a half-on, half-off white sweater, handing in a blanket.

Dree helped Franklin spread the blanket over him. Marguerite climbed in and, cradling Jake's head, held a wrap-around ice pack to it. The young man was absolutely silent and still, not even a moan.

C. J. "Country" James

13

Night Run till Morning

THEY MADE IT TO SOMEPLACE called Clark Fork Valley Hospital in a wild ride that had Dree repeatedly holding her breath on the curves as Franklin drove like someone demon-possessed. He didn't say a word, just kept his eyes locked on the road. Only when something in the car went 'ping' did Franklin talk, and that was a call to warn the hospital they were minutes away, then the same to the sheriff.

Marguerite didn't say anything, either, the whole trip. The only sound was Dree's own breathing and an occasional whine from one of her dogs.

Emergency personnel were waiting as Franklin pulled in. So were sheriffs deputies, including the sheriff, himself. Marguerite sat with Dree in the waiting room until Franklin returned over an hour later, the deputies and sheriff with him. Then, the sheriff began questioning her.

It was after midnight by the time they got back to the ranch. "You're not to go out alone, anymore," Franklin said. "I'll send a man I can trust with you if you think you need to go out for a walk."

"I'll stay near the house."

"Even near the house or the outbuildings. You are not to go out without somebody along to protect you. Understand?"

"Yes, Mr. Jarvis. ...I can go home tomorrow morning, instead of staying on another night," she offered. "I won't be in the way, then."

"And put me two men short with Jake down and you leaving, too?" he said.

Dree blinked at the word 'men'. It was a compliment, and she knew that he knew that she'd understood him. Her face betrayed her with its burn. "I–I don't want to be a bother."

"Just don't go outside alone, and you won't be."

◆

IT WAS A NIGHTMARE. She knew it, but she couldn't wake herself up. Dogs growled and barked. The deep rumble, then woof, of an angry grizzly sow....

Coming awake with a start, she realized it wasn't a dream. Chip and Laddie were at the door, crouched and growling, their hackles up. Outside, men's voices, one of them Franklin's, one she didn't recognize....

A knock on her door. "Dree?" It was Franklin

"I'm awake."

She got up and, pulling on her bathrobe, went to the door...started to turn the deadbolt.

"Keep it locked. Stay inside. No matter what. You hear?"

"Yes."

"Obey me, now. Do not open this door until someone comes get you in the morning. I've stationed a man out here. Bear's out here, too." He paused. "My mastiff, I mean. You can go back to bed, now."

"All right."

She couldn't get back to sleep, though. Her brain whirled, wondering what had brought all the ruckus. She finally got up and sat in the chair. The clock read three.

◆

OLIVIA WAS THE ONE who tapped on Dree's door at five, calling out her name several times until Dree, fallen asleep in the chair, was awake enough to answer her. Dree scrambled to pull on jeans and a clean shirt, then tidied her hair and took her dogs out. Franklin appeared at the front door, looking just like he usually did, like he'd gotten a full night's sleep. He crossed the turn-around. "I said, no matter what, you are not to go out without somebody along. What about that is hard to understand, young woman?"

Dree felt her face flush. "S—sorry."

"Just *do* it."

She picked up the dog poo, then fed the Aussies while he waited. She fed Cougar, but abandoned any idea of saddling him. Franklin escorted her back to the house.

"You think it's my fault Jake got hurt, don't you," she said softly.

He stopped, turned, and looked down at her a moment, then shook his head. "No. It's mine."

Something clicked. Jake Jarvis, bareback on his big black following her wasn't his own doing. He'd been sent to keep track of her. It wasn't Jake who Franklin Jarvis thought was dangerous enough to post his big guard dog outside her bedroom door. It was somebody else—the somebody else who'd attacked Jake. Luckily, she was staying only one more day, and that only because of her promise to help move the cattle.

Franklin Jarvis kept looking down at her.

"What?" she asked.

"How well do you know Larry Carter?"

So he thought the Ag Agent was the one who accosted Jake?! Dree frowned. Larry did have a bad history during his teen years, but he was supposed to be over that, now. "Ah.... He's one of my cousins, related to my mom's side of the family. Carter was her maiden name. Why?"

"How do *you* know him?"

"I don't, really. He comes to the family picnics, but—" She just managed to stop herself. Men didn't take kindly to snide. "But I never really had much contact with him until Glen DeWalt asked me to come here to do this with Mike."

She caught Franklin Jarvis's look, and, kicking herself, explained those relationships, too. "Glen and I are friends. Ever since I was in FFA. ...I know Mike...have worked with him before, doing this kind of field education stuff with Glen. He's good crew."

"Glen's a good man." Silent for a moment, his eyes gone far away, he stared out into the trees west of them. Then, shifting back, he shook his head. Again, he looked down at her. "Why the hell do you pick up your dog's business?"

Dree winced. But, when he kept watching her, waiting for an answer, she stammered, "N–nobody likes stepping in dog poo. ...Me especially."

He nodded. "Got a call from the doctor half an hour ago. Looks like Jake's going to be fine. No bleeding in his brain or under that thick skull of his, so far. Another forty-eight hours will tell. Thought you'd like to know."

C. J. "Country" James

Dree nodded…put on a smile. She was happy for the man that his grandson was going to be okay…told him so, but, even as she said it, something crashed inside her, because she knew it was just all lip service. Inside, she just didn't care one way or another—not in her heart. It was callous of her—she knew it was—but she just didn't feel anything—never had—not when someone got hurt, not when somebody died. The only exception she could remember was when her grandfather passed a couple years back. She'd felt something, then—something strong that hurt horribly.

14

Killer Storms

PISSED OFF TO BE STUCK in a hospital bed, Jake surfed the channels, finally settling on a documentary about some South American tribe. Then he watched *The Farm and Ranch Report* when it came on at six.

Eight brought nurses and a couple of doctors. After long minutes of questions any four-year-old could answer, then a check of his ribs, back, and head, them shining a light in his eyes over and over, they drew blood, then wheeled him down for another trip into the tube—another MRI.

Eleven brought boring, again, so he surfed till he settled on another documentary, this one about armadillos.

It went on like that all day.

His mom, his Uncle Rick, and Aunt Jenny showed up after his dinner tray was taken away, but no Franklin or anybody else from the ranch. "Did they get the cattle moved?" It was thundering and lightning outside, with bouts of hail and heavy rain. The storms had hit a full twenty-four hours early.

"Haven't heard," Uncle Rick told him. "You just worry about gettin' yourself healed up. You look like a 'coon."

The rain lashed the windows, the wind howling. Jake fretted.

THE RIDE UP INTO THE HILLS had gone easy, the cow-calf pairs moving along like they knew the way. The whole time, thunderheads kept rolling in from the west, big, black, and noisy, but the clouds didn't break.

The ride back turned ugly. Lightning lit up the sky, the close crack of thunder, coming right after, making even Cougar jumpy. Then the hail came, along with gusts of wind that whipped the trees till they bent almost in half, some breaking. The ice hit hard enough to make her mule squeal. It battered Dree, stinging any place where it struck. And it started to rain, the water pounding down so hard it snapped as it hit leather, hide and rain gear.

The footing turned treacherous, with slippery ground and rushing torrents where dry gullies had been on the way in. Dree was soaked through despite her slicker.

Darkness fell before they even made it down into the foothills. By the time they reached the flats, she was shivering. She clamped her teeth shut when they started to chatter.

Lights ahead—two rigs bouncing toward them. Franklin called a halt as trucks from the ranch pulling stock trailers rolled up beside them. "Load 'em up."

Dree was never so happy to see the black Jarvis trucks with their shiny brands in her life. Inside, they had the heaters on full blast.

She didn't remember the trip to the ranch. Jostled awake, she climbed down, her dogs pinned to her leg, just in time to grab Cougar as they unloaded him. She got him settled in and both him and the dogs fed, then made her way to the house.

Told to change and get back on the double, they ate buffet-style in a long dining room that lay hidden between the garage and the kitchen. It had a built-in table running down its center—where the crew ate, Dree realized.

Dinner was thick, hot soup, grilled bacon-cheeseburgers—huge—fried potatoes and onions, along with stir-fried veggies. There were biscuits and bacon-flavored, cream-style gravy to pour over them. The men ate like they hadn't seen food in ten days. So did Dree. It was after eight-o-clock when she stepped into the shower, eight-thirty when, finally warm, she came out to flop into bed, her dogs brought in on leashes by the girl named Olivia. "Thanks," Dree told her when she slipped them into her room.

The girl, who'd never once spoken to her during the whole time Dree'd been there, nodded and left.

J AKE CAME AWAKE with a start to a hand touching his shin.

"Missed having you," Franklin said.

The clock on the wall read almost eleven. He sat up and turned up the light with the bed's doohickey. "You got them moved in time?"

His grandfather nodded. "We did. The ride home was bad, though. One man with a broken leg when a horse went down in a wash. Just wanted to stop in to check on you. Can't stay, though. Tomorrow we're heading over to Heron." He tipped his head toward the door. "Your mom will be by to pick you up Sunday if the doctors release you."

"Sorry about all this. I didn't even see him coming."

Franklin nodded, put his hat back on. "You just keep easy."

Jake watched his grandfather leave, his broad, straight back disappearing around the open door, his boot-steps fading down the hall. Franklin was 'dad', not 'granddad', to him, truth be told. The man mattered. A lot. "*Damn* it!" Jake had failed him, again.

15

Cinnamon Rolls & Bull

SATURDAY MORNING AFTER BREAKFAST, her bags packed and loaded, Wil Strakes having stepped along to help, Franklin asked the three of them—Larry, Mike, and Dree—into his office. It was a comfortable room all done in the same varnished wood as the rest of the house, but with lamps that let off a yellow glow—old fashioned, incandescent light bulbs. Franklin handed them each an envelope, and Dree saw a frown cross Larry's face when he opened his.

Apparently, so did Franklin. "I know you said you'd pay your crew, but I'd rather do it this way. I called Glen, and he approved my decision, and he *is* still your boss. I'm not taking the calf tables. The crew has them loaded in your truck bed."

Now, real trouble darkened Larry's face. He folded his envelope, jammed it into his back pocket, then turned and stalked out the door.

Dree ripped hers open, and gasped. "Mr. Jarvis—"

"Franklin."

She hesitated, then said softly, "This is more than twice what I contracted for."

Franklin slapped a hand down on the desk. Dree jumped at the sound. "I *knew* it!" he said. "Thanks for confirming it."

Mike was staring at Franklin. "You mean this?" he asked, nodding his head toward a check and a typed piece of paper.

"I do."

Mike stepped forward and reached his hand across. "I accept. I need to give notice, though—two weeks."

Franklin nodded, then turned to Dree. "I'd like you to stay the weekend, if you can. I'll pay you, of course. I need you to come castrate a few calves on a small spread we own over near Heron."

Dree said yes after she called her dad to get his okay.

◆

THE DRIVE OVER TO HERON WAS PRETTY. Dree had never seen this part of Montana. Wil Strakes drove, Franklin riding shotgun, with Dree in the back. They pulled a big, empty stock trailer.

Wil and Franklin talked numbers—tag numbers— Franklin checking off items on a hand-written list Wil had given him. Finally, they turned and crossed a river. A little while later, they pulled up a road that led to an old house, some barns, and some livestock pens. Bulls, some mature, even old, some only yearlings, fed at long bunks. Further on, there were mares with new foals at their sides. Wil parked beside a barn where about forty cow-calf pairs were feeding from round bunks scattered around a small pasture.

A women wearing a billed cap similar to the one Dree wore when she worked came toward them. Franklin got out, gave her a hug, then, when Dree climbed down, introduced her. "Dree Blake, meet my daughter, Francine Schultz. Fran, Dree."

The woman reached a calloused hand out, and Dree shook it. "So, you're the one Wil here's been worryin' over, holding his crotch whenever he gives you a mention!" she said, laughing.

Dree felt herself turn red, saw Wil turn away and stalk off into the barn.

"Fran, behave," Franklin growled.

"Where's the fun there, Dad?"

The man groaned.

"Come on up to the house. Coffee's hot, and I've got fresh cinnamon rolls." She turned and hollered into the barn for Wil.

Half an hour of listening to the joking and catching up between Wil, Franklin, and Francine had Dree coffeed out and stuffed full of butter-dripping, hot cinnamon roll. Feeling the buzz of too much caffeine and sugar, Dree followed them back out to the barn. Inside, a small bunch of calves, all of them already tagged and branded, bawled for their mommas. The mother cows, most of them older, seemed unconcerned, standing or lying leisurely around in a pen outside, some of them even chewing their cuds.

Franklin tapped Dree on the shoulder. "We'll run 'em into that squeeze over there for you, unless you still prefer doing them on the ground."

"Um...the squeeze, please," Francine said.

"The squeeze will work," Dree agreed, though, really, she preferred doing them down.

There were only twenty-some head to be done, but getting them into the squeeze proved difficult. It also provided some interesting entertainment as Franklin and Wil tried to run the calves in as usual. The animals backed, balked, bawled, and bucked, some bracing themselves, legs jammed against the uprights. One even leapt up and over, bouncing off a side board to use Franklin's back as a ramp to escape.

Francine, standing off to the side, was laughing so hard she had tears running down her face. Finally, she called a halt. "I keep telling you, you don't handle my babies that way, Dad."

She stepped forward. "You boys back on out of there, now, and let a woman show you how to get the job done right."

Both Franklin and Wil looked daggers at her, but, brushing themselves off, retreated.

"Come on, Babes. Come to mama." Putting her hand through the rails, she held what Dree swore was an oatmeal-chocolate-chip cookie. The calves eyed it, eyed Franklin and Wil. One of them stepped forward, sniffed, then stepped in and began sucking on it. With a pull of its head, it snapped it off to gum it a bit, then spit it out to begin sucking on the remaining piece Francine still held. Fran closed the squeeze, rubbing the calf on the head, chin, and poll. "Go on ahead, Dree. Just try not to hurt him too much."

Dree use her anesthetic spray, waiting the full two minutes that allowed the topical to penetrate to its deepest, fullest numbing effect. The calf didn't do more than wiggle a bit as she crimped. The job took over an hour, but the calves came out as if nothing had happened.

"We've always been cutters, but I think I actually like this better than cutting," Fran said, picking up one of Dree's burdizzos. "How early can this be done?"

"As soon as both testes are down and you can feel the spermatic cord. Usually that's about a month old."

The woman looked at her, looked at her father. "Have you managed to convince Granddad?"

Franklin nodded. "Yep. Finally."

Francine laughed. "What's it taken, now? Twenty years?"

"'Bout that."

"I want her back here next spring, early, so she can teach me this."

He nodded. "We'll see" Then, "Dree? With me. Wil, get your rope."

They headed over to a line of pens full of yearlings.

"Ah...Mr. Jarvis, these are too old for me to—"

He stopped and turned to look down on her. "You're not castrating, just looking."

"Ah...okay."

Wil jogged by on a sorrel, pulling up to sidle the animal up to one of the gates and let himself in, the horse backing around easy through the opening, then snugging back to it on the other side while Wil latched the gate shut, again.

Franklin climbed up to sit on the rail. Dree joined him, careful with her leg. "Pick one," he said.

"What?"

"I said pick one. Let's see if your eye for stock is all that Glen claims it is."

"Um...okay." She wondered why the test. Didn't ask. This was a man whom you didn't question, so she just watched as Wil moved slowly through the pasture of twenty-some yearlings, the virgin bulls moving away from the horse as it ambled along easy.

Thinking of Glen's good word and his reputation, she wanted to make sure she actually picked best, so she took her time. She saw four she liked, though all of them were top quality. Of those four, she finally picked the one she thought looked...richest, like good quality chocolate. He was even the color of milk chocolate, though color didn't make the bull. "That one." She pointed.

"Good choice." The man's voice was tight. He whistled and pointed, but Wil was ahead of him, already throwing a loop.

Franklin turned to her. "This is my thanks for you saving my Jake when you *should've* run. I'll hear no argument, girl." He jumped down from the fence, leaving Dree to just sit and stare after him. She found herself suddenly breathless, working real hard to pull air.

C. J. "Country" James

16

Homecoming

DREE WATCHED AS HER BULL was driven in last behind a barrier Wil Strakes anchored in with pins. In front of that barrier were another dozen bulls. All of them, including hers, wore rope halters.

Fran came over and handed them each a lidded travel mug and a plastic-wrapped sandwich, along with another cinnamon roll. "For the trip home. Drive safe. There's dumb-assed four-wheelers out there being crazy, y'know."

Franklin laughed, gave Fran a one-armed hug, ruffled the bunch of brown curls sticking out the back of her billed cap, then ducked as she swatted at him. He climbed in, and Wil put the truck in gear, easing down the drive in a granny low crawl.

They pulled into the Jarvis ranch by four, some of the hands joining them to help move the bulls into a waiting pen. Hers they stuck off by himself. "Brand inspector'll be by Monday morning," Franklin told her.

"Best call your dad and tell him you'll be another day late."

Dree did, and then explained why.

"You got your own brand?" Franklin asked her at dinner that night.

"Dad's got—"

"I didn't ask you about your dad's brand. I said 'yours'."

Dree blinked at him, realizing that the bull was to become her sole property. Again, she felt her face go red, a curse from her mom, just like her figure was one thanks to her dad's side of the family. "Ah...no."

The man nodded, then turned to Wil. Get out the freeze branding unit and make sure that darned tank's still okay."

"So, what's your plan for him," Old Man Jarvis asked her.

Dree took a small breath, held it, then, despite knowing they were just being polite, told them, "I'm going to try to pull a few mother cows I think are best from Dad's herd and run them with him, probably in one of the pastures near the house to keep them separate from the rest."

The elderly man grinned, then, with a nod, went back to forking up slices of roast beef.

Nobody else even paused their fork-to-mouth movements. Better, nobody chuckled. Olivia did shoot her an angry glance, though, and Dree couldn't figure out what she'd done to the girl.

FINALLY RELEASED BY THE DOCTORS, not Sunday, but Monday around eleven after yet another MRI, Jake talked his mom into running him over to the ranch instead of her taking him home with her to Missoula. "You're not supposed to ride or work for another four-to-six weeks, Jake."

"I won't," he assured her, and, when she shot him a disbelieving look, said, "Promise."

"I'll tell Lane to take a bull whip to you if you do," she warned.

"Yes, Mom."

Franklin, Lane, Wil, and his great-granddad were waiting, all grins, when they drove in. Jake got out, and a whinny rang out—Coal. With a quick look to Franklin, Jake put fingers to his lips and let out a shrill, double whistle.

The colt circled his pen, bouncing into a lope, then launched himself over the fence to come running as Franklin groaned and his great-grandfather laughed his gleeful 'hee-hee'.

"You're going to be real sorry one day that you taught him that," Wil said, but he was grinning, too, as the horse trotted up, tossing his head, then stopping up short to shove his nose under Jake's armpit.

Jake scratched. "You keep saying that, Wil, but I don't notice you stopping your mare doing it."

"Not illegal to have a mare running loose on open range, Jake. A stallion, it is. Now, if you want to geld him...."

Jake scratched Coal, rolling an eye toward the foreman. "No thanks. I'll just build him a taller fence if it winds up being a problem. So far, it hasn't."

"Lunch is ready," Marguerite said, poking her head out. "Welcome home, Jake. You look like a coati," she added, referring to his still blackened eyes, nose, and cheek.

"Thanks, Marguerite."

Olivia, standing behind and to the side of her mother, gave him a big smile. Jake's eyes glued themselves to her neckline that showed way too much cleavage. Frowning, he turned away and whispered to Franklin. "I think I've got a problem."

"Oh?"

"Olivia."

Franklin dropped his head, hat shading his eyes. He kicked dirt. When he raised his head, an odd smile played around the corners of his mouth. "So you just noticed, did you?"

"And what did you say you did to win you a good bull like this?"

Dree watched her dad eyeing the animal as she ran him out into a pen. "I helped his grandson get home after some man beat him up."

"What? Is the kid six?"

"No. He's...probably my age."

"Real tough man if he has to get rescued by a girl. I'd say you came out on top of this deal, though."

"I want to bring a few cows in and run Chocolate here with them in the horse's winter pasture, if that's okay. It's time the horses went out to summer grazing, anyway." She watched her father's face, but he didn't react. "I've got plenty hay enough still stored."

He shrugged. "Chocolate, huh?" He sighed, shook his head, then, pushing himself away from the fence, went back to the house.

♦

It took Dree all of April and part of May to select which cows she wanted, then drive them and their calves into the field where she would feed them till she knew they were bred. Driving the cow-calf pairs away from their herd wasn't easy, but, with the dogs' help, she got it done.

She settled for thirty-four cows she thought were the best—less than she'd hoped for, but all of them decent animals. "A bit less quality than you'd hoped for, huh, Chocolate? Sorry about that." The bull, trained to lead and quite friendly, actually, now came for treats and scratches through the fence when he saw her approach.

She was mowing her first cutting way early, the second week in May, when she saw her small herd run past, Chocolate with them. Her dad was hazing them, riding his buckskin.

Getting off the tractor, she ran, but they were gone by the time she reached the fence.

That night at dinner, she asked what had happened.

"I ran them out where they belong, Dree."

"You said I could—"

"No, I didn't. You assumed."

"He's my bull."

"Maybe. But he's on my ranch, and those are my cows. If you don't like it, you're welcome to go round up your...Chocolate and haul him off to the sale yard."

DODGING OLIVIA PROVED HARDER than Jake expected. The girl didn't seem to understand the word 'no'...which was the same in her native language as it was in his. Unlike Franklin and his great-granddad, Jake couldn't speak more than a couple of phrases in Spanish, so he was pretty much reduced to 'no' and the word '*vete*'—'go away' in Spanish.

Still, the girl went out of her way to be near him and, him being stuck at the house, she was hard to avoid. Finally, desperation drove him to saddle up and head out to where he knew Franklin was working with a crew to reset the center pivots. He kept Coal to a walk, going easy. He still got chewed out for it, though. "It's Olivia. Won't leave me alone."

"I'll have a talk with Marguerite," Franklin said with a heavy sigh. "All right. Since you're here, see if you can get that darned computer in there to do what it's supposed to."

Jake laughed. "Sure."

It was Olivia who brought them out lunch. Franklin headed her off before she could get to him, though. That lasted till after dinner. Then, the girl ferreted him out in the barn as he brushed down Coal.

Turning on her, he frowned. "Olivia, leave me the *hell* alone. Stay away. *Vete*! I *mean* it."

Franklin came in, said something to the girl in Spanish—hard words, by the sound of it—and Olivia fled, tears streaming down her face. "She's off to Mexico come summer break from school. Just keep trying to steer your way clear till then. I had a word with Marguerite, but she tells me she's got little control over the girl, now that she's turned fifteen. In her culture, fifteen is considered adulthood and twelve is the age of consent."

Jake paused his hand and turned to his grandfather. "Twelve?!"

Franklin didn't respond.

"…Maybe she needs to go live someplace else."

"I can't turn the kid out, Jake."

"You'd fire any man here if he acted like that."

"They aren't kids."

"According to what you just said, she's considered an adult by Mexico standards."

"I didn't turn you out at fifteen when you started sewing wild oats, did I?"

Jake felt his face burn. He dropped his eyes away.

"*Did* I?"

"No, sir." *You practically hog-tied me.*

17

Chocolate

DREE WOUND UP loading Chocolate into her trailer and hauling him to the barn to have the vet stitch him up after her father's mature bulls ran him off through the fence. Then, she spent a day mending the broken fences.

The following week, after calling Franklin Jarvis and once she got the last of her bales shipped off on the hay broker's trucks, she loaded the bull into her trailer and started the long drive up to the Jarvis ranch. Her trailer broke an axle right after turning onto the old highway, now a county road, again, that led up to the Jarvis two-mile-long drive. She was some eight miles short of the ranch entrance. As usual, cell service was nil, nor were there any houses in sight. It was after five.

Working out how many hours she had until sundown and wishing she'd brought Cougar along, she slapped a note on the dash, slipped some nose tongs into her backpack just to be safe, then, calling the dogs, locked up the truck.

Unloading Chocolate, she started walking, the bull willing and calm, even when somebody's horses galloped up to the fence.

It was hot, and she cursed herself for not bringing more than one small bottle of water. Still, eight miles was do-able before dark, and she'd be darned if she was going to spend a night hunkered down in the truck, only to face the same problem come morning, all of them thirsty and hungrier.

"THOUGHT YOU SAID THAT BLAKE GIRL was going to be here by dinner time," Old Man Jarvis said, eyeing Franklin.

"Well, she said she'd be here around five-thirty or so," Franklin said, not lifting his eyes from the paper.

"She's not here, yet."

Jake rolled his eyes. One of the funny things about his great-grandpa was the way he used the obvious to press home a point that he expected you to act on. But he never got around to spitting out the actual point. "Maybe she had a breakdown," Jake offered.

Old Man Jarvis twisted his head to squint over at him. "Yep. My thinkin', too."

Franklin put his paper down. "I've got her number. I'll give it a try," he said, and, pushing himself out of his chair, went into his office. He came out about five minutes later. "She's not answering. I called her dad's place, and he said she left sometime around noon he thinks. We'll give her a little while, yet. She could've been held up by the construction."

"Why's she bringing the bull back?" Jake asked. He knew about Franklin's gift to her of the animal.

"She didn't go into detail, and I didn't ask."

"Not good enough for her?"

"Jake."

Marguerite held dinner till six-thirty, but the girl still hadn't shown up. Franklin ate fast, then, instead of pouring himself a whiskey, got up and pulled out his keys. "I'm going looking."

"We'll hold the fort," Old Man Jarvis said.

"You want company?" Wil asked.

"Nope. You go on home. I got it."

DREE PULLED CHOCOLATE DOWN off the road and called the dogs as a truck came in sight. The bull got busy eating, then, with a pull, headed toward where the dogs were getting themselves a drink from some water running into a culvert that ran under the road.

The truck stopped. "A little late to be walking your big, brown dog, Dree."

Dree looked up to see Franklin Jarvis sitting above. "I broke down. Trailer axle."

"And you thought you'd just hoof it the rest of the way, did you?"

"I didn't see much choice."

"Where's your rig?"

"Back a ways."

"Well, leave him here," he said, tipping his hat toward the bull. "You and your dogs hop in. We'll go get a trailer."

Dree unsnapped the lead, and let Chocolate go, giving him a fond scratch in his favorite place under his chin. Then she climbed up the bank and got in, the dogs scrambling up to lie on the floorboard at her feet.

The bull climbed up the bank, too, following as Franklin turned the truck around.

The man frowned. "What's he doing?"

"Um…probably trying to follow us."

Sure enough, when Franklin headed down the road, the bull galloped after them. Franklin slowed, and, with a sigh, said, "Okay. He comes, too. We take it slow, I guess."

"Thanks," Dree said, a catch in her voice. Her eyes were stinging bad.

By EIGHT, FRANKLIN WASN'T BACK. Jake eyed his great-granddad, and Old Man Jarvis nodded, got up, and went to get his boots on. "Hook up to one of the stock trailers, Jake," he said as he climbed in the passenger seat. "Just to be on the safe side, mind."

They found them crawling along in granny low about a mile from the bottom of the drive, the bull walking along beside the passenger-side window. "Well, would you lookee there," Old Man Jarvis called out the window, his voice gleeful. "It's a Jarvis bull, pretty as you please."

Jake pulled to a stop beside Franklin. "Need a ride?"

"Need that trailer."

"I'll turn around."

Jake watched Dree Blake call the bull and walk him into the trailer, no lead, no nothing, him just following her like a dog. He saw the stitches on the animal's head, brisket, shoulders, and legs, vet wrap on one of them just under the animal's left knee. He itched to ask her what happened, but kept his mouth shut.

Back at the ranch, they unloaded 'Chocolate' into one of the pens, and threw him some hay. "Can I get a small can of grain for him?" the girl asked. "It keeps his mind off me changing his bandage and putting salve on his stitches."

Jake rolled an eye toward Franklin, and Franklin returned the look. The girl cared about the damned bull. And he *was* a darned good-looking animal—one of the best of last year's crop. But, still. This was a pet, not an animal fit for the range, anymore.

Jake braved the question as, grain poured, the girl worked loose the vet wrap to expose a nasty, long cut, neatly sutured, obviously by a real veterinarian, not just a farm job. But the wound was a long way from healed. "How'd he get hurt?"

It took her a long time to answer. When she did, it came out slowly, him teasing it out of her with 'why's' and 'how comes'. Franklin waved him silent when the girl gave a shuddering sigh and laid her head against the bull's belly, just leaning there.

Franklin put his hand on her shoulder, took the tube of antibiotic salve from her hand, and urged her to her feet. "Marguerite saved you a plate," he said. "Come on. We're done here."

◆

"WHY THE HELL WOULD HER DAD take all her hard work of roundin' up those cows and just throw it to the wind? And what fool turns a yearling bull out with growed up senior range bulls?" Old Man Jarvis demanded. "It's his daughter, for God's sake. Don't he care?"

Jake agreed. His granddad, though, just shook his head...didn't respond.

"It ain't right."

"We don't know her dad's side," Franklin finally said. "There's always at least two sides."

"What are we going to do with him?" Jake asked. "He's too tame to turn loose with a herd."

"Take him back to Heron. Use him for the next generation."

Jake frowned. "You going to linebreed with him, then?"

Franklin nodded. "I'm thinking on it...have been. We're running out of good sources for fresh blood. In fact, I think we're running the widest heterozygous blood pool of heavy marblers in the U.S. and Canada, so, unless we import Herefords from Britain or move to adding in Devons, we're going to have to start crossing back."

Predictably, Old Man Jarvis opposed both imports and adding Devon blood. He shook his head. "No. Not so long as my feet stay 'bove ground. We stick with Herefords—U.S. of A., All-American-bred Herefords—like we always have. You don't mess with what's workin'."

"He's a darned fine bull," Franklin said. "I was hoping she wouldn't pick him when I took her out to the Heron place. Glen's right. She's got a good eye. Real good."

"And, now, he's ruined," Jake said. "Leave it to a girl."

Old Man Jarvis turned in his chair. "Francine's a girl, and she can rope a greased hog and you can't, Jake Jarvis, never mind how good she runs stock. What you got against that Blake girl, anyway? What she ever done to you?"

Jake shrugged, but his great-grandpa just kept staring. "She's...she's just...a girl."

"Seems to me, son, you owe her your life. If she'd run like she shoulda, if her dogs hadn't taken a piece out of that Carter fellow, chances are he'd a kicked you till you didn't have nothing left but mush for brains."

Jake frowned and sat forward. "I didn't know we had any proof it was him. I–I thought it was him, but, afterwards...well, I couldn't say for sure if it was or not. Everything just got jumbled."

Franklin eyed him. "You remembered enough to set the police on his trail. He confessed after the doctor who treated him for dog bites got suspicious and reported it. The deputies questioned Carter again, and he confessed."

His granddad shifted his eyes away, what Jake knew was anger making his face a sudden mask as his index finger tapped the chair's arm twice. Over it that fast, Franklin brought his face back. "Judge only gave him six months in jail, though, then two years on parole when he agreed to take something they call 'anger management'. He'll be out by Thanksgiving."

He sighed. Then: "Good thing to come out of this, Glen's postponed his retirement indefinitely. State canned Carter."

"So, back to the bull," Old Man Jarvis said, leaning forward. "I like him. And I don't mind at all that he's full on tame. Most of our stock is tamer than average, anyway, cuz of Fran and that we handle 'em more here. I admit, the name 'Chocolate' gives me a chuckle, but I'm bettin' we get some darn good stock by him."

Franklin nodded. "Agreed."

"We'll wind up having to pen him up separate, though," Jake argued.

Franklin rolled a glance his way. "So? We do that with Number 843 and old Number 9, too."

"That's because they're valuable. ...And old. This bull's not even proven, yet."

"He'll prove. Mark my words," Old Man Jarvis said. "He'll prove."

C. J. "Country" James

18

Trade Up

O VER BREAKFAST THE NEXT MORNING, after Dree pulled out Chocolate's paperwork and signed him over, Franklin told her what they planned for him. It was more than she'd hoped for. He'd have a better life than what she could ever give him.

Out at his pen, she dressed his wounds one last time. "Okay. You're officially home," she told him, scratching his neck.

Then, with a promise to mail the trailer title and signing a bill of sale for it for a buck so Franklin could junk it, she called her dogs, got in her truck, and headed for home.

◆

H E LEANED ON THE COUNTER, too close, watching her. "You just *gave* him back?"

Dree focused on scrubbing a blackened pot her dad had burned trying to heat himself up some dinner the previous night.

"That bull was worth at least a couple of thousand dollars, Dree! What happened to all that learning you got with that fancy degree?"

She poured more Bar Keeper's onto her sponge and went back to scratching at a particularly burned-on spot. Giving up, she got out a pad of steel wool.

"Okay. I admit. He was yours to do with as you please."

Finally, he retreated to the living room just as the last bit of burn let loose its grip on the stainless steel. She put the pot in the dishwasher with the rest of the second load and started the machine. Then, instead of going out to check fence, she decided to vacuum.

From the corner of her eye, she watched his mouth say something, but ignored him, taking her time going over and over a particularly heavily-traveled spot on the living room carpet. Finally, he snapped off the TV with the remote and stomped out the door. From the window, she watched him drive off down the county road.

She finished the vacuuming, then threw a load of clothes in the washer. Done, she took a walk, her dogs coming with her, her feet pulling her over to check on her fields before she headed down to the creek. She loved this place. She loved the life. What she didn't love was the struggle, but, no matter how hard she tried, it just didn't work out. "Day late and a whole dollar short; too late and too little"—her Gram Blake's sayings. Then, getting a wild hair, Dree got up and headed back to the house. Time to buy a new trailer. "And a new truck."

SURPRISED, JAKE PULLED OVER and parked, then just sat watching. It was the Blake girl's pickup, pulling a brand spanking new, white stock trailer. It was parked in front of the Jimmy lot. He waited over a half an hour, then shrugged and reached for the key.

A man came out, walked around her truck, then disappeared back the way he'd come. Jake sat back and decided to wait a little bit longer.

He was rewarded a few minutes later when Dree Blake got into her truck, started it with a sputter of black smoke, and drove into the lot. Fifteen minutes later, she drove out pulling the trailer with a shiny red, used GMC 3500, a 2007 diesel by the look of it. "Good choice, Ms. Blake."

He grinned. Maybe he wouldn't wind up stuck behind her struggling up the hills when he had to go rescue his uncle from Derrick Jones' place.

Following a second whim, he trailed her out of town, staying well back. Predictably, she headed south out of Missoula, following the Bitterroots. Then, exiting the four-lane, she turned down the old highway where he'd all but run her off the road.

Another hour, and, finally, she turned off on a county road. He drove on by.

Stopping at the next town to top off his tanks, he asked a man at a run-down station and snack store if he knew where the Blakes lived.

"Which Blake? There's four of them around here."

"They run cattle."

"They all run cattle, son," the man who was his grandfather's age told him with a laugh. "Except for old Gram Blake, anyway."

"The girl rides a mule?"

"Oh. Jim Blake's place. That's just back up the road here a little ways. Let me give you directions. What's your business?"

"The girl's trailer broke down, and I've got some salvage money for her."

"Good. They can use it. Rough times for them since the missus—"

"George!"—a woman's voice. Jake looked up to see a white-haired woman standing, pen in hand, in a backroom doorway. She was frowning.

The man drew a crude map on a piece of notebook paper. "Anyway, just turn here, and follow the road till you can't go no more, then turn right. They're the first place you'll come to...an older style farmhouse, white, two-story clapboard. Name's on the mailbox."

"Thanks." Jake folded the paper and stuck it in his shirt pocket, then paid cash for the diesel.

◆

'OLDER' DIDN'T DO THE PLACE JUSTICE. It was pure antiquity, from the heavy-railed, late nineteenth- or early twentieth-century corrals to the weathered old outbuildings, all of them run-down and sagging. The only thing close to new on the place was Dree Blake's freshly bought pickup and trailer, and one large, open metal shed where what looked like a couple of old tractors were parked. The house, its windows still single-paned glass, needed paint. Badly.

Jake saw the mule standing in the shade of the barn. It was swatting flies as it pulled hay from a bunk. Off in the distance, he saw a center pivot working—just one.

Shaking his head, he pulled some money out of his wallet—what he figured her old trailer had yielded in scrap, then drove on in and, clipping a note to it, got out and dropped it on the seat through her truck's open driver-side window.

DREE SAW JAKE JARVIS just as he dropped something into her pickup. Waiting until he backed out and drove off, she went to look. Three one-hundred dollar bills with a note attached lay there—a note signed 'Franklin'…except it wasn't Franklin's signature. Of that she was pretty certain. She checked, finding the copy she'd made for her records of the check Franklin Jarvis had given her. No. The note was not signed by Franklin.

She sat down, reached for the phone, then stopped herself. No, she decided. She'd leave it alone. She stuffed the bills in her pocket, wadding up the note and tossing it into the overfilled garbage can sitting next to her dad's desk.

It bounced out.

With a sigh, she picked it up, and, pausing, straightened it out and stuck it into a folder in her file cabinet. Then, she went and did chores, dumping the trash from the waste paper basket into the burn barrel.

19

Girl Trouble

"Y OU CALL WHEN YOU'RE GOING to be late," Franklin said, getting up from his favorite chair. "We waited dinner for you. Now, it's probably ruined, and I ought to let Marguerite skin you."

Franklin stalked past him and headed into the dining room. Waiting for his great-granddad, Wil, Lane, and the rest of the top hands to go in ahead, Jake followed.

Once the food had been passed around, Franklin took up, again. "Where were you?"

Jake toyed with lying, but Franklin always saw through it, said the eyes gave it away. He settled on a hedged truth. "Saw the Blake girl in Missoula. She bought herself a brand new trailer and a used Jimmy— a good one, by the looks of it. Diesel."

Franklin frowned. "That's why you didn't call?"

"That's why I'm late."

"What? You helped her pick out the truck?" Wil asked.

Old Man Jarvis chuckled.

"No. I just saw her rig parked, and watched."

Franklin sat back and, putting his fork down, wiped his mouth, then just waited. When Jake didn't go on, he said, "And?"

Jake shrugged. "Ah...."

Franklin just kept watching him, not eating, just staring him into an answer.

"I followed her out of town."

"Why?" The question was hard-voiced, his grandfather's face stern.

"Just curious, I guess."

"How far?"

Jake sighed. He shouldn't have said anything. He should have made up some excuse. "All the way to her...her dad's ranch."

Franklin's eyes had that hooded look that always reminded Jake of a rattlesnake ready to strike.

"The place is really run down." He was trying to deflect with reasons or, at least, information, what he knew was boiling up in his granddad.

"Is that any of your business?"

"No, sir." Jake's eyes shifted to Wil, then to his great-granddad. They kept their eyes on their plates, as did the rest at table, everyone's forks almost mechanical in moving food to their faces. No help anywhere. Jake worked on cutting his meat. "There's a pretty new center pivot in one of the fields, though—still shiny— so they can't be doing too bad." He was trying for nonchalance. "Looks like one big enough to cover a full quarter sect—"

"Jake!"

Getting angry, Jake put his knife and fork down, then sat back. He didn't dare look at his granddad. He'd blow if he did. "I didn't do anything wrong, sir. I was just curious. She didn't even know I was there."

There was a long silence, the only sounds that of cutlery clinking on china. Jake waited, staring straight ahead at the opposite wall. His jaw had gone rigid. So had his hands. He fought for easy, but couldn't get there. "I didn't do anything wrong."

Silence.

Jake waited, damned if he was going to apologize, bargain, or beg.

Finally, Franklin broke it. "She's not one of your *floozies*, Jake. She's a *good* girl. Glen's known her since she was a young kid. You stay *away* from her."

Jake flinched at 'floozies', but, biting his temper down, turned straight eyes to his granddad. "Yes, sir."

♦

B UT HE COULDN'T. Maybe it was because Franklin ordered him not to, forbidden fruit being that most desired, but Jake found himself any excuse to head south—tracking down machine parts, mostly. Any time he managed it, which, admittedly, was rare, he found himself rolling past the Blake's driveway, once on the way down, then, again, on the way back, no matter how much he swore to himself that he wouldn't. One thing he did manage, though: he always made sure he was back home before dinner. No questions asked, no excuses to make or battles to fight.

When the Blake girl's slate eyes invaded his dreams, though, he stopped going. Then, one of his dreams woke him up.

Breath on his face, a hand on his thigh near his groin…. Sitting bolt upright, he froze. "What the hell?!"

"Shhhhh."

He flicked on the light and let out a yelp. *"Vete! VETE!"*

Feet in the corridor…his door slamming open. The girl clutching herself, a filmy, short teddy barely covering her nakedness. Franklin stormed in, grabbed her, and hustled her out, only glancing back long enough to bark, "You lock your door from now on!"

Jake's whole body was rigid. Jail was not an experience he ever wanted to have. Not for anybody. Especially not for some girl.

Franklin came back a while later, tried the door, then knocked. "Jake? Let me in."

Dressed, now, Jake unlocked it. "I'm going to Mom's, Grandpa."

"I need you here."

"She...she." He shook his head and turned away. "I don't *need* this. You already think I'm a sum bitch. I'm not. I haven't been out with a girl, haven't *had* a girl, since you caught me drunk in town. I quit 'em. Cold."

He turned. "For *you*. But you still think I'm a— Never mind."

He pulled his travel bag from his closet, opened drawers, and started stuffing in underwear, socks, and tees.

A hand clamped down on his shoulder. "Stay. I've given Marguerite notice. She and Olivia are gone at first light."

Jake sank down on the bed. "It's not just that. I haven't told you. I've been...." He sucked in breath, then let it out slow. "I've been having these dreams."

Franklin sat down beside him. "About?"

Jake sighed, again. "Okay. I'm going to be honest with you. And I don't want you bull butting me, cuz, damn it, I don't need or deserve it."

Jake waited for some kind of acknowledgment and finally got it. "All right," Franklin agreed, the first time Jake could ever remember his granddad agreeing to a deal with him Franklin hadn't himself brokered.

"I couldn't not go. Maybe because you told me not. I kept going down past the Blake's place anytime I had some excuse."

He heard his grandfather breathe out hard.

Jake got up, backed up, stood facing the man he respected most in the world. Looked him straight in the eye. It was the only way. "Then I stopped going. Had to. She—the Blake girl—she's been showing up in my dreams. Her eyes…. Only her eyes. And I don't even *like* her."

Jake wanted to bury his head. Just like he had when, as a little kid, he'd buried his face in his pillow when his dad came home drunk, raging at his mom. "I don't even like her."

The silence between them lasted for longer than seconds. Jake heard the old grandfather clock down in the great room strike the half-hour. He just stood, his eyes pulled to the window where, faintly, light was just thinking about coloring sky above the Black Badger where his great-great-grandfather had built the first Jarvis ranch house. "I don't know what to do."

Franklin blew a huge, heavy sigh. Jake heard him get up. Then, Franklin surprised him when, instead of leaving, he came over and slid a hand, then his whole arm, across Jake's shoulders, his hand grasping him hard. "I don't know, either, Jake. ...But, maybe, you better find out. I give you my blessing to go get it sorted."

The man turned him to face, then. "Just promise me to keep your fly zipped and your hands to yourself."

"I will."

C. J. "Country" James

20

Groceries & Ice

HER DAD HAD TAKEN HER TRUCK. Again. Didn't even ask if she needed it. And she did. They needed some groceries from town, and she needed menstrual pads and tampons, both.

She dialed his cell…got no answer and left a message on his voice mail, not that he'd probably check it. Then she went searching to try to find the keys to *his* truck—no luck. "Probably still in your pocket!"

"So, I'm supposed to, what, Dad? Drive the 40-40 to town?" She sank down on the couch, thought about saddling Cougar, nixed that idea, and called Sheila Goldsmith, down the road.

The old lady answered on the fourth ring. "Can't today, Dree. I'm sorry. I've got some sort of bug keeping me hugging the toilet."

"Is there anything I can do?"

"No, honey. 'This too shall pass.'"

Dree chuckled, catching it. "Okay. Call if you need me."

The crunch of gravel on the drive caught her ear, and, hanging up, she burst out the back door, expecting that it was her dad back earlier than usual. She stopped dead. It was Jake Jarvis's black truck. The young man got out, lifted his hat to her, then just stood there. "Hi."

"Hi," she said cautiously. "What do you want?"

"Nothing. Just in the neighborhood and thought I'd say hi."

He was wearing 'Sunday clothes', if all black, though it was only Saturday. "You come from a funeral, or something?"

"No." Then, "Where's your truck?"

"Which one?"

He paused, his eyes shifting to scan the drive and turn-around, catching on her dad's blue Ford. "The white one."

"I got rid of it."

"Oh."

"I bought a newer one."

"Oh? Where's it?"

"It's not here, right now."

"Oh."

This was ridiculous. "Jake Jarvis, I don't know who you think you're fooling with, but I know you know I have a different truck. I saw you when you dropped that money into it the very day I brought it home...not twenty minutes after I brought it home. So, what do you want? Why are you here?"

He shook his head. "I told you. I was in the neighborhood and thought I'd look you up."

"Okay. You've come. Now go. Goodbye."

She turned and was halfway through the door when he yelled, "Wait!"

She paused to look at him. He'd moved closer. "You need to leave."

"Aren't you even going to ask me in for iced tea or something? Lemonade, maybe?"

"No."

"Can we sit on the porch?" He tipped his head toward the veranda on the front of the house.

"No."

He took a step back. "Okay. I'll leave."

Dree's mind was whirling. "Hang on. There *is* something you can do. You can drive me into town. I need to get groceries and, as you can see, Dad took my truck."

"Okay. Be glad to," he said.

"I'll get changed. I'll be quick."

Why she was doing this, she didn't know...except that she desperately needed the pads and tampons. Jerking on clean jeans and shirt, she brushed her hair and twisted it up, anchoring it with a jaw clip. She looked like she felt—terrible. She let it back out and settled for it loose.

Scribbling a note for her dad in case he came home, she called the dogs and headed toward the barn.

"They can come, you know."

She turned around. "Okay. Thanks."

♦

D REE HAD NEVER SAT on leather seats before. Well, she guessed she might have in Franklin's car that awful night, but she hadn't noticed them. Sitting on these, she was surprised by their comfort. The whole rig was tuck-and-roll top-of-the-line. "Nice," she said.

"What?"

"The truck."

"Oh."

"Is that all you say, anymore?"

"No."

She turned to look out the window, suddenly uncomfortable.

"What grocery store do you go to?"

Her discomfort vanished in a bolt of laughter she couldn't stop. "There's only one grocery store in town, Jake Jarvis. Three bars, two churches, one grocery, a dry goods, the farm store, and two gas stations, only one of which sells diesel and DEF. The drug store is part of the grocery store, but only open two days a week when a pharmacist comes down from up north."

"Oh."

Dree turned her head, studying him from the corner of her eye. His hands—both of them—were white-knuckled on the wheel. His head was cocked oddly forward and tipped her direction so that the brim of his very expensive black Stetson obscured all of his face except his mouth and chin. This wasn't the cocky, full-of-himself guy she remembered from spring. He was almost sullen, where, before she'd asked him to run her to town, he'd been hesitant, but still.... What? Open? Probably resented taking her shopping. Typical. She turned to the window, again.

"Is there a café?"

She looked over at him. "Yes."

"Do they serve sundaes?"

Dree blinked at the question. "Yes."

"Do you want.... Could we stop and.... How about we stop and have one...two...you one and me one. It's hot."

Again, Dree found herself laughing. Grabbing a hold of herself, practically hiccupping, she said, "Sure. I'd love to. They make them the old-fashioned way in the old-fashioned tulip-style glasses. They even put nuts and a cherry on top. Suit you?"

"Yeah."

"Okay."

Silence. He was driving really, really slow, she realized. Then figured out it was to preserve the truck's pristine paint job. Oh, the all-important Boyz Toyz. Her father was just that picky about his new TV when she tried to dust it. She had to go real slow and easy. Might scratch it.

"Grocery store first or sundaes first?"

Jolted, she said, "Grocery store. They close early on Saturday."

"The cold stuff will warm up."

"I'll get ice."

"Okay."

21

Hot Fudge & Rabbit Holes

JAKE WANTED TO KICK HIMSELF up side of the head. She didn't want him coming into the store with her, and he didn't blame her. Even to himself, he sounded like an imbecile. He just didn't do girls well, not unless they came onto *him*. And they always had. Then, it was easy—just stand back and let 'em. It helped that the Jarvis brand was painted on the side of his truck. This, though, was a lot harder.

He didn't feel anything, though—not when she'd come out of the house, not in the truck. So why was he cold-sweating? Why did her eyes keep haunting him?

She was coming out.

He got out, and, taking a couple of the bags out of the cart, opened the truck box and started putting them in. She handed him the next couple, and he slid those in, too. All of them were tied neatly shut…with square, not granny, knots. That sort of impressed him.

"Here's the ice," she said, handing over a plastic bag holding a solid, square block of it.

He slipped it in next to the groceries and shut the lid. "Where's the café?"

"Across the street." She pointed.

He nodded. "Let me park over down by those trees. ...Shade for the dogs. Hop in."

♦

THE CAFÉ WAS ALMOST EMPTY—a couple of kids playing the game machines and a white-haired couple having a meal. Jake let her pick where to sit, sliding in across from her in the booth she chose. "You hungry?"

She looked at him, those slate-colored eyes reaching down into him, making him feel like she was seeing him naked—not his body, but himself, some scared little kid. He didn't like it. He didn't want her to stop, though. He wanted to either get used to it or get over it, her haunting him.

"Yes, I guess I am," she answered, finally.

"We can have the sundaes after, if that's okay. I haven't eaten since breakfast."

"Okay."

They ordered from the menus stuck between the sugar dispenser and the napkin holder when the waitress came around offering water, soda, coffee, hot or iced tea, lemonade, hard cider, beer, or wine. Jake got water and ordered a steak.

"Don't," Dree said. "You're too spoiled on your own beef. You'll hate this. Try their lasagna. It's great."

He took her word for it, and, when it came—when both platters of it came, because she ordered it, too—he wasn't sorry. "This is really good."

"It is, isn't it?"

She smiled as she said it, and she was almost pretty when she smiled…which usually wasn't too often, he remembered. "How come your dad took your wheels?"

He saw right away that it was the wrong thing to ask. "Sorry."

"It's okay. He just does."

"That year 3500 diesel Jimmy is a really good truck."

"How come you're driving a RAM, then?"

He laughed. "Because that's what Franklin likes. He bought it for me."

"I like Franklin. He's…straight up."

Jake couldn't help himself. "He's the absolute best," he blurted, and saw her blink at him oddly. "What?"

"He's your granddad, right?"

"Yeah."

"Where's your dad?"

Jake sat back and looked out the window. "Probably down at the bar, right now, soused on his ass."

"Oh."

Again, he was sorry he'd said it. Dodging a glance at her, though, she didn't seem shocked. "Sorry."

"Why do you keep apologizing? My dad drinks, too. Too much. In fact, if you look down the street, you'll see my truck down there, nosed in at Trixie's."

Jake didn't have to look, but he did anyway, just so it didn't look like he'd already noticed...which he had when he'd driven through town. "I think it's a thing for their generation."

"And ours. And the ones before and after ours," she said. "Uncle Bill's truck and Cousin John's truck are down there, too. The bar is their regular meet-up. ...And my mom drank."

"Your mom and dad, are they divorced?"

He watched her eyes drop, her face get stony. Again, he said, "Sorry," but this time she just looked away. He picked up the thread. "My mom doesn't drink. She just works and goes home. She's an R.N. Works in ICU."

He let it sit, waiting her out, pretending to watch out the window between bites of lasagna.

"How come you don't live at home?"

It was fair—her touching a sore spot since he had. He pulled a breath, kept his eyes out the window. "Franklin pulled me out of there when Dad put Mom in the hospital. He tried to get her to come, too, but she's old-fashioned that way—stick to your man, and all. Franklin wouldn't let me go back, not till I was sixteen, and, by then, I didn't want to."

"How old were you?"

He looked at her. "Six."

She nodded, started to say something...stopped.

"Say...or ask. What?"

"Does your dad still...hurt your mom?"

Jake shook his head. "No. Franklin took care of that. I don't know how, but I don't think Dad has ever touched Mom since. Not any way, at all, ever. I'm an only."

"They still live together?"

"Yeah. But Mom owns the house and the cars. Dad doesn't own anything. Signed something Franklin had drawn up. Franklin.... Well, he kinda rules the whole clan." He sat back and grinned, then. "We're a tough bunch, and it's good he does, even if it sounds bad."

"It doesn't sound bad. My Gram Blake is almost the same way, but she does it with money."

The waitress came back, and they ordered their sundaes. He got himself a banana split. She ordered hot fudge. "You like chocolate?" he asked.

"I love it, but only the really good kind that's way too expensive. I do love hot fudge sundaes, though."

"I don't much eat chocolate, except for hot cocoa in winter when Marguerite— When Marguerite used to make it."

"Used to?"

Jake sighed. Told her what happened.

"What's going to happen to her?"

"Who? Olivia?" He shrugged.

"Marguerite. She lost her job."

"Franklin got her one with some doctor over in Missoula who was looking for a cook-housekeeper."

"Oh. That was nice."

"Yeah."

D REE FELT LIKE SHE'D FALLEN into Alice's rabbit hole. She, Dree Blake, was sitting in a café having an early dinner and dessert with a man who was handsome, polite, and heir to a small cattle empire. This was not the real Dree Blake. This was some imposter, some schizophrenic double sitting here while she, the real Dree Blake, cowered in a corner of herself.

But she liked it—really liked it. Even though she knew the man sitting across from her could be a real jackass...or at least a brat. She had firsthand experience with that side of him. Still, this was *some* life out-take. She could almost think herself pretty if she didn't know better. "So why are you here?" she asked, reality completely and suddenly landing hard on the heels of the 'happy'.

He stammered. Finally said, "You were on my mind."

"Why?"

He shrugged...looked out the window. "Just were."

Dree scraped up the last of her sundae. "You should finish," she said, pointing at his half-eaten split.

"Would you step out with me? Maybe dinner...a real dinner out and a movie or something?"

'Step out'—it was an old-fashioned phrase Dree hadn't heard coming out of anyone's mouth except, maybe, her Gram Blake's. Her knee-jerk response was "no, never." She managed to squelch it, and, rearranging her words, smiled first. "I don't date, Jake. Haven't since once in high school, and that was the prom."

"Oh." Then, "Why not?"

Dree fought an impulse to tell him, "None of your business!" Instead, she just shook her head. "I just don't."

He took a bite of his split, licking the spoon. "You could maybe make an exception, right?"

"No."

"Is this because I acted like such an ass in the barn or are you still mad that I almost clipped you?"

Dree watched his eyes—no humor there. He was serious. "I don't hold grudges. You apologized, and I accepted that apology. That's history."

He sat quiet, watching her in a way that irked her. Did all the Jarvis men do this? Franklin sure had it mastered, and it looked like Jake did, too. She drew a big breath, sighed it out, then, reluctantly, shared more history. "I don't date because the one date I went on wound up with my dress ruined." And it was her turn to look away. She felt her face burn, rolled her eyes at herself, then, schooling herself, faced forward, again.

He was frowning...stirring his ice cream around until the rest of the strawberry was thoroughly mixed with the vanilla and chocolate. He stabbed a piece of banana and ate it. "I'm not like that."

"Maybe not, but I'm done. I'm perfectly happy without all that kind of drama. If I want drama, I'll go act in a play."

His eyes reached for hers—incredulous, disbelieving. "Serious?"

"Serious."

Something seemed to switch in him. He got...bolder, more like himself like he was during branding. "How about a horseback ride? ...Just on your ranch. I could bring Coal down—"

She got bolder, too...felt herself find herself. "No."

Again, he looked out the window, his eyes far away. "Okay."

"Are you done with your banana split?"

"Yeah." He stood up, grabbed the ticket.

"I'll pay my half, please." She took her wallet out.

He just looked down at her—shades of his grandfather—then shook his head. "No." His voice was ice. He went to the counter to pay, came back to drop a couple of tens on the table, then stood waiting.

Dree let him escort her out to where the truck was parked, actually let him lay a light, guiding hand on her back. She wanted to run. She felt like the whole damned town was watching her from behind their sheers, drapes, and curtains. The gossip would be flying tonight— *"That dumpy Blake girl out with some tall, handsome stranger What brand was that on his truck?"*

Grumpy Dree, Dumpy Dree, frumpy, dumpy, grumpy Dree—the childhood taunt rang in her ears on the stone silent trip all the way back to the ranch. At least she had groceries and her personal necessities. ...And a memory keepsake—her first dinner out with a man. *And last.*

FRANKLIN WAS WAITING UP when he got home at nine. "How'd it go?"

Jake flopped down on the couch across from him, threw his hat on the coffee table. "Okay, at first."

"And?"

Jake shook his head. "And she says she doesn't date. Won't step out with me. Won't even go for a horseback ride on her own place. ....I offered to bring Coal down, even."

His granddad didn't say anything.

"I guess somebody roughed her up on her prom night. Says that was her first and last date." He kicked off his boots, and put his feet up. "She let me buy her dinner at the café in town, though. And take her grocery shopping. Her dad took her truck and left her to walk. He was down at one of the local watering holes when I drove into town."

Franklin still didn't say anything.

Jake got up and got coffee from the kitchen, then settled back in. He was real glad *this* was home.

"Are you over her, now?"

Jake rolled his eyes. "I don't know. I guess. ...Maybe."

He heard his grandfather sigh. After another minute or so, Franklin got up. "I'm going to bed."

Wide awake, Jake stayed up watching movies till two.

22

Dust Up

H E WASN'T OVER HER. He knew that by
Tuesday. Her eyes, the feel of his hand on
her back, even her smile and the way her
curls lay soft on her shirt kept coming bright to his
mind. "I'm going back. Going to try, anyway."

They were rewashing the dishes the new help had
slopped through. "We need to can this new guy," Jake
said.

"I know. He cooks well enough, though."

"He burned the steaks."

"He did."

"I'm glad the crew comes in, now. I like having a
big table."

"I do, too, though I'm not used to having the table
stretched its full width and length. We're going to have
to knock out the wall."

"Takes forever to get the rolls passed back up, even
with two baskets of them."

"It's real hard finding a male cook and housekeeper,
Jake."

Jake laughed. "I should think...unless you hire in somebody out of New York or L.A."

Franklin cleared phlegm from his throat. "No."

Jake practically bent double, he was laughing so hard, now. He turned around, planting his butt against the counter edge for support.

"It's not funny, Jake."

"Yes, it is. 'Sex and the Country'."

It was too obvious that the reference went right over his grandfather's head. Jake worked on sobering...failed. They did have a problem, though. The house was beginning to show pretty bad signs of neglect, and Jake hated having to help sweep, mop, vacuum, dust, and do his own laundry. So did the hands. "Isn't there some kind of service out of Missoula?"

"No. I've checked."

"Even if they came once a week. Just to clean up the house and bunkhouse."

"I've called them all. They say it's too far. Not worth their while."

Jake turned back to the sink, replaced the dishwater, then pulled another set of plates, remnants of food glued on them by having been run through the dishwasher without being scraped. "Do they make better dishwashers?"

"Ours is top-of-the-line, Jake. They don't come any better. Are you serious about visiting Dree Blake, again?"

Jake scrubbed. Finally, he answered. "Yes. Just once more. Maybe she just needs a little more coaxing. Like Coal did."

"Why pursue it?"

Jake turned to face. "Because I can't get her out of my mind, even when I'm awake, now."

It was the first time in his life he'd seen his grandfather's eyebrows raise in surprise. Then, the question: "Are you serious about this girl, Jake?!"— incredulity.

He didn't know. "I just want to get to know her a little better."

"Why?"

"I don't *know*."

"She doesn't strike me as your type."

Jake rinsed a plate and stuck it into the drainer. His granddad traded out his damp dishtowel for a dry one as Jake kept his mouth shut, biting down a surge of bitter words. Franklin was right, and he knew it. "She's not arm candy, you mean," he finally said.

"That, yes. And the other."

Earned reputation, branded for life, was the saying, and Jake had the brand, seared pretty deep. "I just...." He shook his head. "I don't know. I told you I didn't know why from the start."

"Is it the challenge? Because she won't have you?"

The answer trued in his mind the minute his grandfather said it. "No."

"You're *sure*?"

It wasn't a question. More like something Franklin was suggesting he think on. And, no, Jake wasn't sure about the challenge part. But he knew he definitely wasn't hankering to lay with the Blake girl. "I'm not interested in *fucking* her, Grandpa."

The man groaned and smacked him up side the head with the dishtowel.

DREE WAS PULLING WEEDS in the garden when Jake Jarvis's truck rolled in about ten. Saturday, again. She stood up and watched him climb down. Today, he was dressed in a white shirt and blue jeans. He wore his everyday boots, but they were shined. He wore the same fancy black hat as last week, though. He walked over. "Hi."

She stared at him, then, finally, said what she wanted to know. "What are you doing back?"

"Came to see you. Can I help?" He tipped his head toward the weeds.

"No, thank you."

"Why not? Two pair of hands work faster than one, and I know the difference between what's vegetables and what's weeds."

"That's surprising, but, no, thank you."

An odd look crossed his face, his head tipping off to the side. Dree felt her resolve wobble and stiffened it back just that fast.

"Come on. Give me a break, would you?"

That sealed it. Same words as prom night! Dree picked up her hand tools and let herself out of the gate, switching the electric fence back on that, for all its strands, didn't keep the deer from getting in.

She put the tools away in the little garden shed, then headed for the house. He trotted to catch up. "Dree, at least can we talk?"

Up the back stairs at a trot, she bolted into the living room, grabbed her twenty-two, and went back to the door. Kicking the screen door open, she stepped out on the landing. "Get gone. Now."

He eyed the gun, eyed her, stepped back, then stopped. "You wouldn't."

She chambered a round. "Try me."

"Dree—"

She pulled the trigger, the bullet catching dirt off toward the tractor lane. In the corral, Cougar jumped, then trotted to the far side and turned to face.

"Leave." From the corner of her eye, she saw her dad come out of the equipment shed.

Jake held out his hand. "Can we just talk?"

"Leave."

"I'm not leaving till you hear me out, woman!"—anger.

Just that fast, she chambered another round, raised, aimed, and fired. His hat blew off, tumbling over the gravel and dust behind him.

He backed up fast, his eyes wide—incredulous—grabbed his hat and, turning his back on her, walked slow and stiff over to his truck. He got in, and, starting it, gunned it, slewing around, spitting gravel. It peppered her. It hit the siding and windows. A rock hit her foot hard enough to sting through her boot and her sock. She watched him spin out the driveway, almost losing control, then tear up the road. She kept watching till his truck disappeared from view.

Her dad walked up. "Good thing you didn't hit him, Dree. You could have hurt him real bad...or worse."

He reached up, his hand asking, and she handed over the rifle. She was shaking all over.

23

9-1-1

HE HIT ADAMS, and, deciding to, pulled in at the first bar he saw—a dingy place that reeked of years of tobacco and spilled beer and whiskey. He didn't care. He didn't care that his best hat had a bullet creasing the crown. "Whiskey straight," he said when the bartender came up. "Give me a double."

The man poured. Jake tossed it back, then pointed. "Another."

He tossed that back, too. "Hit me, again."

The bartender's eyebrows arched, but he poured.

Jake nursed this one, though what he wanted was to down the whole bottle. Reaching bottom, again, he waited a bit, then got one more, this time with a beer chaser.

"Hey, Cowboy."

Jake ignored her.

She sidled up to him, easing herself onto the stool right next to him. He shifted sideways away from her, eyes on the wall. Anger boiled up even worse.

"You look like you could use a friend," she said, her voice soft. She reached her hand out, but didn't touch him, just left it near, resting on the dirty bar. "...Name's Maddie. Maddie Somner. You're not from around here, are you?"

He wasn't going to answer. He just wanted her, everyone, to leave him alone. "No."

He said it hard, spitting the word out low and long. He felt his jaw working and stopped it. He unclenched his fist that had balled up. He realized that he wanted to hit her.

"Your truck's pretty. What's the FJJ5 license plate mean?"

He twisted to stare at her, wanted to piss in her face. "Franklin Jacob Jarvis." He said it slow, precise, terse.

"And the 5?"

He sighed...turned back to his whiskey and beer. "The fifth of that naming."

"Oh. Wow."

Jake rolled his eyes. Then, deciding, he turned back to her. "You want to go somewhere?"

"Su-ure."

♦

HE TOOK HER TO THE MOTEL that sat off behind the bar. He got as far as stripping her down to her bra and panties, her getting his shirt off. Then, he stopped. "Get off me."

"What?!"

"I said get off me."

He practically threw her off the bed, got up, and pulled on his boots. Grabbing his shirt and his hat, he pulled out his wallet and stepped over to drop a fifty on her exposed belly. It was all she was worth. Then he got in his truck and headed southeast.

He fought it all the way...didn't stop, though. It was near dark by the time he pulled into the drive. Her truck was gone. He tried the door, anyway. It was open. He walked in. "Dree? Dree Blake?"

S HE SAT BOLT UPRIGHT, tossed the book, and, grabbing her jeans, tried pulling them on, her toes catching.

Her dogs growled.

She fumbled her pants up and ran to the door.

Opening it, she heard his boots on the stairway.

The dogs launched themselves into the hall. She slammed the door, locking it...grabbed her extension.

"Dree Blake?"

She dialed 9-1-1, the line ringing, ringing.

Chip started barking. There was a yell. Something crashed. A thump—loud and hard. ...Growling. Like a cornered badger—her Laddie, always the silent, aggressive one.

"911, what is your emergency?"

"He's in the house. On the stairs. My dogs—"

"Who, ma'am?" an irritatingly calm voice on the other end asked—a man, of course.

"JAKE JARVIS," she screamed into the phone. "He broke into my house."

"Stay calm, Ma'am. I've got your address. I'm dispatching deputies, now."

"Hurry!" She was practically passing out, red-blackness rolling across her vision. She couldn't catch her breath. Her ears roared.

"Stay with me. What's your name, Ma'am."

"Dree. Dree Blake. ...Oh, *God*! *Hurry*!"

Silence beyond her door, now. Occasionally, she heard a growl, maybe a moan. She wasn't sure. She got the window open, was ready to try to climb down the rose trellis. She was shaking all over, the man on the phone asking her stupid questions—her date of birth, her full name, who her father and mother were, what she did for a living.

It seemed to take hours before she finally heard sirens. Four rigs came flying down the county road. The man on the phone wouldn't let her hang up.

"Stay with me, Adrienne. Stay on the line." Then, "Okay. The deputies want to know where you are in the house. Can you tell me?"

"In my bedroom."

"Is that upstairs or downstairs, Adrienne?"

"Upstairs."

"Where exactly upstairs?"

She sucked a breath, closed her eyes, trying to figure directions she already knew by heart, but now were all jumbled up. "West end of the house. The very end of the hall. I'm in the southwest corner bedroom. I've got the window open. I–I'm going to try climbing down, now."

"No, Adrienne. Stay where you are. Please stay where you are, honey."

She hated 'honey'. She wasn't anybody's 'honey'. Not now. Not ever! "My name's *DREE*!" she screamed at him. "Not 'honey', not even 'Adrienne'! *DREE!*"

"Okay, Dree. Please try to keep calm. Okay? Just a little bit longer while the deputies work their way to you."

"Oh, *God!*"

She heard the back door bang open. Then there was a crack as something broke. The front door banged open, crashing against the cabinet that was behind it. Dree heard glass break. "Oh, God!" They were trashing the place. She went to the door, stood there, angry that she was too chicken to open it.

"Dree? Are you still with me?"

"Yes," she whispered into the phone.

Chip started to bark. Someone yelled.

She dropped the phone, and, jerking open the door, she hollered down. "Don't shoot my dogs." Then she screamed it: DON'T YOU *DARE* SHOOT MY DOGS!"

Voices. Then, "Can you call your dogs off, Ma'am?"

She walked down the hall, her fear for herself turning to fear for her dogs. She saw Jake, bleeding and sprawled on his back, fallen in the stairwell's corner landing three steps from the top. Laddie was crouched right beside him, close, growling. Chip was back, sitting on the top step, watching. "Laddie, come. Chip, come," she said. "Come on. Back, now. Leave him alone."

Chip came to her almost at once. She grabbed his collar...squatted down, petting him. "Laddie, boy. Come. Please come."

The Aussie angled his head just enough to catch sight of her...growled, then, inching backward in a slow crawl, hit the edge of the stair and stopped.

She eased forward toward him. "Good boy. Come."

He rose, and, with a last glance toward his mark, turned, climbed the three stairs up, and skulked toward her. She grabbed him...hugged him. "Okay. I've got them. You can come up, now."

"Stay where you are."

"I am."

A deputy stormed up the stairs, and, black automatic leveled on Jake, snarled, "Put your hands on your head. Slow and easy."

She saw Jake obey as another deputy eased by to come toward her. He eyed the dogs.

"Let me put them in the bathroom," she said.

He nodded.

She got up enough to work her way backwards, her hands gripped hard on her dogs' collars. "In," she ordered. And, shoving them, she pulled the door shut.

The man grabbed her arm and pulled her down the hall to her room...closed the door. Spying the phone, he picked it up, said something into it, then stepped over to her nightstand to put it down in its charging cradle. "Are you okay?" he asked her. "Did he hurt you?"

She shook her head.

"Did he *touch* you?"

"No. He didn't get near me. I locked the door."

The man—older...about her dad's age—visibly relaxed. "I'll be right outside your door. You need to get dressed.

STRIPPED OF HIS WALLET, his keys, his watch, and even his boots, Jake was handcuffed, his legs shackled, then transported in the caged-in back of a Ford SUV to a hospital emergency room. There, he suffered having the dog bites cleaned and bandaged without even the nicety of a topical anesthetic. Then they took him over to the Sheriff's Office, took his picture and fingerprinted him. They hauled him into a room and tried questioning him.

He demanded a lawyer.

They threw him into a bare cell. "Don't I get a phone call?".

Nobody answered him.

Morning came. He knew because a deputy came in carrying an ugly breakfast of bad-tasting mush and a hard piece of toast, no coffee, just water.

"I want my one phone call, and I want a lawyer," he said to the deputy who brought it.

The man just gave him a dead-eyed look.

He asked for aspirin. His head was splitting.

The man turned and left...didn't come back.

Hours passed. He just paced or sat on the metal bunk. There wasn't even a mattress or pillow. He used the toilet, again—stainless steel and strange looking. The thing flushed itself. He washed his hands, threw cold water on his face, but there wasn't anything to dry with.

Somebody else brought in lunch—one sandwich, bologna on white, no mayo. Not even butter to grease it. The bread was dry, the meat cheap.

There was no way to tell time. There were no windows. Jake desperately needed a painkiller. His leg and his arm where the dogs bit him were swollen and throbbing.

The door opened, somebody talking about charges. Jake stood up.

Franklin walked in, along with a man in a suit—not Powell, the ranch's regular lawyer, but some other. A short, heavyset man came with them whose name badge identified him as the sheriff. Franklin threw in his boots. "Get 'em on."

C. J. "Country" James

24

Brokered Deals

H IS GRANDFATHER DIDN'T SAY one word to him all the way home. Jake didn't care. He stared at the window, his focus on specs of dried water and dirt marring its surface. Behind them, Lane drove his truck, Franklin having thrown the keys to the man once Jake signed for his stuff, him released to his grandfather's custody.

Home, finally, Jake trailed his grandfather up the front steps. The man opened the door and stood waiting. Jake went on in. Behind him the door slammed. He jumped.

"You stink like rotting, sour mash from old John Grady's still. Get to showering, change your clothes, then get yourself to my office."

Jake went to his room and locked the door. Sometime later, a hand pounded on it. He rolled over, burying his head with the pillow.

"Jake?"

Moments later, he heard the sound of the lock turning. He hunkered in.

"Jake!"

His grandfather sat down on the bed, the stiff mattress adjusting itself with a hiss. A hand touched his back, and he jerked. "Easy, son. Easy."

That hand began stroking his back, small movements...kept at it. Jake wanted to scream, to sit up and punch the man he cared most about in the world. He took his fist and shot it out, hitting the headboard. He kept hitting. The pain felt good—real good.

A hand grabbed his arm. "You're getting blood all over. Stop."

Jake sobbed. Once.

"Jake, I don't know what you were thinking, but, whatever it was, you were taught better. Now, we've got to get this sorted, one way or another. You're facing serious jail time."

He didn't care. "Let 'em," he mumbled. "Bring it on."

Hands pulled him out, pulled him over. He struck out...connected, heard his grandfather grunt. Then, strong arms wrapped him up, locking around him like a vice. "Quit! Right now! Or I'll call Doc Perkins and have you sedated."

"I DON'T *CARE*!" he bellowed, and tried to fight free.

The arms crushed harder. "Yes, you *do*. That's the *problem*. That's the *whole* problem. Now, *quit*."

A knock at the door. "*What?!*" Franklin demanded.

"There's a man here asking for Jake." It was Wil's voice.

"He can't come."

"Says he's Jim Blake, Dree Blake's dad."

Jake froze.

He heard his grandfather sigh. "Get Lane in here," he called out.

"No," Jake said. "I–I'll…be okay."

"I can't trust that, Jake."

He pulled away, and his grandfather let him. "I'll be okay. I promise."

There was too long a silence. Jake glanced up, saw his grandfather watching him, Franklin's face drawn, too white, the eyes black-brown, hooded, and sad. Franklin had blood on him—Jake's blood—and a lump was beginning to swell on his cheek.

Guilt hit him, bludgeoning him, roiling his guts. "I'm okay. I'll be okay, now. I promise."

"You're not going to do something stupid like you did when Lea got hurt?"

Jake shook his head. "I promise."

"You're only as good as your word." Franklin stood up. "I'm trusting you keep it. Get a shower."

H ER DAD FORCED HER HAND. He made her drive into Adams, him riding along to make sure that she did what he told her. She dropped the charges. So he wouldn't kick her out of the house.

"You shot at him, Dree. Came real close to killing him. I told that to his dad. Told them I'd testify to that fact. I explained.... Never mind."

"What did you ex*plain*?!"

He kept silent.

"And he doesn't even *live* with his dad."

"Franklin Jarvis!" he snapped.

"That's his *granddad*." But she was mortified. "What did you *tell* him?!" she demanded, again.

"That you're broken. Damaged goods. Will probably never be right in the head. And you aren't and won't. Don't argue with me, because I'm right, and you know it."

Dree stormed upstairs, locked herself in her room...screamed. She didn't bother with chores, didn't go down to fix supper. He could starve, for all she cared. So could all of them. She heard her truck drive away around nine.

Getting up, she washed her face, then went out to the barns and fed and watered the stock, knowing he hadn't.

JAKE WATCHED AS THE LAWYER handed Franklin back a cashier's check for the bail money. He watched Franklin write out a personal check for just under five grand, and winced. "I'll pay you back," he said, after the lawyer left.

"You can pay me back by staying clear away from that Blake girl."

"I can't."

Franklin leaned his head back on his desk chair, blew a breath, closed his eyes. "Jake—"

"No. I can't shake loose of her."

His granddad spun around to face the window, stared out at their mountain. "Why not?"

"Because she's like Mom, that's why. Because she's special like Mom, and that's what I want in a girl."

Franklin turned back to look at him. "You don't even know her. You can't say that."

"I want to know her...to find out. But I think that.... I think—"

"You're talking marry her?"

"I don't know. Maybe."

"God save us from hormones."

Jake shook his head, not even angry. "It's not hormones, Grandpa. I don't get a hard-on being around her."

"Jake!"

"I know. Don't talk about it. Don't say the words—not fuck, tits, hard-on, screw—nothing."

Leaning an elbow on the armrest, his grandfather buried his eyes in his hand. "Just one big headache," he muttered. "I wish Larry Carter had never brought her here."

"Well, I'm glad he did! I'm glad that I met her, got to work with her. Now I want to find out if I want to spend the rest of my *life* with her. You ought to understand that. You loved Grandma that way!"

"Jake!" Franklin bolted upright, put his hands on his desk, arms spread wide, bending toward him, eyes hard. "She won't have you."

Franklin had him there. Jake turned his face to the window. "I know."

The man sat down. Silence stretched. A sigh. Then, softly, "If you're serious, if you're *dead* set on this, Jake…and you *better* be, then you court her proper. The old way."

Jake's eyes locked on his granddad. Franklin watched him, measuring him, he knew. Jake waited.

"You start by sending her flowers every darned day. Every one, not just weekdays, but every day. And not cheap ones, either. You send roses, lilies, whatever the florist thinks best. And you keep sending them. …Then you start sending boxes of candy, too, probably chocolates. Women love chocolates."

"She does. But only—" Franklin waved him silent.

"You bribe the delivery boy…girl…whoever, to see how she's taking it…to not let her return them. And when you finally get some kind of signal it's time, and it's probably going to take months, you send her an invitation to…."

Franklin flipped through his old-fashioned Rolodex. "The Red Bird. …She'll refuse, but you just keep sending the invite. And the flowers. And the chocolates. You've got one year—one year, only. Then you promise to quit."

Jake stayed silent.

Franklin stood up. "Shake on it. Now. …One year."

Jake rose, stepped forward, and, his hand shaking, he clasped his grandfather's warm, calloused one.

The man came around his big desk, and, grabbing him up, gave him a squeeze, then let him go. "Good luck, Jake. ...I mean it. Because I like her, too, and I can't think of a better woman to help you run this place when I'm dead and gone."

Jake ducked his head. "Don't say that."

Franklin laughed. "And you say I'm tetchy about private things. You are, too. We all die some day, Jake, and you gotta face that."

25

Roses & Chocolate

D REE WASN'T EXPECTING to come in
from baling to find roses on the porch. A
glimpse at the attached card showed "Jake
Jarvis" as the sender. She grabbed them up, intent on
throwing them in the garbage, then, with a sniff,
decided why waste them? They were beautiful and
delicious-smelling. Nobody had ever sent her a dozen
roses. Besides, it was just an apology. Not that she
had any intention of forgiving the S.O.B.

But the next day brought another dozen. And the
next, too. On the fourth day, she met the delivery
woman at the door and told her to take them back.
The woman eyed her, gave her a piece of her mind,
then set them on the porch, anyway. Stung, Dree
watched the woman drive away. Her dad came up and
said, "She's right, you know."

Dree stomped upstairs.

Days turned into weeks. The flowers kept coming,
a bouquet a day, each one more elaborate. They
overflowed the living room, the bedrooms, the dining
room and kitchen. Even the bathrooms had their
blooms. Luckily, the cut flowers only lasted about a
week to ten days, so, once Dree had established a

pattern and a plan, she was able to rotate out the faded for the fresh. And, in time, she got used to it. She especially liked when rose petals fell into her bath water. The whole house smelled good.

Then the candy started—boxes of expensive chocolates coming along with the bouquets. These she threw in the freezer so they'd keep. She refused to even open one box.

"He must be spending a small fortune," her dad said.

Dree grumbled.

Week after week they came, the flowers and chocolates. She had one of the freezers topped nearly full of boxes of the expensive candy, so full that she had to shift them to get at the bacon beneath. Then, in came an envelope with the daily delivery. It was a card showing a reservation for two the following Friday at the Red Bird in Missoula. Dree dropped to a chair and groaned. This guy just wouldn't quit! She scribbled out a note saying "No, thank you. Dree Blake," and stuck a stamp on it after figuring out the return address by digging out the copy she'd made for her records of Franklin's check.

The next day, a similar envelope arrived with the flowers and chocolates. Angry, Dree sent this one back, too, with the same refusal. And day three...four...five.

The following Monday, when Dree came home from getting groceries in town, her dad was waiting for her with the recurring envelope in hand. "Seems to me," he said, "that Jake Jarvis is pretty serious."

"Dad, please don't start on me about this."

"Well, you are accepting the flowers and chocolates."

"No. ...Well." *Damn.* "The woman delivering them won't take them back! She's called me dumb, ungrateful, spoiled, stupid, and a whole bunch of other things. He's got some sort of agreement with the shop. Has to. She absolutely *won't* stop bringing them or take them back with her. I've *tried*!"

"Dree, you're yelling."

Plopping down in an armchair, she let out a frustrated sigh. "Sorry."

"You need to settle this," her dad said.

"I thought I had. ...I made it crystal clear to him to stay away. You know it. You used it against me to get me to drop the charges I filed against him!"

Her dad was silent, but, when she rose to go start chores, he said, "Some men want an answer that makes sense to them, not just a brush off."

"And putting a bullet through his hat, then having him arrested wasn't clear enough?!"

He laughed. "That just makes it more of a challenge, Dree. You need to give him a solid reason why." Then he said something that set Dree back on her heels. "You know, I can't figure out why, Dree. Because, you know, he's called me and asked. And I don't have an answer. Can you tell me? He seems a good man."

"Boy, you mean," she spat.

"Just like you're a girl, Dree, but that's not an answer. Can you give me one so, if he asks me again, I can give him an honest reason other than telling him all our private, personal family history?"

Dree couldn't. Or wouldn't. How could she tell her own father that it was because of him and her mom that she didn't want to have any brook with the idea of marriage. Much as he was a drunk and a hardass, she wouldn't for the world do more to hurt him, not more than she knew he'd already been hurt, than they'd both been hurt.

"Why don't you accept the dinner invite? Tell him to his face that you really mean 'no' along with your version of 'why'. The 'why' is the important part."

Dree stared, her thoughts churning. She felt cornered, especially when her dad just kept watching her. Finally, an answer formed, almost on its own, and she blurted it out: "Only if you come along. That's the only way I'm meeting Jake Jarvis face-to-face."

"All right. I can do that."

♦

T HE HARDEST PART WAS CALLING. A woman answered and asked her identity.

"Dree Blake."

There was a sharp breath intake, then a rustling. Seconds later a muffed "She's called. She's on the phone for you, Jake."

Another line picked up, and Dree stiffened at Jake's hello. She heard a click as the extension hung up.

Blurting out her terms, Dree expected argument and objection, but, instead, Jake Jarvis said, "Okay. I'll pick you and your dad up at three-thirty this Friday." His voice was low, soft, and steady. "See you then."

Dree didn't even say good-bye. Just hung up, and, knees shaking, she sank into the chair underneath the wall phone and just drooped, her heart pounding in her ears, her hands quivering in her lap. Then it hit her. He was coming here!

She had planned on meeting Jake in Missoula, not letting him come to the ranch to pick them up. She wanted to call back and tell him 'no', but, when she reached for the phone, she couldn't do it. She couldn't face the prospect of calling him all over again. Instead, she went out to do chores.

" Y EEE-HAAAAW! SHE SAID 'YES'," Jake shouted. Then, pounding into the great room, he took his mom in his arms and danced her around, spinning her this way and that. "She said 'yes'. You coming up to help brought me good luck. He kissed her cheek, smothering her with a hug."

"Jake. Jake! You're crushing me," Loretta objected, but she was smiling when he finally let go.

"She said yes, Mom!"

"I–I heard you the first *and* the second time, Jake."

Franklin came out of his office, grinned, then headed over to the liquor cabinet.

"What are you going to wear?" his mom asked.

"My black pearl-button shirt, a black string tie—the one with the onyx—and some black jeans," Jake answered.

"Let me polish up your good boots, okay?"

He grinned at her. "Thanks, Mom."

Franklin handed each of them a glass. "For luck," he said, tossing his back. "Jake? We need to talk about what's next. My office."

"I'll start dinner," Loretta said. "You've really got to find some help, Franklin. I love being here, but I need to find a real job."

"I offered to pay you."

"No. You need to find a replacement for Marguerite, preferably somebody older with no kids."

◆

THURSDAY, Jake went to a jewelry store and bought a delicate necklace that had Dree's birthstone in it—a long, faceted, teardrop amethyst. He didn't get a big one, about the length of the end of his thumb, only. Franklin had warned about that. But he got a nice one, set in platinum, glad that Dree's dad had shared the birthday information when Jake, on his granddad's prompt, had asked a month or so ago. That Jim Blake was in on the campaign had surprised him, Jim Blake, Franklin, and he meeting for lunch in Missoula. Jim Blake had driven Dree's truck.

Jake had his pickup detailed after getting the Dodge dealership to attach a fancy fold-down step to the passenger side. He sat four solid hours while they polished it up and cleaned every tuck-and-roll seam, crease, button, and crevice. Then, he got the corsage.

C. J. "Country" James

26

Dinner Out

S HE WAS CAREFULLY IRONING the rayon
scarf she planned to wear. Her dad walked in
and eyed her dress where it was hanging, freshly
pressed, on a cabinet knob. "You're wearing *that*?"

"Yes, I'm wearing *that*. '*That*' is my best formal
dress!"

Her dad's eyebrows arched. "It looks more like
something you'd wear to a funeral."

Dree shook her head and shut the iron off. She *had*
bought it to wear to a funeral—her Grandfather
Blake's funeral. He should know that.

♦

S HEILA GOLDSTEIN SHOWED UP Friday
morning just as Dree was finishing chores.
Maneuvering her way into Dree's bedroom, she began
poking through the closet. "This one is sort of pretty."
She held out a flowered summer dress that Dree hated.
The woman turned back to the closet. "Let's see what
else is in here."

"Did Dad call you?"

Sheila mumbled something that Dree couldn't hear. The old woman had her head buried at the very back of the closet.

Dree watched her emerge and hold out the empire-waisted bronze-colored dress with shirred satin bow that she'd worn to her grandmother's 50th wedding anniversary three years past. "It looks brand new."

"I only wore it once."

The woman reached up onto the shelf. "Oooo. Shoes that match. Heels, even." She pulled the clear plastic zip sack down, held them up near the dress in its equally clear dry cleaner bag, and nodded.

She looked over at Dree. "I've got an idea. Hop in the car."

"I've got work to get done."

"Yeah. In town. With me. Come on. Don't make me pester you all day about this. The sooner you go, the sooner you're done."

Sheila hauled her all the way to Adams, herding her into a too-fancy beauty shop. Dree hadn't been to a hair salon since that horrible day of her senior prom. She didn't want to go in, but it was impossible to fight Sheila's arguments. Retired school teachers, especially ones who raised goats, were a stubborn pain. So was the salon, it turned out.

What Dree thought was going to just be a shampoo and updo turned into a wax job on her eyebrows, a facial, styling her hair, and, then, *after* the updo, a make-up job, along with her nails buffed and polished.

When they finally let her look in the mirror, she practically didn't recognize her own face.

"You really need to let us do more than just a French manicure. We've got some wonderful acrylics that—"

"No. This is way more than enough," Dree said, getting up.

When she tried to pay, the shop told her that the bill was already covered. "Your dad," Sheila told her on the way home.

Dree stared out the window, wondering what the hell had gotten into her dad. He *never* paid for stuff like this—didn't believe in it. Suspicious, she sincerely wondered if she was being set-up by her own father. *He wouldn't. ...He never had. Not like him.*

HAT IN ONE HAND, the box with the corsage in the other, Jake approached the Blake front door. He really didn't know Dree Blake from anything, but the vivid memory of her soft voice, her struggle to get him onto Coal, to get him home, her hand on his leg keeping him on when he just wanted to fall into blackness.... Brave, strong, smart, willing, even after he'd been such an ass to her. He'd never known a girl his age who had that kind of guts, that kind of compassion and fearlessness. Yes, he wanted to know her better.

He knocked, and, moments later, the door opened. Jim Blake, dressed up in a western suit, stood there, a thin smile playing across his face. The man winked at him, invited him in.

Women's voices upstairs—Jake heard Dree's voice. Footsteps on the stairs, careful and sharp. She rounded the corner, an older woman behind her carrying something. He sucked his breath in when he saw her. She was beautiful. He blinked. This was Dree Blake? Where was the short, sturdy girl with the frowny eyebrows dressed in jeans and an over-large shirt? "Hi."

Her eyes touched his, then dropped. "Hi."

He held out the flimsy plastic box with the corsage, glad he'd taken the sales matron's advice and gotten a traditional orchid. He watched a frown cross her face as she saw what he held. The older woman took the box from him, clucking and crooning as she neatly slit the seal and removed the delicate bloom. Nimble fingers attached it to Dree's dress, Dree's cheeks flaming up.

Jake grinned—couldn't help himself. Dree Blake was something to look at when she was all prettied up!

After the older woman draped a wrap on her arm, Jake offered her his, and she surprised him when, with only a hint of hesitation, she took it. Jim Blake followed them out, the older woman telling them to have a good time.

Jake opened the passenger side door while her dad got in back. He pulled down the step he'd had installed, then stood, his hand there to steady her as she climbed in.

He felt like laughing. She wasn't used to the heels she was wearing, and, somehow, that made him feel special. She'd done this for him.

DREE FELT LIKE GOODS. Anger boiled up. It mixed with embarrassment and shyness. The boy…man…next to her smelled good, and she was angry at herself for liking it. She was angrier still at her dad who was obviously having a good time at her expense. And she'd seen Jake's grin at her clumsiness as she'd tottered her way down the porch steps and then fumbled getting into the pickup.

Heels were hobbles, and she felt like a moose prancing around trying to act like a fairy queen. Damn Sheila Goldsmith for making her wear this ridiculous outfit. Damn her dad for insisting she go through with this farce. She only had herself to blame, though. She should have—what should she have? She didn't know.

Stayed home. And locked the gate.

THE TRIP WASN'T LONG ENOUGH for Jake. He could have driven all the way to Bozeman, even Billings, with her sitting there next to him. She smelled like something fresh—fresh air and sunshine with just a touch of the scent let off by the wild honeysuckle up on Black Badger. And he was glad Jim Blake was along. It somehow made things easier—a *lot* easier. The girl actually scared him some, not because she'd blown his hat off or got him arrested, but because she was so darned keep-to-herself.

He'd made it his business to look her up...and found nothing—not on Facebook, not anywhere. The only thing he'd found was a couple pictures of her where somebody named Caroline Tailor labeled a picture of Dree as her BFF. It showed a heavily made-up Dree playing Viola/Cesario in *Twelfth Night*. He also found one with her sitting at a piano when she'd been Caroline's accompanist at a singing recital in Helena. There was the MSU college graduation notice—BS in Ag Applied Economics. That was it—nothing else on the Internet, except a couple of hits leading to Adrian Blakes in the Montana online obituary database. By the ages, he figured one was her grandfather or a great uncle, the other some cousin who'd died young.

She was unrecognizable playing Shakespeare, but she looked almost the same in the recital pictures as she did now. Well, not *now* as in the shapely beauty sitting next to him, but the Dree who'd impressed him on his grandfather's ranch. He chuckled to himself and started whistling softly. The woman next to him was no 'Dree'. She was all 'Adrienne'.

"What's funny?" she asked.

Startled by the question, he looked over at her. "Nothing's funny. I'm just happy."

She looked away out the window, again. He went back to whistling until her dad said something about cattle futures, and the rest of the drive was spent in solid talk about this coming fall's stock prices, Dree becoming animated when she ponied up her take.

The woman knew a lot about futures and trends, Jake discovered—surprisingly a lot. She also had strong opinions about where agriculture was headed, opinions he didn't quite agree with...or maybe just didn't like—that ranches like theirs were doomed, that meat would be grown in Petri dishes. "I've got an AgBiz MS, and I think you're wrong," he said.

She started rattling off statistics, social movements, scientific advancements, and historic trends in price and demand for the last several decades, and that muzzled him, not because it proved her point, but because he wondered how the hell she remembered that kind of stuff.

By the time Jake pulled into the Red Bird's parking lot, Dree's reserve had vanished and Jake's own hesitancy was history. He did hurry around so she wouldn't try to get down without help, though, and, without hesitation this time, she grabbed his hand. She still caught a heel on the lip of the truck step though, and Jake was right there to catch and support her.

"Thank you," she said, once she got her feet under her. She was pink with embarrassment all over again. For Jake, it seemed a perfect moment.

"Would you accept a thank you for at least agreeing to come, even if I never see you after tonight?"

He'd planned his words carefully, working them through with Franklin. He'd wrote them out and memorized them. And they seemed right. She looked up with a curious tilt of eyebrow. He held out the gift-wrapped box with the necklace.

"I'm sorry. I can't."

"Yes, you can. There's no strings attached. It's just a thank you for finally letting me at least apologize face-to-face. I apologize for barging onto your ranch and frightening you by invading your house. So, will you accept my apologies and this small token? Call it 'a sorry stone'."

She turned beet red as he spoke and, finally, finally, she raised her eyes and met his. She nodded—just once—and Jake knew he'd hit a home run.

Slipping the ribbon off, he opened the box, and heard her sigh out a breath. "It isn't much. Just a little thank you. Can I put it on you?"

Head ducked, she nodded, and taking the delicate chain with its faceted, tear-drop-shaped lavender stone out of its velvet mount, Jake latched it carefully around her neck, his fingers easy and gentle, well-skilled now from Franklin making him practice doing it over and over on his mom who he'd talked into staying on at least through rest of the month. But, man, he wanted to kiss this neck, the small curls laying there. He sucked in a breath and stepped away to offer his arm. And she took it.

Jake saw Jim Blake grin and nod at him.

DREE CHOSE SOMETHING ITALIAN she couldn't pronounce along with a red wine; Jake Jarvis and her dad predictably both had the biggest bison steaks and got brandies. Dinner was a continuation of ranch talk which made her comfortable, but, this time, it was stories about mishaps with cows, bulls, and calves, rank horses, tractors breaking down, or center pivots getting bogged in the mud. Jim was full of tales from his youth, and Dree felt proud when he talked about participating in the Great Montana Centennial Cattle Drive with her granddad, whom she realized she desperately missed.

Jake asked why she rode a mule, and, honestly, she told him. "My knee's metal and plastic. I can't afford a horse slipping and falling on it," she said, her dad's face going dead-pan. She reached out and touched his hand, then caught Jake's eye, again. "If I go down, I'm probably lame for life, maybe even an amputee, and I don't much like the idea."

At the end of the evening, and they stayed to close the place down, Jake drinking water, her dad drinking whiskey, Jake asked to see her again. "No. This has been nice, but, no. And please stop the flowers and candy." She watched his face freeze.

"Can I ask why?"

"I told you before, I'm not interested."

He sat very still, then surprised her when he asked, "So, there's nobody else, right?"

She couldn't help herself. She laughed out loud. "No. There's nobody else. Never has been, never *will* be." She saw her dad dodge her a quick, frowning glance. Then, again, she reached to touch his hand.

Her dad pulled his hand away and picked up his whiskey, bolting it.

27

Lit Fuse

H E SAW JIM BLAKE'S EYES rake his daughter's face. Those eyes were a mix of angry, hard, sad, and, somehow, even tragic.

Thinking fast, he said something just for the hell of it to watch her reaction. "So you're a lesbian?"

Her eyebrows reached toward the sky. Then she grinned, mirth dancing in her eyes. A chuckle erupted from her throat. "If I said I was, would you finally take 'no' for an answer?"

That was exactly what he needed to hear. "Mr. Blake? Your place is in high need of some work—a man's hand." Startled by himself—his own words coming out, not practiced with Franklin, he forged on. "I'm willing and able to do that work, when I'm not needed on the Jarvis spread. The price is room, board, and a chance to get to know Adrienne, here, a little better. What say you?"

He saw Dree's mouth drop open, but, before she could get a word out, Jim Blake, who also looked like he'd just been hit by a two-by-four, honored him by saying, "Done," stood, and reached a hand across the table.

Jake stood, too, and shook it, and they sealed the deal that fast.

Dree went silent, just stared at him, then at her dad. Abruptly, she stood up and disappeared toward the restrooms.

Jake blew breath.

So did Jim, then he started laughing. "She's a stubborn one, Jake. And she's got a temper, once riled. I think you...we just lit the fuse."

Jake thought so, too.

SHE WANTED TO TEAR THE AMETHYST off her neck...throw it at him. She wanted to take her fists and pound them into his face. Her dad's, too. She stood at the sink looking back at herself in the mirror—her face white despite the makeup and her deep tan, her eyes hard and flinty like they got when life was going wrong. And life had just really gone wrong. A man she didn't like—well, maybe a little, dinner and sundaes at the café coming to mind—and she didn't *want* to like, a man who didn't seem to understand the word 'no', had just wrangled his way into her stronghold. She had two choices—stay or leave—and she didn't know which to choose. Staying would mean serving up meals and working beside him, and the mere thought sent her into a rage.

She *could* go live with her grandmother. But leaving would probably mean losing the ranch. Her dad couldn't handle the place alone. Heck, even with both of them, they were losing ground, and they couldn't afford to hire help.

But here was *help,* her rational brain said. *You don't have to like him. You don't have to cater to him. Don't pander to him. Just feed him and treat him like he's just another hired hand. Ignore him, like you did the boys in high school and college who jeered and taunted. You can* do *this.*

But at what price?

"*That's pride speaking,*" said her grandmother's voice in her head.

But the price to be paid to *this* hired hand was him insinuating himself into her world. Whether she wanted him there or not. His words echoed: "To get to know Adrienne, here, a little better."

She ran her hand under the faucet, the sensor turning the water on, and washed her hands. "Damn it, Dad," she swore, then pulled some towels and wiped her hands dry, her anger and shock transmuting with the act into resolve. She'd make this work for the ranch's sake, but it would be with a brook-no-bullshit bitch of an attitude. She'd work Jake Jarvis into the ground. He'd beg to never come back.

Returning to the table, she didn't sit down. She stood behind her chair and just waited.

The men got up, silent and careful-moving. She turned and headed toward the door, Jake Jarvis catching up and passing her to pull it open.

She took off her heels and got in the back for the drive home, spurning Jake's offer of a hand up into the passenger seat.

Watching her, his eyes wary, her dad got in front. The men starting to talk about needed repairs as they headed toward the interstate, her dad occasionally asking her what she thought.

Leaned up against the side of the crew cab, she pretended to sleep. Sometime later, she woke to the truck idling and something soft being draped over her. Grateful, she snuggled into it and went back to sleep. "Thanks, Dad."

JAKE SMILED AND CAREFULLY TUCKED the blanket in around her. This was a woman he could see himself with—not some empty-brained pretty face with a nice figure just meant for breeding. This was a solid woman like his mom and his grandmother, a real beauty when she did herself up who really had heart, mind, and guts. And, man, did she have guts, more than him, in a lot of ways.

Getting back behind the wheel, he talked low, asking questions, but got no answers much from Jim Blake. When it came to the why's and the wherefore's, the man just clammed up.

Turning into the drive just after one, Jake watched Jim Blake wake his daughter. She looked like a child while asleep, her face relaxed out of its perpetual sternness. He wondered about that. Why didn't she smile more? Why so stiff and reserved? And why did she dress like a field laborer, as beautiful as she was when she got prettied up?

Getting out, he walked around to the passenger side and opened the crew cab door to help Dree down.

She ignored him, spurned his hand and padded, barefoot, high heels clutched in her hand, up the front porch steps.

"You staying or leaving?" Jim asked him.

"I've got gear with me. I can do either."

"Best get the worst over first. Park your truck in the open bay of the equipment shed," Jim Blake said, "then come up to the house. Use the front door."

Jake did as bid, then jerked his emergency tote and kit from the storage cubby under the back seat. He hadn't planned on staying, but he didn't think he was going to get a second chance.

Jim had left the door open, and, through the screen, Jake saw Dree come from somewhere, her arms loaded with a pile of bedding. "Here," she said, shoving them at her dad. "Give these to your new hired hand."

Jake stepped in, and her eyes caught his. She frowned. Yep, she was mad.

Jim Blake said nothing, just took the bedding and watched her turn and climb upstairs. Jake watched, too, his eye catching at the soles of her bare feet as they padded up the wooden treads. When they disappeared, he stepped over to his new boss and took the bedding. "So, where's the bunkhouse?"

Jim Blake shook his head. "You're not staying in the bunkhouse. Place hasn't see a body or a broom in more than a decade. You'll stay upstairs in one of the guest bedrooms, not that it's been used, either, for quite some time, but I know it's clean. Bathroom is in the middle of the hall to the left. Wanna drink before we head up? I sure could use one."

"Me, too. Will it take her long to get over her mad?"

Jim Blake cast him a sideways glance, then went over to a wall cabinet. "Dree, 'get over'?" He laughed as he poured, then turned and handed Jake a tumbler with two fingers of Jim Beam. "Dree doesn't 'get over'. Dree punishes with silence until she wears you down or gets even."

And Jake wondered what 'getting even' would bring, because Dree ought to have figured out by now that she couldn't wear him down. He had his boot in the door, and he planned on keeping it there till she let him in.

C. J. "Country" James

28

Little Surprises

MORNING. DREE HADN'T SLEPT, not a bit. She took a walk, then did the chores, starting breakfast at the usual time, her dad and Jake's footsteps and cursing loud overhead as they scrambled around.

Her dad made it down first, Jake, still buttoning his shirt, hard on his heels. She served up bacon, eggs, hash browns and toast, pouring orange juice into the glasses she'd set in front of their plates. Then she retreated to the kitchen to eat by herself.

The men came through, carrying their plates, flatware, and glasses. Her dad went back for the coffee. "Ain't right you eatin' all alone in here," he mumbled.

She didn't reply, just turned her face to the window where the sun was smiling. She heard them sit down at the kitchen table and dig in.

Grumpy Dree, Dumpy Dree....

She finished her food and loaded the dishwasher, then headed out to start her workday.

"**H**OW ARE YOU with servicing equipment
...tractors and the like?" Jim asked.

Jake eyed the man. "Pretty good."

"That's this morning's job. Dree's going to mow
her fields again today, and I want to make sure her
tractor and mowing unit aren't going to break down on
her."

"*Her* fields?"

Jim nodded. "Yep. All hers, though she gives the
last cutting and most of the money to the ranch. They
were a college project financed by my mom. ...Against
my advice. Took some of our winter pastures and
turned them to irrigated timothy and alfalfa production,
and it proved out for her...for us. It's the only thing
making money here." The man's voice, proud before,
turned bitter. "...The only thing keeping us from
bankruptcy."

The single center pivot Jake had noticed.... "How
many acres?"

"Quarter of a section, total."

It wasn't a lot. Still, if she got two to three cuttings,
it would add up, depending on the quality.

Jake followed Jim's example and loaded his
breakfast dishes into the dishwasher, then followed the
man out to the equipment shed. Two tractors sat
there, both John Deeres, one small and almost a relic,
the other, also old—a 40-40 built sometime in the
1980s. All the equipment was decently maintained,

though. "Air filter needs cleaning," Jake said as he checked the 40-40, all its fluids, lotions, hoses, and fittings. "Could use a new fuel filter, too."

"Air compressor's in there." Jim Blake pointed left to a small door. "Parts are on the shelf above the work bench."

Jake found the replacement fuel filter, then, opening the door, saw the compressor—*really* ancient. After a quick check of the drain valve, then the oil level, he flipped the switch, eye wary on the pressure gauge. The machine began coughing and sputtering, then, after a few minutes, leveled out and began building pressure in the tank. Fitting an air nozzle, he blew out the air filter.

"She wants to turn all the bottom land to hay, but I'm against it," Jim said, his voice breathy as he struggled with something on the 930 mower/conditioner. He stood up, wiping his hands on a rag. "This is a cattle ranch—always has been—not a farm," he said with a laugh, but Jake heard the underlying resentment. "Her great-grandfather would climb out of his grave and come haunt us if I let her do it. The only reason I let her keep the one field was I was tired of having to buy hay. The dry land fields don't produce enough. As it is, one cutting of her field keeps the stock easy through winter."

"She gets three cuttings, you said?"

"Some years four. Probably will get a good four this year. ...I don't agree with her growing the timothy, though. Our horses do fine on the wild hay we bale up. Don't need that fancy stuff."

Jake eyed the baler. Traditional, small, rectangular bales, not the big round or square bales now the norm. He wanted to ask, but didn't. Jim Blake clearly disapproved of his daughter's project. Jake knew the feeling. He despised farming, too—dirt-scratching— but knew it often paid better...except for his grandfather's operation. But that was all Franklin's doing, Franklin's diversification—specialty ranching and butchering, shipping out beef all year long to supply a specific clientele, most of them located in the biggest cities around the nation. Hauling that frozen beef was all that his uncle and his cousin did, their big refers grumbling in at odd intervals during any given week on the feeder spread north of Great Falls, then grumbling back out to disappear for three to fifteen days at a time.

They'd finished checking and servicing all the equipment by nine, and Jim set him to working on mending some corrals and a big swing gate. Happy to be out of the equipment shed, Jake cut and bolted in sister rails where the breaks were. The swing gate proved troublesome, and he wound up taking the whole thing down with the aid of the 40-40. The cable needed shortening, and the take-up was frozen. Fixing it, he lifted the gate back onto its supports and adjusted it so it actually swung closed with a little shove.

Happy with the job, Jake went to wash the dust off at an outside hydrant. It was nearing eleven and, spying what had to be the bunkhouse, he looked inside. He expected dust, cobwebs, and clutter, maybe even hornets, and, while there was dust, the place was tidy and neat. He closed the door and went to look in the barn, surprised to see an open stall door. He frowned, walked out back to check the corral and horse pasture, then scanned the fields—no mule and so no Dree.

Trotting over to the house, he checked inside. Jim wasn't there, and Dree's truck was gone. Something didn't feel right.

He waited another fifteen minutes, then headed back to the barn and, cornering a sorrel in the pasture, brought it back, saddled it, and took off the way he'd seen Dree head out. An hour later, he found her, but only because one of her dogs barked.

She was on the ground beside a cow hung up in the fence, her mule set back on his heels, anchoring the head which Dree had looped on a slip halter, made out of twisting the lariat, so the cow didn't choke. The cow's hind feet she had tied to the base of a fence post. Dree was struggling to work on the animal's front half.

Jumping off, he expected the sorrel to ground tie. The sound of the animal galloping off behind him made him want to curse as he ran over to help. "Got worried," he said.

Dree gave him a glance…said nothing. She had a cut on her cheek, the blood-run dried and crusty. Her shirt was torn and her jeans covered in dirt and manure.

"Got another set of cutters?"

She nodded toward the mule, and, easing up to the animal, he patted it, talking soft, even as the mule, rotating just one ear, kept his attention on Dree. Jake checked the near-side saddlebag, got what he needed, then rejoined her.

Together, it took them ten careful minutes to finally free the wire from its wrap around the cow's front legs. Then, throwing a piggin' string around the cow's front hooves, Jake held her while Dree cleaned her wounds and stitched up the worst of the tears. "I've been at this for hours," Dree said. "I thought for sure Dad would come. He usually does if I'm not in by ten-thirty or so."

"We were servicing the equipment," Jake said. "Then I guess he had to go to town. Your rig's gone."

"Oh. Yeah. His meeting with Uncle Bill and John. I forgot."

Done, she went over to her mule and pulled something from the offside saddlebag. She returned with a loaded syringe. She injected it into the cow's rump. "Go ahead and let her up."

Jake jerked the leather thong loose from the front legs, released the hondo on the hind ones, Dree whistling to her mule who immediately let up the pressure as Dree pulled the loops of rope from the cow's head. The cow rolled to her brisket, then kneeling up, got her hind legs under her and stood to her damaged front legs.

"She's one of our better-bred cows," Dree said, "but she's always getting herself hung up somewhere. This is the third time this year. ...And the worst."

Jake started splicing fence back together. "Calf okay?" he asked. He didn't see it.

"Yes. I've got her hog-tied over under those trees. Wouldn't leave me alone." She mounted up and, reining the mule over, jogged over to some small pines. Moments later, a pretty good-looking four- or five-month-old heifer calf came bawling up to the cow, sidled up and banged on her udder. The cow twisted her head around, owning it, then, when the calf had gotten in a couple of good sucks, limped away, the calf following close. "I think I'm going to have to convince Dad to cull her," Dree said. She rode away.

Jake wasn't surprised that she left him to hoof it back. It was in keeping with the 'get even' formula Jim Blake had warned him about. What astonished him was when, about five minutes later, she came loping back. "I thought maybe that Brodie had stopped at the creek like usual, but he's gone. Probably back at the barn by now."

As she talked, she unbuckled the saddlebags behind the cantle and moved them in front of the saddle, tying them there with the saddle strings. She scooted her butt over the cantle, then looked down at him. "Climb on, but don't hit him with your boot, please. ...Or me."

Jake didn't question. He eased up to the big animal—sixteen-one easy, as big as Coal—and, with his right foot rather than left, stepped up, put his butt in the seat, and, kicking the stirrup off, swung his right leg up over the mule's neck, real slow. He'd never ridden a mule, but figured it couldn't be *that* much different ...except for the ears and the short, choppy gait.

It wasn't. And the animal's gait wasn't choppy. The mule walked out nice and long. For all intents and purposes, if you took away the head, maybe fluffed out the tail a little and broadened the feet, Cougar looked and moved like a horse at the walk. Her mule wasn't at all like the pack mules he'd seen his nephews bouncing around on up at the hunting camp a couple years back. "He's almost a horse, this mule," Jake said.

"Well, what did you expect? An overgrown donkey?"

"Ah...yeah."

"Sur-*prise*."

29

Suspicions

JAKE SMILED TO HIMSELF. He heard pride and not even a hint of snide in the lilt of her words.

"Can we move it? We won't even make it home by dark if we don't get going."

Jake squeezed the mule into a jog, expecting rough, but getting another nice, easy smooth. He thought Dree would at least hook her hands in his belt or, barring that, grab the cantle, but she didn't, just kept her hands laid on her thighs, all relaxed.

When they got to the creek, instead of trying to balk and then jumping into and through it like the sorrel had, the mule just walked through. "Who trained him?" he asked.

"I did."

Jake felt just the slightest twinge of resentment surge up. What was she, some sort of all-round hand? It was beginning to seem so. But, then, it made sense. She was an only child just like him by the pictures on the mantle, so she'd have had to get good at a lot of things, especially since her dad was so poor. "I saw the bunkhouse. How long since you've had help here?"

"A while."

In other words, none of his business.

DREE WAS TOTALLY MAD at herself by the time they finally got to the house. She liked the smell of him. She liked the smell of him better sweaty than clean, and that was just *wrong*. The whole ride home, she had to battle an urge to slip her hands around him, to lean against his back and breathe in. When they finally got to the house, she slid off over Coug's butt instead of waiting for Jake to dismount. "I've got to get us some lunch and get dinner in the oven. Can you put Cougar in his stall for me? I'll come unsaddle him once I'm done."

"Yup. I'll round up Brodie, too. I think I saw him over by the back fence as we rode in."

"Take a can of grain with you, or you'll never get near him."

She practically ran to the back door, bounding up the steps and into the kitchen. She wanted to run to her room and bury herself in the closet like she had as a kid. She didn't though. She just washed her hands and face, then got the oven started and the roast out of the fridge. Her dad wasn't back, yet...probably still at Uncle Bill's. Or else he'd stopped at the bar early.

It was past two and she was hungry. That meant Jake was, too. She pulled out sandwich makings and went to work building some for them both, then got some of her homemade chicken soup from the freezer, popping the plastic container into the microwave and setting the machine to defrost.

Back to the barn at a trot, she found Jake brushing an already unsaddled Cougar down, the mule contentedly chewing on hay. She grabbed a quarter can of grain and threw it into his trough, then leaned on the top rail and watched. "You get Brodie?"

"Yep. Put him back in the horse pasture where I found him. He busted a rein. I can fix it, though."

"Next time take the bald-faced gelding. He's a better horse and not herd-bound. Don't take Dad's buckskin, though."

"I think I'm going to go get Coal, if that's all right with you and your dad."

"Fine. He can use the big stall on the end. It's got a good turn-out."

"Thanks."

"Lunch is in the house when you're done."

She left and went to check the pigs to make sure they hadn't flooded their pen with the water nipple. They hadn't, so she went back to the house.

The microwave was beeping when she got there, and she pulled the soup out, stirred it, then put it back in on high to finish warming up. Footsteps up the back stairs cued her, and she got out bowls, spoons, and a ladle.

"I'll take some of that." It was her dad.

"Hi. How was your meeting?"

"Fine. You haven't started the mowing yet?"

"One of the cows got herself hung up in the fence, and I had to stitch her up."

"Well, there's plenty of daylight if you get started now." He grabbed a sandwich from the plate of three of them she'd made.

"There's soup in the microwave. Some of it's for your hired man. So are two of the sandwiches," she said, grabbing a chunk of cheese from the fridge and heading out the back door to get started.

She stopped twice to check on the roast, the last time to slice some carrots in with it. She put some potatoes in to bake. She stopped again at six, did the chores, set the table, then, with a yell, called the men into dinner. Not stopping to wait for them, she was back on the tractor by seven and doing her final pass by eight-thirty.

Done, she parked and went to reset the center-pivot's position so she could start tedding tomorrow. She couldn't get it to budge though, and, trekking along its length, she couldn't find the problem.

"Need some help?"—Jake's voice.

She turned and, with a sigh of exasperation, nodded. "Thanks. It won't move, and I can't figure out why."

Jake went to the tower, then, coming back out, walked the length, checking hoses and fittings. He bent down to a wheel about halfway down the length of it, and, fiddling there, hollered at her to try it.

She ran to the tower and hit the switch. It moved, and she got it positioned just where she needed it.

It was dark twilight when they headed back to the yard, the tractor's lights making an eerie effect, warping the lane. Jake hung onto the side of the cab, his feet on the steps. She'd latched the door open, and, again, his proximity disturbed her.

"You go eat. I made you a plate and put it in the microwave," he said. "The rest is in the fridge. I'll put the tractor away and get it ready for tomorrow."

She let him, grateful he'd offered. She was exhausted and starving. But she'd gotten almost everything done that she'd planned...except house cleaning and wash.

When she got to the house, her dad was asleep in the chair, the TV blaring. She nuked her plate and sat down at the kitchen table. Two bites into her dinner, she heard Jake's truck leave.

SOMETHING WASN'T SQUARING. Jake couldn't put his finger on it as he drove north to the ranch. Every time he thought he got a handle on what it was, it faded, again. It drove him home, the road, the miles, the hours disappearing as his brain churned, trying to pinpoint what exactly was bugging him about the day. He was no closer to finding out by the time he turned up the drive to the ranch house than he had been when he'd left the Blake's.

The lights were on—Franklin waiting up for him. "I didn't call to warn you I was driving in tonight to have you wait up," Jake told him.

"You home for good?"

"No. Just getting Coal."

"You're not driving back *tonight*."

"No. Tomorrow."

Franklin nodded.

Instead of heading upstairs, Jake sank down in the armchair across from Franklin's, then just sat.

"Hungry?"

"Not much."

Franklin got up, and Jake wanted him not to. But it was late, and morning didn't wait, so he just watched his granddad walk off.

Franklin surprised him by bringing a couple of plates back, handing him one and keeping the other for himself. The food was hot and smelled good. Jake set the plate on his armrest and tucked in.

They ate in silence. Then, with a rush, Jake found his mouth open, words tumbling out. "I think he lets her do most of the work. I don't know that for sure. It's just a feeling. But she checks the stock, she mends the fences, she does the chores. She does all the cooking, too…and, probably, the housekeeping. He disappeared into town all day. Took her truck. …I guess he had some sort of meeting or something. But he wasn't back even by two. Then he set me to fixing a couple of holes in the barn roof after she went out to mow. I saw him head back to the house, and he didn't come out, again. He was sleeping went I went in to ask him if he had a sawzall."

"Did he?"

"I didn't wake him up. Just found some snips in the equipment shed that doubles as a shop."

Franklin didn't say anything. Just sat watching him.

Finally getting uncomfortable with the stare, Jake picked up his plate, grabbed Franklin's, too, and headed for the kitchen. He was washing up when Franklin came in, picked up a dish towel and started drying.

"Every family handles things a little differently, Jake," he said after awhile.

Jake chewed on that. Then, draining the dishwater, he turned and leaned his butt against the counter. "Yeah." Then, looking his granddad in the eye, said, "Reminds me of Dad."

Franklin's already grim look didn't shift. He didn't even blink. What he did do after a few long, silent seconds was nod.

30

Scratching the Surface

"I GUESS THAT DIDN'T WORK OUT for you," Dree said at breakfast.

Her dad paused his fork, his eyes glancing her way. "What?"

"Jake Jarvis, hired hand."

"He said he was going to collect his things and bring his own horse. Would be back this afternoon."

"Oh."

Something inside her bounded. Something inside her sank. "What if I don't want him to come back?"

Her father put his fork down, wiped his mouth with his napkin, then stared down at his plate for a moment. Then, his head came up, but he didn't look at her, just stared straight ahead. "Dree, a deal is a deal, and, whether you like it or not, whether you think we don't need the help or not, this was my decision. I'm happy to have him here for the price. He's already done more in a day that I could have managed in two or even three." And, picking up his fork, again, he went back to eating, his signal that the conversation was over, and she'd better not backtalk him.

JAKE DIDN'T LEAVE THE RANCH when he planned. He'd slept through the alarm and nobody'd bothered to wake him. Once on his way, he punched up the Blake ranch on his quick dial.

Jim picked up.

"Running a little behind. Should be there by three."

"Haven't had enough of her, yet, huh?"

Jake tried to laugh…hoped he sounded convincing. "Nope. Haven't even scratched the surface."

"See you when you get here."

Dree was still out on the tractor when he pulled in at two-forty-five. He parked, unloaded Coal and put him in the stall Dree had told him to, then hauled in his saddle and set it in the aisle.

Jim Blake came out to the barn, leaned in to take a look at Coal, then whistled. "Some horse."

"He is."

"Put your saddle in the tack room," he said, pointing, and Jake nodded. "You can park your trailer in the lean-to the other side of the equipment shed."

Jake had to clean the junk out of the lean-to, then rake up miscellaneous bits of metal, nails, and binder twine before chancing backing his trailer in. When he got close, he looked at the heights, convinced his trailer was a little too tall to fit. He backed it next to the lean-to, instead, after raking that clean, then carried his travel bag to the house.

Jim was watching TV.

Jake went upstairs to his room, changed clothes, then went back down.

Jim didn't even turn around, not even when Jake stood outside on the step and, watching, let the screen door slam. Perplexed, Jake went back to the pile of junk he'd pulled from the lean-to and put it all back inside. Then, seeing a couple of gaps he'd missed on the barn roof, he went to fixing those.

Dree chugged in on the 40-40 about five-thirty. She glanced up at him. "You're supposed to be wearing a safety harness," she called after shutting down the engine.

"I didn't bring one."

"They're in the equipment shed."

"I'll remember." He grinned down at her. She cared enough to not want him to fall.

She started the tractor back up, parked the tedder, then drove over to the fuel tanks. From his perch on the roof, he watched her fuel up, check the fluids and lotions, then, when the pump quit, hang up the hose and head the tractor back to the shed. She backed it in smooth and sure. Then she went to the house.

She came out fifteen minutes later as he was climbing down from the roof. "It looks good," she said, pointedly looking up to where he'd been working.

"Thanks."

She headed for the barn, and, after stowing the extension ladder, he followed. She was filling the water buckets, Coal, Cougar, and the three horses from the pasture all munching grain. "I only gave Coal a taste," she said. "I have no idea what or how much you feed him."

"A three-pound can of Co-op ration."

"Oh. Same as us. Okay. You want to get him a can, then? I only gave him about a cupful."

"I did bring my own feed, you know."

"No. I didn't."

"Brought a bale, too. Can I store the grain in with yours?"

She chuckled. "Of course, silly. The hay, too. Take the wheel barrow."

"I think it'd be easier to just dump the bale outside," he said, then grinned at her frown.

That frown turned to surprise when he backed up his pickup. "I guess I'd better go get the tractor back out."

"No need," he said. "Just get out of the way."

She stepped back, and he pumped the pedal on the hydraulic wedge Mike Guthrie had rigged underneath. He stopped when the bale started to roll. When it settled again, he gave it a couple more, then stopped as the bale rolled off nice and easy.

"What happened to your tail gate?"

"It's in the trailer. I'll put it back on in a minute."

"That's a whole half ton, isn't it?"

It was a statement, like she already knew that, just wanted his say so. "'Bout that."

She nodded, then went over to the equipment shed and disappeared inside. Seconds later, she came out with a tarp.

He got up on the bed and slung it over the bale, then jumped down to help as she began tying it down. "I wasn't going to tarp it," he said.

"It's going to rain."

He looked over at her. "Okay. Sure." There wasn't a cloud anywhere, and the weather forecast said no let-up of heat and sun.

"You don't believe me."

"Ah...."

She looked at him, her slate-colored eyes looking almost lavender as a reflection from the evening sun glanced off his truck's chromed bumper to light her face. "My knee tells me. I've got to get the hay baled and picked up tomorrow, because, by Tuesday, it's going to rain."

Tuesday, it rained.

31

Heaven & Hell

I T TOOK HIM A COUPLE OF WEEKS, but Jake settled into a manageable routine. Keeping up with Dree, who was used to just about doing it all, took him some effort. She went to bed way after sundown and got up even before first light, so he did, too. Except for weekends. She went to bed early on Friday and Saturday and got up Saturday and Sunday at a more normal hour of four-thirty instead of three. Two nights a week with a full night's rest after getting maybe five a night the rest of the time was killing him, though.

He took over feeding the hogs for her, and cleaning the chicken coop, but he had no idea how to milk her cow, her laughing at him when he tried. "Didn't even know they did it that way, anymore," he told Franklin when, called home for a week, he helped run bulls back to the ranch.

Happy for the relative cool of his granddad's spread, Jake felt like he was on a vacation. He wallowed in the luxury of sleeping till five and hitting the sack at eight-thirty or nine. It was a relief to work a normal day's labor, good, willing hands, Mike Guthrie, included, doing their all, every one.

"Still haven't found a good replacement for that jackass in the kitchen, huh?" Jake asked after breakfast his second day back.

"Nope."

"How about asking Mom to come back? The hospital cut back on their staff, again, and she got axed for cheaper, younger nurses, not just laid off like last month."

Franklin shook his head. "I wouldn't put your mom through this kind of hell. She doesn't need to work, Jake. She's plenty set for life from company shares."

This is a far way from Hell, was Jake's thought. *This is pure heaven.*

Jake called his mom, and, next morning, Loretta was fixing up griddle cakes, bacon, and eggs before Franklin even got up. Jake let her in, getting up early to meet her and hand her Marguerite's old key ring he got from the office.

Franklin canned the creep cook that very morning…didn't even give him a severance check. "Good riddance," Jake's great-grandfather said. "I *like* a woman runnin' the house. Makes a man feel special, wouldn't you say, Jake?"

Jake agreed. Especially his mom doing it. She always seemed happy, no matter what.

"What are you frowning about, Jake?" Franklin asked, walking in from just having showered the day's dust off.

"Nothing."

"That wasn't nothing. Spit it out."

Jake gave a glance over at Wil who was reading the paper, Lane, Mike, Shawn, and the rest of the hands sitting around watching the tube. He let out a breath. They all knew about his stay over at the Blake place. Couldn't not. "I was thinking about Dree. Mom's always happy. Dree's always sad…or, at least, troubled."

"That'll change."

Jake jerked a look up at his granddad. "Why do you say *that*?"

Franklin just nodded, then repeated himself, but with a different slant to the words—even more sure— as he headed on into the dining room. "Dinner!"

JAKE'S ABSENCE REALLY HURT. She hadn't realized how much she'd come to depend on him, his even helping with housework—folding up his own clothes, grabbing the vacuum or a rag when something got spilled.

He was faster than she was at fence mending, better at sorting out, then immobilizing cows needing doctoring, and he was definitely better at figuring out how to fix the barns and corrals, something she'd just given up on completely. It was his hand bringing the place back, and she knew it. She was glad to buy him the cement and any posts, lumber, fencing, or roofing he asked for. She was glad to cook for him and clean up after. It was a small price to pay, and, unlike she'd feared, he made no demands on her. He pretty much kept to himself and let her alone. For that, she was grateful.

What really was strange to her was that, unlike her dad, he always seemed cheerful, no matter the job, even the awful ones...like when she stupidly drove the 40-40 over the septic drain field and broke it, her dad frantically waving at her. She'd stopped, shut the machine down to be able to hear him, and heard the crack. Then, not knowing better, she backed out and around the wrong way, breaking more pipe.

Luckily, they still had the old outhouse, grandfathered in, but Dree had a porta-potty brought in, anyway, while her dad and Jake dug up and fixed all the damage. No bath and doing dishes all by hand with bucket and tub for two solid days and three nights was her penance. Sheila Goldsmith kindly let them use her shower to clean up at night.

She also missed Jake when her dad disappeared for long hours with her truck, him sometimes leaving before ten and not getting home till way after she'd gone to sleep. Being alone wasn't the problem; having her plans to run down to the farm store for grain or needing some groceries was. With Jake around, he'd just hop in his truck or even throw her his keys to drive herself. Her dad never saw fit to leave his keys home.

Friday, when her dad didn't come home, she got angry. By Saturday mid-afternoon, she started calling around to her uncles, her cousins, and even the sheriff—no Jim Blake. And no Gram, either. A house-sitter answered the phone at Gram Blake's, but refused to give Dree any answers about where her grandmother was. The woman didn't know her dad, she said, but, no, Gram Blake wasn't with anyone when she left.

Monday, her Uncle Bill called. "Found your dad," he said. "I'll be there in half-an-hour to pick you up. Tidy yourself. We're heading up to Missoula." That's all he would tell her.

Fretting, Dree showered and got on clean clothes, then waited outside, climbing into her uncle's fancy new pickup when he finally rolled in. "What's going on, Uncle Bill?" He was dressed up like Sunday-going-to-church in a tan-colored suit.

"Your dad's in the hospital up there. It doesn't sound too good, Dree."

Her first thought was that he'd been in an accident. Her second was that he'd ruined his liver with drinking. It was neither one. Her dad had a brain tumor. The doctor told her it was probably malignant. They'd know more after the results of the biopsy came back.

They'd already removed the growth. He was in ICU. She could see him for ten minutes only.

His head was all bandaged up, tubes coming out from under the gauze. He was groggy, his speech slurred. Dree held his hand, and, his eyes on hers, he took off his wedding ring, then, when she held out her hand, he closed his into a fist. "Mooo."

He tried again, and, confused, Dree just stayed passive. That seemed to please him. He picked up her hand, set it on his leg, then worked his ring onto her left ring finger. Then he closed his eyes and seemed at peace. Her eyes burned.

"He's still confused. He needs to rest," the male nurse told her. "You can come back for a short time tomorrow."

"Do you have his belongings? He's got my truck keys."

The man opened a closet and pulled out a bag that included her dad's wallet, some change, his two key rings, her keys, and his watch. He pulled out another containing his clothes. "You should take these. He's not going to be needing them, not for awhile."

◆

DREE FOUND HER TRUCK in the parking lot, found the parking stub tucked in the visor that would allow her to leave. He'd checked himself in early Friday afternoon, according to the time-date stamp.

Home, she did chores, then tried Gram Blake's again—still the house-sitter answering, or, more the truth, *not* answering. The woman was absolutely tight-lipped about where her grandmother was.

"It's an emergency!" Dree told her. "Her son's in the hospital, critically ill!"

"I'm sorry. I've got no way to reach her. Don't even really know where she is. If she calls, I'll tell her to contact you."

The answering machine blinked, and, hoping, by some miracle, it was her Gram, she punched the button. It was Jake. He was going to be another few days. "Expect me there probably Friday, Jim. Franklin needs me another week. I'll be there as soon as I can get away. Sorry. Tell Dree hi for me."

"Hi back," she said, missing him, then caught herself…scolded herself. "Dammit."

C. J. "Country" James

32

Cornered

THEY DIDN'T LET HER DAD OUT of ICU till Thursday. Dree drove into Missoula every day after morning chores and a fast check of the stock. Then she drove home, getting back in time to do the evening ones. Thursday, she had to track down her father's new room. The main desk didn't know. "Room 211," they told her up in ICU.

Her uncles, both of them, were there when she walked in. So was her Cousin John. Her dad, looking better and laughing at something her Uncle Bill said, sobered the minute he saw her.

Her uncles and cousin excused themselves, closing the door behind them as they left.

"How are you feeling? What do the doctor's say? Have the results from the biopsy come back?"

"I have brain cancer, Dree."

She sat down, her breath caught somewhere down below by her heart. Huffing a little, she grabbed onto the chair arm. "Can't they do something?" she asked, when she finally got her chest working. "Chemo? Radiation? I know—"

Her dad waved his hand at her. "Shush, Dree. Yes. They've already started. They think that.... Well, let's just see how it goes."

"Okay. But—"

"Dree. Listen to me. Carefully."

She waited.

"I'm signing the ranch over to my brothers." He held his hand up before she even had a chance to get her mouth open. "Don't bother arguing with me about this. I've already signed the papers."

"You *can't*! I want to run it! It's my right. I'm the only one left! I *care*! ...I'm *good* at it."

"Dree! Don't do this to yourself. Don't do it to me. A women has no place running a ranch. It's too much. She's meant to marry and have kids." Then, "I'm sorry."

There was no talking to him. He got hard-eyed, harder-lipped, and silent, glaring at her. Finally, he ordered her out. When she refused to go, he pushed the button to call the nurse, and, when a woman came, told her to make Dree leave. "I don't want to see her."

Outside, her uncles and cousin stood, backs to the wall, hands in pockets, talking. They glanced her way, then her uncles shifted themselves so she couldn't see their faces. Her cousin just stared at her with his usual insolence. John and she did not get along. At all. Nobody said anything to her—no words of assurance, no words of compassion.

As she waited for the elevator, she saw them file back into her dad's room. "Cowards."

J AKE KNEW SOMETHING WAS UP as soon as he turned in the drive. Two pickups, one new, one older than Dree's old white beater, along with a brand new Lincoln sporting a magnetic Realtor sign were parked in the drive. He left Coal in the trailer and made his way to the house.

Through the kitchen window, he saw Dree backed up to the sink, her face tight and haggard-looking.

She glanced out the window, saw him, but turned back to whoever was talking to her.

He took the steps two at a time and went in. He didn't remove his hat.

Four men, three older, one about his age, but fleshy with a very white face, looked his way and the talking stopped. The man wearing oxford dress shoes and a suit was the one Jake guessed owned the Lincoln. "Hi," he said. "I'm Jake Jarvis. I help out around here. Can I help *you* with something?"

One of the older men—the one wearing a good suit and boots—reached out and shook his hand. "I'm Dree's uncle, Bill Blake," he said. "Pleased to meet you."

Jake turned to Dree. "What's going on, Ms. Blake?"

She blinked in surprise, then her eyes registered, and Jake gave her small nod, encouraging her with his eyes. He saw her pull air, then settle, her eyes—desperate— on him. "Dad has brain cancer. He's in the hospital. He's signed the ranch over to—"

She turned away to face the sink, her hands gripping hard.

Jake didn't move, just shifted his eyes to the men and waited.

Bill Blake spoke up. "Jim thought it best," he said.

"You're selling the place? Is that why this Realtor fellow is here?"

The man in question stiffened, but kept his peace.

"Ye-es."

"Dree's being difficult," said the youngest man— sandy-haired with strange, pasty white skin and a softness, especially around the middle, that reminded Jake of a botfly maggot. "I'm Dree's cousin, John, by the way." He reached out, now, extending his hand.

Jake took it...felt the sticky, cold sweat in the palm. "Jake Jarvis," he said again.

"I'm Dree's Uncle Pete," the other man said, now also reaching a hand out. Dressed in cheap work clothes and boots run over at the heel, he seemed the straightest of the bunch to Jake, but his eyes—slate eyes like Dree's—wouldn't stay still. They shifted around constantly from face to face and place to place. He was afraid, his nervous sweat stinking of it.

"Pleased to meet you," Jake said, purposely saying it as he shook Pete's hand. This would be the only possible ally, but a weak one. The others were snakes, all of them, especially the youngest. Pete was the go-along-to-get-along type, easy to bully, easy to sway—no backbone.

The Realtor shifted, cleared his throat, and, purposely Jake tipped his hat toward him. "I'm sorry. We weren't introduced," he invited. He didn't smile when he said it, though.

"Jeff Townsend," the man said in that practiced 'always your friend', 'trust me', stock-in-trade-of-the-business voice. He reached out his hand, and, again, Jake shook.

That seemed to do it. The men relaxed, their backs losing stiffness, their faces gaining a measure of ease. Jake looked at Dree, who had since turned back to watch, and held his hand out toward the dining room table. That broke it, and, relaxing further, Bill Blake pulled his hat off and turned to lead the way.

Jake flashed a glance at Dree, and, with the smallest twitch of his head, tried to cue her.

She got it and moved into the dining room.

Jake followed her in, sitting her down at the opposite end of the table from Bill. He pulled out the chair next to hers, swapped it around backwards, and sat down, arms crossed to lean lazy over the back. He wasn't quite *at* the table, but he was party to it—no threat, no stake, or so he hoped they would read it. "So, John there mentioned that there's some sort of difficulty?" Jake prompted before anyone else grabbed the floor. "What seems to be the problem?"

"*Dree's* the problem," John said, bluntly.

"John. Go easy"—Bill Blake. The man's eyes eked grateful toward Jake, his manner that of someone who'd found a mediator to talk sense to his niece. "Like you heard, my brother has signed over his place to me. ...A-And to Pete, of course. And, to cover Jim's care and hospital bills, we've decided the best thing is to put the ranch on the market."

He tipped his head toward the Realtor. "Jeff, here, already has buyers interested who are ready to sign. We should get a very good price that will keep Jim comfortable. Dree, too."

"But she's got to leave, and she's refusing to," John said, jumping in, his eyes hard and accusing.

Bill started to reach his hand out, but stopped. He nodded. "That's about the gist of it."

So John was Bill's son, Jake guessed. He turned his face to Dree. She was looking down at her hands which were clasped, skin red, knuckles white, in front of her on the table. He looked back at Bill. "Well, I think this is probably a bad time to be asking Ms. Blake to think about anything, as worried as she's got to be about her dad. Why don't you give it a few days?"

Cousin John's ears were turning beet red, even as Jake said it. The Realtor kept glancing toward Bill. "Because we have buyers, right now!" John snapped. "She's just holding up—"

"I think you're right," Bill said, cutting in. He shifted his attention to Dree. "I'm sorry, Dree. I know this is a hard time for you. But, honey, you have to face facts. Your dad's just looking out for your best interests."

It was clear to Jake that they had this whole thing sewn up, and, walking in on it cold, he didn't have enough knowledge or facts to head things off for her. "What are your terms?" he finally said.

"She's gone by Monday. Or, better, before. She takes her own personal property, and the junk that's in the house, here...whatever belonged to her mom along with her dad's personal effects."

"The stock?"

"The cattle will be sold. The center pivot, too. And the tractors...all the equipment. If she wants the hogs, horses, and whatever, she's welcome to them. They won't bring much."

It was all John speaking—hard words, viciously spoken.

Jake stood up. "You've had your say and laid your claim with whatever legal rights you say you hold to force Ms. Blake from her home. You've made yourself pretty clear, here. Now, I think you should probably go."

"We need to get started—"

"Sixty days is the law, isn't it?" Jake asked.

All of them stilled. John's ears turned color, again.

The Realtor leaned forward. "We'd hoped—"

"Sixty days is the law, *isn't it?*"Jake repeated, cutting the Realtor off, and all of them flinched, even John.

It was Bill as well as the Realtor who both finally nodded when Jake kept cold eyes on them.

"Then sixty days it is. Not before. Now, for Ms. Blake's sake, I think you ought to make your goodbyes and get off the place, because, until that deadline is up, this is *her* place, not yours, and I think a judge and the sheriff will back me up on that."

"We'll hire you," John said, his voice now a touch desperate. "To take care of the stock till we auction them."

Jake looked at him—the young man's pale, watery blue eyes, his cheeks now a blotchy mottled pink on the pasty white skin as the flush of rage waned from his ears. "I'll be here working as long as Ms. Blake stays. Stock won't go lacking," Jake told them.

Bill put a hand on the young man's shoulder. "Come on, John. Time to go."

Jake followed them outside, watching until the last of their rigs disappeared down the road and made the turn toward town.

"Thank you. John scares me. So does Uncle Bill."

He turned to see Dree standing there. "You should've called me. I would've come."

She didn't acknowledge him, just stood meeting his eyes, her slate ones strangely dark and too full of sorrow, too full of defeat. She turned her head toward his trailer. "I'm glad you brought Coal. Cougar missed him."

C. J. "Country" James

33

Breaking Point

S HEILA GOLDSMITH WAS THRILLED to have
Dree's chickens, and Dree was touched that Jake
offered to build the woman a coop for them. He
did it in an afternoon, even piping the water over and
wiring in the power. Dree helped dig, hammer in nails,
and hold boards, then staple up wire heavy enough to
keep varmints out.

"They probably will quit laying for a couple of days,
maybe a week," Dree told Sheila when she and Jake
brought the chickens over in burlap sacks after the sun
went down, putting the sleepy birds on their new roosts
as quietly as they'd taken them down from their
perches at home.

Dree brought in their feed, feeders, and waterers,
Jake setting them up as Dree explained nesting boxes,
egg collection, feed rations, and the necessity of
infrared heat lamps for warmth along with DayLites to
keep them laying in winter.

"I'll get some books from the library. I've never
had chickens, but they've got to be easier than goats,"
Sheila said. "Don't you worry. I promise to take the

best care I can of them, Dree. They're beautiful birds. I love that fancy rooster. He's something."

The woman grabbed her arm as she started to get in the truck. "Dree. I'm so sorry. If there's anything I can do...."

Dree forced a smile. "Thanks."

♦

DREE HAD THE MOBILE SLAUGHTER come early, even though the pigs were forty to sixty pounds light of her preferred weight of two-eighty. "Would your dad take the meat?" Dree asked.

Jake nodded.

The day that the shop called to tell her the fresh meat was ready, they loaded up Jake's truck bed and made the drive, the boxes packed in dry ice. "I'll bring the hams and the bacon up later, once it's cured," Dree told Franklin. "I hope you like smoke cured."

"What's going on, Dree?" Franklin asked.

She turned to Jake. "You haven't told him?"

"No. Didn't think it my place, unless—"

"Told me what?" Franklin demanded.

Dree swallowed. "I have to leave the ranch."

"Why?"

Dree shook her head, her breath catching, her chest locking up. She turned away and tried to find air. She couldn't...wanted to scream at herself for being so weak. Red-darkness flooded her, and she tried to find a grip on the truck. Hands grabbed her, a shoulder— Jake's—catching her under the arm as she felt her knees turn to water.

"*DREE!*"

"I–I'm okay. I–just–need to–catch my breath."

"On the ground. Sit! Head between your legs. Now!" Franklin snapped. And she felt him put her there.

That made it worse. "I can't—"

Chaos erupted around her, the blood-red darkness filling her eyes, the roar deafening her ears. Explosions...faces. Adrian's bloody body, no face. She was smothering, hot, suffocating slime drowning her, a weight on her chest. She couldn't *breathe*. And, through it, she heard screaming...screaming, not sure if it was hers or just the kind that bounced around inside of her head. All she wanted was for everything to just stop. But it wouldn't. She couldn't *breathe*.

"WHY DIDN'T YOU TELL ME?"

"I wanted to get Dree's permission, but, every time I started to broach the subject, she'd brush me off. I don't even know the whole story, just that her dad's in the hospital, got brain cancer, had surgery, and is undergoing treatment. He signed over the ranch to his brothers, and they're selling. I managed to get her sixty days. They wanted her out last Monday."

Franklin dropped into his desk chair and spun it around to face out the window. Jake took his usual chair and waited. The space, the silence, let his mind ease, and he pieced together what else Dree had told him and what he knew from months back when they'd sat down for dinner and sundaes.

He offered it up, the two other small bits of information he had. "She has a grandmother—Gram Blake, she calls her. Gram Blake is like you—rules the family. But she does it with money, Dree says. So, when this happened, I asked her if she'd talked to her grandmother about it all, and she said that she couldn't. Her grandmother's been out of town since before this happened, and the house-sitter staying at the lady's place says she doesn't know where she is."

Franklin had slowly spun back around as Jake talked.

"Okay. This is beginning to make some sense, then."

Jake frowned. "How?"

"I don't know, yet, but I do know one thing. Dree needs a lawyer, and we're going to get her one, right now." He picked up the phone.

There was a knock at the door. "Come in," Franklin growled, putting the receiver back down.

Doc Perkins poked his head in. "I've got her sedated."

"Come in. Sit."

The man stepped in, closed the door, and sank into the big, leather, antique "King's" chair that had been Jake's favorite when he'd been a kid.

"What was that? Some kind of fit?" Franklin asked. "Is she epileptic?"

"No. That's what is known as a panic attack."

Jake sat forward. "You mean like real bad hyperventilating?" He'd never seen anyone have hysteria like Dree had, not even Jack's girlfriend when the star high school quarterback died on the field of a broken neck.

Perkins shook his head. "Sometimes that happens, but no, not what you think. Usually, the opposite— hypoventilation. It's related to...or even a symptom of PTSD. Sometimes mimics a heart attack, sometimes an asthma attack, sometimes both. Sometimes choking."

The man rolled his eyes from Jake to Franklin, then back. "It's very serious. At least it is as bad as this young woman exhibits it. Something very, very bad, very traumatic, happened to her sometime in her life. This was a very violent episode. I'm glad I was in the neighborhood."

"Is there a treatment?" Jake asked.

Doc Perkins blew a breath. "Psych evaluation, anti-depressants."

"You mean like Prozac," Franklin said, his voice scalding.

Perkins nodded.

Franklin waved a hand, shook his head.

"Inositol, an over-the-counter supplement, can help sometimes, and, actually, beta-blockers—heart medication—too, but I don't recommend beta-blockers. Mostly, prevention through managing the triggers is best."

"The girl's under a *lot* of stress," Franklin said.

"Well, the first thing is to get rid of what's triggering the attacks. The more she has them, the more frequent and worse they'll get."

Franklin stood up. "Okay. We take away the stress, then."

How the hell do we do that? Jake wondered.

He found out moments after Doc Perkins left as Franklin hollered out the door for Wil and got on the phone to Fran, then Loretta. Finally, he called the ranch's lawyer.

"Get back to the Blake place tonight, Jake. Take Mike Guthrie with you. And you're both to take rifles and your sidearms. You're holding the fort. I'll be down tomorrow with help."

DREE RODE WITH FRANKLIN—alone— nobody else in the truck. He explained his plan, explained the law as he understood it from talking to a man named Powell. "I trust what he says," Franklin told her. "He's gotten us through a lot of legal scrapes."

"I'm sorry," she said. "I didn't mean for you to get involved."

The man cast her a quick sideways glance. "You think you've got such big shoulders that you can just waltz your way through this all by yourself?"

Dree looked out the window. "...No. I–I.... Dad...."

"Dree, you just concentrate on finding the paperwork proving what's yours."

"I have to pack up the house."

"Loretta and Fran drove down early with a crew of movers and a truck. I called around, and there's a building you can rent for the stuff that's your Dad's. Jake tells me you were told to take all the stock, except the cattle. Is that right?"

"Yes."

"Legally, or, at least as legal as can be determined, right now, that transfers their ownership to you. Jake heard them say it, and that, according to Powell, is good enough as things stand. We load 'em and haul 'em out of there. Today. Along with everything else that's yours."

"I'm going to lose my fourth cutting."

"So? Unless we can get this thing stopped, there's not a thing to do about it. Accept that, hold your head up, cut your losses, and get to work starting over again."

Dree's eyes started burning. She had no place *to* start over again. She'd always thought the ranch would be home, no matter what. *You were wrong*, she told herself. *You should have known he wouldn't give it over to you. Dad, you're turning me out of my* life. *And all because I'm a girl! How* could *you*? "Sexist pig!"

"Me?"

Startled, she looked over at Franklin. "No!...I'm so sorry. *No!* I–I was thinking about Dad."

She saw him pull a deep breath, sigh it out. "Dree, men in this country are hard men. We're raised hard, we live hard. And we try to protect our women—" Again, he drew a breath. "Well, a lot of us...the right ones among us do. It's in our blood, part of our...call it part of our nature. Your dad probably thinks he's doing what's best for you."

"Like shoving me at *Jake*!"

He rolled an eye her way. "No. That was Jake's doing. Jake's in love with you. Has been since right after he first met you."

"Oh, *God*! You can't know that!"

"I do know that. Found him hysterical in the barn. Knew the symptoms. I had them myself when I met…when I first met the woman I still love, even now as she buried up at the ranch, rotting in dirt."

She shut her mouth.

"And what's so bad about that, Dree?" Franklin asked. "Jake's a good boy. I should know. I raised him up."

The sound in his voice, that broke something inside her. "I know," she said softly. "He told me."

"You don't have to love him back. You don't have to *have* him. But don't blame your dad for what's all Jake's doing." He paused, then said, "…And mine."

Jolted by that revelation, her every thought dried up. Except one—betrayal. Franklin Jarvis was party to it all, a man she had believed to be trustworthy, straight up…honorable. Did still, though she fought that, even as the thought rolled through her mind.

She shook her head and finally found a place for her eyes and her hands—a trustworthy place—on her dogs sitting curled at her feet.

C. J. "Country" James

34

Pulling Up Stakes

WITH MIKE GUTHRIE'S HELP, Jake had the center pivot broke down and ready to move.

Next, they tackled the hay stored up in the loft, moving the bales to the loft doors, ready to load onto the flatbeds Jake knew were coming.

"Where's the rest," Mike asked. "This can't be all from those fields."

"She sold it as soon as she baled it, I think."

"Good. I hate these little bitty bales."

"Horse people love 'em, I guess."

"Horse people, maybe."

"Yeah, but they've got a point. Can't just pull off a leaf and throw it into the feed bunk with ours."

Mike laughed. "No-oo."

The grumble of a semi truck got Jake looking. "J.D.'s here," he said. Then, "And his kid's right behind him."

"We're going to need more than two trucks," Mike said. "This is more than one load all by itself."

"Yeah."

Jake climbed down. Mike continued to move bales.

Reaching outside, he saw three more rigs coming up the road—not J.D.'s. These had System Transport, Inc., painted on them. They pulled up short, parking in a line along the county road, nose-to-tail, their air brakes releasing as they shut down. His uncle, J.D., and his cousin, J.D., Jr., walked up. His cousin grinned and pushed his Stetson back, then reached out and grabbed Jake's hand to give it a shake. His uncle gave him his usual slam on the back, followed by a quick bear hug, his stiff, handlebar mustache pricking Jake on the neck. "Jake! Long time no see!"

Jake grinned. "You still got that stupid alley cat with you?"

"He ain't no alley cat. He's my Grade A, Number One foot warmer."

Jake tipped his head toward J.D.'s fancied up tractor with its extra long cab, even a skylight. "I thought you had air conditioning and heat in those portable condos."

"Do. But nothing beats a warm body, you know." He smacked Jake on the arm—hard—and grinned. "You *do* know that, right?"

"Get a wife."

"No way. Just got rid of the last one. Cat's way cheaper and don't whine and complain. ....Well, not much. 'Sides, there ain't no honey-do list." The man winked. "What we loadin' up first, Jake? We pay by the hour, not just the mile, so time's money, boy."

Dree was startled to see the line of semi-tractors pulling flatbeds lining the county road. She was more surprised when Franklin pulled in, weaving between two more semis to park up on the lawn, out of the way. There was a moving van—yet another semi—with "Hernando's Moving Co., Inc." painted in big red letters on its side. It was backed up to the veranda with a carpet-covered ramp running from her front door up into it, men, most of them Hispanic, carting blanketed furniture out of the house. Drop-jawed, she stared. "I don't know if I've got enough money to pay for all this, not and put a down payment on...someplace."

"We'll worry about that later. Remember. You cut your losses, and get to work starting over again. You do what you have to as the doing needs done."

Something about him, his outlook, made Dree want to weep. She didn't. She wouldn't. But the warmth rose in her, pushing itself into her throat, into her eyes. She pulled a breath, caught Franklin dodge a quick glance at her, and let it out in a long, slow release. "Okay. What do you need me to do?"

"We—you and me—need to get to any kind of paperwork you know of that'll help us prove your ownership of the property we're pulling out of here."

She nodded. That was easy.

"And I'd like to see anything you can find on title, deed, land patents—anything. Even a plat map can help."

That wouldn't be as easy. Her dad's filing system was to shove everything willy-nilly in boxes. "Okay."

Inside, she heard women's voices upstairs. She frowned.

"I told you. That's Francine—my daughter you met at the Heron spread," Franklin said, "and Jake's mom, Loretta. I figured you'd want women doing the packing up, since, well…."

Again, Dree nodded. *Don't look a gift horse….* "It's fine," she said. "It's…wonderful of you…you all. I don't know how I'll repay you your kindness for all of this." And she meant that, even if the idea of strangers touching her things rubbed on her nerves.

Franklin stood, hands jingling change in his pocket.

Pulling herself out of her dead-zone, she said, "Sorry. The office is over here."

He followed her in, stopped, looked, then settled in a stiff-backed chair, the wood creaking.

She grabbed the desk chair and pulled it out. "Here. I need to get to the filing cabinets behind you."

He got up and, with an uneasy look, sat himself down into her dad's big, rolling, desk chair.

Unlocking the cabinet, she pulled out the folder holding her bills-of-sale and equipment and truck titles, handing it over to him. Then she grabbed the portfolio she'd gotten from Gram Blake granting her use of one of the deep wells and a quarter-section of hay ground, plus the loan repayment book that went with it.

Franklin was busy leafing through the first folder, so she laid the portfolio and loan file off to the side.

Finally, she pulled out her pay books. "Do you want these?" she asked.

He looked up. "What are they?"

"Receipts, copies of checks, and the records I made of my expenses and profits from my hay."

"Give 'em here." He held out his hand, his sleeve brushing the pile she'd put on the desk corner.

The portfolio and loan repayment file hit the floor. He frowned. Took her record book and the AR/AP/GL folders, then reached down and grabbed up the slewed stack from the floor. He opened it—the portfolio—its shiny black surface and gold-embossed lettering shimmering as it reflected the overhead light. He reached out and turned on the desk lamp, then sat back and began reading.

Dree started pulling out boxes containing her dad's records and papers. Opening the oldest she could locate, she began leafing through the pile of unsorted, miscellaneous sheets inside. Already she knew this was going to take hours, maybe days.

She was two hours into it, starting her fourth box, when Franklin called a halt. "Dree, close those up. Fran and Loretta are ready to start in here."

Gratefully, she slipped on the lids and got up, her butt numb from sitting on the hardwood floor. Her knee was a little stiff, too. She worked her leg, freeing it up. "I'll help them pack," she said.

He nodded and, taking the stack of files, folders, and a couple of loose pieces of paper she'd pulled from her dad's boxes, went to the door. "It's going to be all right, Dree. Keep your chin up."

"WHAT ARE WE GOING TO DO about the cow?" Jake asked.

"She been milked out this morning?" Franklin asked.

"Yes, sir. Mike did it both last night and this morning. I can't get the hang of it."

Franklin wasn't listening. His eyes were on the door of the horse barn. He pointed. "Cats. Go get Dree."

"I don't think they're hers."

Franklin eyed him. "Ask her."

Jake trotted to the house, found Dree, and she came out with him. "I didn't even think about them," she admitted. "I usually feed them in the barn. Did you?" she asked, her eyes soft on his.

Jake shook his head. "Sorry. I didn't realize—"

"It's okay. Maybe it's better, anyway. Maybe they'll come despite all the fuss because they're really hungry."

"They're wild, right?" Franklin asked.

"Not really. No. They just don't like…."

"Men," Franklin finished for her. "Okay. You catch 'em, we'll haul 'em."

Jake saw her smile for the first time since the whole ordeal had begun. "You have carriers?" he asked.

"In the garden tool shed."

"I'll get them."

When he got back from giving Dree the cat carriers, he found Franklin standing, holding the Jersey, a nice leather halter slipped on her head. "We'll load her up front in Dree's stock trailer. Jake, I need a good piece of plywood."

"For what?"

Franklin sighed. "To protect her udder from getting kicked or bumped by the horses, Jake. She's a milk cow, not a Hereford."

"So? She's a cow."

Franklin pointed down at her bag. "You see that thing? It bruises real easy. Then it's mastitis, and I know you know about *that*."

Jake did.

Dree came out hauling two carriers, the cats inside hunkered down, yowling. "I've got a bra for her," she called. "Don't load her until I can get it on her."

Jake glanced at Franklin, but his granddad just stood, his hand scratching the cow. "A bra for a cow?"

Franklin laughed. "Yeah. It's a contraption you strap on when you let the calf get half, but stop 'em from raiding the two other quarters. You switch sides out every milking while the calf's on. Leave it to Dree."

"Leave what to Dree, Grandpa?"

Franklin nodded toward her retreating back. "She's a smart little gal. You picked a good 'un, Jake. Now, if you can just set the hook and the line don't break."

35

Broken Dreams

FRANKLIN WOULDN'T LET HER DRIVE her own rig, not with the stock loaded in. "I know you're capable, and all, but I'd feel better if you let Mike drive it on in. I want to talk to you, anyway."

Dree breathed a sigh of relief. She didn't want to try pulling the stock trailer, loaded, up the winding long miles of highway that led into Adams before getting to the four-lane. "I'll ride with you," she agreed.

"Good."

Even with the semis long gone with her center pivot, hay, tractor and all the equipment, they still looked like a vagabond caravan heading out, the moving truck, the line of pickups with trailers.... They took everything that was hers by right, and even things that she thought weren't...like the garden tools, saddles....

"How would you feel about living in Heron till things sort themselves out?" Franklin asked her. "Fran said she'd love to have you. 'Course, she'll work you to death, where, at the ranch, you'd be free to come and go as you please. My place is closer to seeing your dad, too."

Dree reached down to fondle Chip's ears. "Dad won't let me come see him. Not since the day he told me about signing the ranch over."

Franklin stayed quiet for a long while—miles. "Well, you think on it."

She did. All the way to the ranch. When they got there, pulling in long after dark, she'd decided to take up Fran's offer. It would get her away from Jake. She was getting way too used to him, and that wasn't healthy.

Franklin seemed sad when she told him the next morning, but he gave his blessing to her choice. Cougar loaded along with the Jersey, she signed her dad's three horses over to Franklin, then followed Fran's pickup down the drive, Jake, Franklin, and Old Man Jarvis watching from the front steps.

She felt a lift as the Jarvis ranch house disappeared. She was free. *Not free. Not nearly, even*, a little voice whispered inside her. But she *could* concentrate on trying to put her life back together, this time in some way that could never make her vulnerable to decisions made by a man. She had a degree. She could find a job. In time, maybe she could buy a ranch of her own. "Damn you, Dad."

◆

LEARNING TO HANDLE MARES with foals at their sides, learning to handle bulls up close and personal—very personal—was new to Dree. Fran's sense of humor helped get Dree over the stumbles and humps that tripped her up time and again. The great thing was that she got to see Chocolate, again, and the young bull remembered her, coming up to the fence for treats and scratches. He was all healed up, and the scar under his knee was barely noticeable.

With the number of bulls being hand fed and handled so regularly, Dree wondered how Fran had the energy, even with the help who drove in every day, leaving come evening. The animals were taught, not just how to lead, but how to mount large, docile steers used as teasers, then to allow an artificial vagina to be slipped over their erection. Fran started the calves on their kindergarten education, as she called it, even before they were weaned, getting them to lead around by a rope attached to their own mothers' tails, then graduating them to leading on a beefed-up horse hot-walker.

The big eye-opener was actually how Fran trained them to mount the teaser.

"Aren't these range bulls?"

"Some of them are," Fran said. She motioned. "Come here."

She led Dree over to the barn where Chocolate was kept. "Number 9 and Number 843," she said. "Old—very old—range bulls, their blood coming down from some of the original Jarvis stock.

"The semen I collect from them is shipped all over the world, now, mostly to specialty herds here in the States, but to Europe, Africa, South America, China, and Japan, too. One straw from either one of them is sold for over two-hundred dollars, and I get anywhere from fifty to five-hundred straws per ejaculation.

"I get fifty- to sixty-thousand straws per bull per year from these boys and they're ancient. I'm getting anywhere from eighty- to one-hundred-thousand from those in their prime and, even though their semen isn't as valuable, only nets anywhere from twenty-five to a hundred per straw, it's still worth the time and the effort, don't you think? Do the math."

Dree thought 'wow'. And she'd thought her hay was a cash crop.

"Franklin built this," Fran said. "Ask me to run it after my Alfie got run off the road by a four-wheeler and got turned to charcoal."

Dree flinched.

Fran noticed. "The dangers of hauling hazmat, Dree. He was pulling a tanker loaded with avgas when some bitch decided she just had to pass on a hill. And, of course, there was somebody coming. And good ol' Alfie, he just had to take the high road, killing himself rather than them. Don't ever marry a trucker, not unless you wanna stay lonely and missin' them for the rest of your days."

"Franklin lets you run this ranch all by yourself?" Dree asked over dinner a couple weeks later after helping Fran with doing the final stage of weaning the calves.

The woman frowned at her. "Of course. Why wouldn't he?"

Dree shook her head. Then, at Fran's continued stare—*must be a Jarvis hereditary trait*—said, "Because you're a woman, and, to quote my dad, 'women have no business running a ranch. They're meant to marry and have kids.'"

Fran burst out laughing. "You're kidding me, right?"

Anger brimming up in her, Dree said, "No."

The woman laughed even harder. Then, sobering suddenly, she said, "What a fucking male chauvinist pig!"

Dree's thoughts exactly.

Then, "No, Dree. We got a saying: 'Franklin's an equal opportunity discourager.' If you can't do the work, you're gone. If you can, no matter what kind of gonads you got, you stay on. I've got the balls and then some, excuse the expression, more than my brothers, even, and Dad's proud of that."

"I NEED YOU TO GO with a crew over to Heron, Jake. There's some fences need mending, and Fran's got her hands full this week with weaning the foals."

Jake jumped at the chance. He hadn't seen Dree in almost a month, not since she'd left with his Aunt Fran for Heron. "Yes, *sir*."

Franklin rolled an eye at him. "You're there to work, Jake."

"I know."

Then, he saw Franklin smile as his granddad went back to assaulting his sausage, gravy, and biscuits.

◆

DRIVING OVER TOOK FOREVER. When they finally pulled in, Fran came out, but not Dree.

Fran saw him looking, and grinned. "She's helping the vet with one of colts, Jake. Horse barn. You remember the way, right?"

Jake grinned and trotted off.

He found her leaning against a stall door, smiling up at a tall, Native American man who had a long pony tail hanging down his back. "Hi," Jake said, walking up.

The man stood away from where he was leaning. Dree did, too. "Hi," she said back. "This is Dr. Warren Jeffries, Jake. Dr. Jeffries, this is Jake Jarvis. His Coal Bar High is the sire of Jake's Charboy Bar, here."

The man held out his hand, "Pleased to meet you."

Jake nodded and shook, a smile freezing on his face. "Likewise," he said…and didn't mean it, at all. Dree's eyes were that lavender that he'd only seen once, and there wasn't a bit of sunlight, reflected or otherwise, to make them that way. She practically glowed. That glow changed to a frown as he stood there, his tongue glued to the roof of his mouth.

He shut his eyes to her, and turned to the vet. "How's the colt, Doc?" It was the only thing he could think of to cover himself.

"He's perfectly fine. They're descended. He just carries them high. It's a trait common in Quarter Horse colts. By the time he's eighteen months, they'll stay down where they should."

So now he knew what was up with the colt. "Good to know, Doc. Thanks. I'll let you get back to it, then." He touched his finger to the brim of his hat, "Dree," and turned on his heel and worked real hard to walk, not run, from what he saw in her eyes.

C. J. "Country" James

36

In The Drink

DREE FINISHED UP WITH THE VET around two and, seeing him off, went to find Jake to tell him the good news. Spying the crew working the fence up over by the south tree line, she headed over. But Jake wasn't there. Unwilling to ask, she headed to the house to get a bite. She hadn't eaten since breakfast, and her stomach was gnawing itself.

Inside, Fran was on the telephone. Dree went and washed up, then headed into the kitchen.

"What happened between you and Jake?" Fran asked coming around the corner.

Surprised by the question, Dree said, "Nothing. He came out just as Dr. Jeffries was finishing up with little J-Char, asked if the colt was going to be okay, then left like he was in a big hurry."

"That's it? That's all he said to you?"

"He really didn't say anything at all to me. Just talked to the vet about the colt."

Fran frowned.

"What's wrong?"

"You didn't say anything…hurtful to him?"

Dree stared at the woman. "No. He barely acknowledged me. I just now went out to find him over where the crew's re-setting the fence to talk to him, but he wasn't there."

"That's because he's disappeared. Nobody can find him, and he's got the keys to the crew cab." Fran approached, put her hand on Dree's arm. "This is going to sound bad, but he didn't catch you kissing Doc Jeffries or anything, did he?"

Dree practically choked on her laughter. "Nooo. Gawd. What do you think I am?! That man must be, what, a dozen years older than me?" Then, seeing Fran was dead serious, she stopped herself. "What are you saying, Fran?"

"What exactly *were* you doing when Jake saw you?"

Puzzled, Dree related their conversation. "Dr. Jeffries and I were talking about Coal when Jake himself walked up. It was perfect timing. I introduced him as Coal's owner, and they shook hands. Dr. Jeffries is thinking he might want to breed a mare to Coal."

Fran was nodding. "Okay. I'll call Franklin back."

What did Franklin have to do with this? "Fran? Why call Franklin?"

"I told you. Jake's disappeared. Hours ago. Probably right after he left you and Doc Jeffries at the barn."

"On foot?"

"Well, he didn't take a truck, and he didn't take a horse or trying riding a bull."

It was beginning to dawn on Dree that Fran and Franklin, both, thought she'd done something to cause this. "Fran. When he came into the barn, he looked happy...great, in fact. Not shadowed like he had been working on my dad's ranch. He just was worried about whether the colt's testicles had dropped okay."

Fran shook her head. "You are so clueless. How would Jake know about J-Char's ball problem? You tell him, did you?"

"No."

"I didn't tell him. I didn't tell Franklin, either. How would Jake know?"

"He asked."

"Did he?"

Dree thought about it. "Yeah. He asked if the colt was going to be okay."

"Specifically?"

"Yes."

"So he asked about dropped testicles, did he?'

Dree frowned at the sarcasm. "No. He asked if the colt was going to be okay," she repeated.

"Right. And *bull*shit. He was covering his ass. You haven't a clue about Jarvis men. Hell, you haven't a clue about men, in general. Honey, Jake saw you with a handsome, highly eligible man, and I bet you dollars to doughnuts you were smiling and laughing and having a good ol' time. And Jake took that to mean you were smitten by him. Now he's gone off, sulking. All we can hope is that he don't hurt himself."

"What?!" Dree felt her breath stop. She caught herself, hands gripping the edge of the table as the red roar came rising up. She fought it back down.

"Franklin's on his way, now. We're going out looking for him."

"I'll find him," Dree said. "I'll do it."

"Dree, no!"

Dree pushed past her and bolted out the door. The screen door slammed. She heard it come open again with its stretching spring sound as she whistled her dogs.

"Dree, get back in here!"

She ran to the barn and grabbed Cougar's bridle, then ran to the pasture where he was lazily swatting flies in the shade. "COUG-," she hollered. He twisted an ear her way. She whistled, and, turning around on his haunches, he trotted over, making his little grunting sounds.

She let him out, and he dropped his head for her to slip in the bit, then buckle the crownpiece over his ears, latching the cheek piece home, then the throatlatch. "Over, big guy. Fence," she said, and, he shuffled sideways so she could use the rails to clamber up on him. "Laddie? Chipper? Find Jake. Fi-ind Ja-ake," she repeated.

Chip barked.

Fran came around the corner. "Dree, wait for Franklin."

Laddie began running in circles, tail up and flagging. "Seek. Find Jake," Dree said, again, shifting Cougar away from where Fran was coming at her, praying the dogs connected her words with her meaning. It had been weeks since they'd seen him or heard her say his name. "Find Jake."

Laddie kept circling, then headed out toward the horse barn.

"Dree," Fran said, walking up to put a hand on her leg."

Dree looked down at her. "If it's my fault, then I'll fix it."

"You don't know him. You don't know about him. Wait for Franklin, Dree."

Laddie was circling, tail flagging. She felt her hope drop. Suddenly, he stopped, his nose glued to the ground, practically inhaling the dust. He lifted his head, looked her way, then started barking—his signal to her that he'd "found." "Seek," she said. "Find him. Good boy. Find him. Where's Jake?"

The dog cast, zig zagging, then took off like a bolt following along the lane that headed down toward the river. Dree backed away from Fran, then nudged Cougar into a jog.

"DREE! *WAIT!*"

Dree pushed Cougar into a lope, then, when she'd almost caught up with her dogs, eased him down slower. Laddie had his nose to the ground, Chip right on his tail. They were making a bee-line along the right wheel track.

Getting to the trees about a mile down, both dogs crawled under the fence and disappeared. Sliding off, she tied Cougar's reins up and left him to graze, crawling through where she saw the underbrush broken.

A few yards ahead, the going got steep and slick, and she had to resort to sliding down on her butt. She missed catching herself on a narrow fisherman's trail and, with a shock, shot, feet first, into the river.

The water was deep and cold, despite it being the last week in August. Chip appeared and, running the bank, began barking.

Paddling her way downstream, she tried to find a good place to get out, but the bank seemed to get steeper and steeper, no shallows. She headed upstream, again, fighting a surprisingly strong current, Chip still barking his head off. "Chip. It's okay. Good boy. Shush," she called to him. He was distracting her, making her nerves fray.

Finding a downed log, she clung to it and tried to figure herself a way up. "Dammit. Stupid," she cursed herself.

"Dre-eeee!"—Jake's voice, far off.

"HE-EERE," she called back. She'd *found* him. ...Well, he'd found her, but he was okay.

Chip started barking, again. "Shush! You're driving me nuts, Chip!"

"Dree!"

She heard Laddie barking, too, now.

Jake's voice was above her. "I'm here. I'm fine," she answered. "Just can't see a way up."

He came sliding down the bank, holding onto the deadfall. "Here. Take my hand." He reached out, his hand inches from her.

"I'll pull you in, silly."

"Take. My. Hand."

"Okay. Don't say I didn't warn you."

She grabbed. He grabbed back, and, with a wrenching pull that felt like he'd jerk her arm off, got her out of the water, his other arm grabbing her around the middle as they fell backwards into the brush...and slid back down to fall over the edge back into the water. "Told you so," she gasped.

He grinned. "And there goes my hat, too. You've really got it in for my hats, don't you?"

"Not really."

"Come on. Grab a hold of my belt. There's a wide spot further upstream, a little sand beach."

"I can swim on my own, thanks."

"Okay. Stay with me and stay close to the bank. That current out there is real strong."

"I will."

37

Not Death, But Forever

THE LITTLE SAND BEACH was actually pebbles. Surrounded by ferns, some creeping, succulent-looking ground vines, some nice, plushy moss, and the gnarled roots of trees exposed by high water, it felt like a private alcove. "There used to be a place like this down by the creek that runs through Dad's place," Dree said. "Then, one year, high water during the spring melt-off washed it gone. I was so sad. It took my favorite tree downstream, too."

"I have a special place at the ranch I like to go sit. You can't see it from the house, so I go there when I want to be alone and think," he said.

"Is that what you're doing today?"

He went quiet on her. She sat watching the water, trying to do what he did—outwait him. It didn't work. "Everybody is worried about you. ...Fran and Franklin, that is. Maybe the crew, too. I don't know."

"Franklin?"

"Yeah. Fran was talking to him on the phone when I went in for some lunch after the vet left. Why'd you leave? Fran thinks it's my fault."

"No."

She looked over at him, his wet hair sticking to his forehead and temples, to the back of his neck. "I think she's right. You thought.... I don't know what you thought, but *something*...and all because I was standing there talking with Dr. Jeffries."

Again, silence. Just as she was about open her mouth to say something more, he spoke: "You looked happy."

He turned his eyes to her. "That's the happiest I've ever seen you."

"Okay. You know why?"

He went back to watching the water.

"Because Dr. Jeffries is a highfalutin equine specialist and, when he saw J-Char, he asked me about Coal. Wants to breed a mare he owns to him. Then, in typical, perfect Jarvis timing, you walked in. I was happy for Coal and for you. ...And, yes, for Dr. Jeffries, too. I was proud. That's why I was happy, Jake Jarvis. Is that so wrong?"

He shook his head. "No."

"Jake." She reached a hand out and just brushed his. "I'm not interested in the vet, if that's what you thought."

She wasn't expecting it. He reached out, fast as a rattlesnake strike, and, grabbing her head, planted his lips on hers, his momentum carrying them both over. She didn't fight—she didn't want to. She was hungry for him, and that shocked her. She found her arms hugging him tight, rubbing his back, her crushed lips willing, even though he was hurting them.

He lifted his head, his eyes, hard, questioning, searching, looking into hers. Then he kissed her, again, softly this time, a tenderness there that made her melt, butterflies bubbling inside her. ...His hand, one gentle on her face, the other stroking her side. She sank into it, into the bliss, wanted more—

"All right, you two. Are you about done?"

Jake leaped to his feet. Dree sat up, turning her face away, the curse of her mother burning her up. Jake's hand grabbed hers, lifting her, and she found her legs. She was shaking, and it wasn't with cold.

♦

FRANKLIN TRAILED BEHIND, and Dree felt like he was herding them. Branded in her brain was the frown on his face when they'd climbed up to the fisherman's path—like an angry, dark thunderhead or a ticked-off bull.

When they got to the lane. Cougar was gone.

Dree panicked. The red-black rose up, but she beat it back down. *Not now! Go away!* "Cougar! COU-GAR! *Omigod! COU-GA-AAR!*"

"Fran took him back," Franklin snapped as he got himself unhooked from a barb on the fence. "If you want to sneak off, don't leave your mule standing bold as you please by your trail busted through the bushes, and don't have your dogs posted like beacons right where you lay," he growled. "Get back to walking. *March.* The mosquitoes are eating me *alive.*"

Jake glanced at her and grinned. She rolled her eyes, shaking her head. He might think this great fun, but she was humiliated.

"**B**E CAREFUL, JAKE," Franklin said on the ride home, the hired hands long since having driven themselves back to the ranch using a spare set of keys Franklin had brought up.

"I just kissed her. I didn't even mean to. ...And she kissed me back. She *wanted* me."

"You remember picking out your first horse?"

"Yeah."

"You remember me telling you to be really sure of your choice, because there was no turning him back once you threw your saddle up on him?"

"Yeah, I do." Jake smirked. He was way ahead of Franklin, this time. "And the next day, I wanted to pick a new one, and you wouldn't let me."

"Why was that?"

"To teach me to make better choices."

"No, not the picking. The feeling you had inside that made you want to trade back for a different horse."

"Fear."

"Right."

"I'd picked for flashy, and he was too hot. I'm not going to change my mind about Dree, Grandpa."

"Not you. *Her.*"

"I'm not changing my mind."

Franklin cursed, a rare thing. "You know," he said after a time. "Sometimes I think a post is smarter than you in some things."

"Y OU SAID I HADN'T A CLUE about Jarvis men," Dree said over a dinner of really good, hot stew Fran whipped up from leftovers of last night's supper. "So why don't you tell me?"

Fran eyed her, spooned in another mouthful, then, wiping her lips, sat back.

Same exact mannerisms as Franklin and Jake, even Old Man Jarvis, Dree thought. *Must be genetic or something.*

"I'm a Jarvis *woman*, Dree. What can I possibly tell you about Jarvis *men?*

Dree felt the test, the older woman's challenge of her to earn it. "Well, let's see. You grew up with how many brothers?"

"Fi— …Four."

"I'd say you qualify."

Fran looked past her, her eyes distant. "Yeah. I suppose I do, and I can. Tell you. But I just don't know if I should."

"I'm a big girl. I can handle it."

Fran's eyes locked onto hers, a strange sadness coming over her face. "I'll just say this, Dree. With a Jarvis, it ain't 'till death do you part. It's forever."

38

Decisions

T HEY SAT AND TALKED, staying up till long after bedtime. Fran was supportive, not critical, when Dree explained that she didn't want to get married, would never have kids—not ever. "I've told Jake that repeatedly."

"Well, for a woman, it's a smart, safe way, especially these days, that's sure." The woman's eyes went far away, then she shook herself. "I wouldn't trade my times with Alfie, though, much as it hurts now that he's gone."

♦

F RANKLIN CALLED HER TO THE RANCH the following Monday...wouldn't say why. Reluctant to leave Fran with all the work they had scheduled, Dree tried to postpone until Saturday. "That way I can go get the groceries we need, too."

Franklin insisted she had to come today.

Driving in, Dree saw two strange cars parked in the visitors' parking. Pulling in next to them, she peeked in the closest as she got out, but no clues presented themselves. By the look of the cars, she thought, *brokers, Realtors, or lawyers.* She was right on her last guess. She was also surprised. "Gram!"

The old woman, looking, for all her years, healthier and more robust than when Dree had last seen her at Easter, stood up to grab her hand, squeezing hard. "I'm sorry about your dad, Dree."

Eyes burning, Dree just shook her head. "He's doing well. I call the doctor every week to keep tabs."

"I mean that he forced your hand, ran you out. That's what I'm here about. That's why I've come."

Dree didn't want the 'happy' to break, yet. She pushed on, desperate to hold off the hurt that was coming. "Where have you been, Gram? You look great."

Gram Blake smiled, her eyes twinkling. She sat back down, and Dree took a seat on the couch beside her chair. "I went all over Europe. I even went to the Vatican and got to see the Pope. Got a blessing from him. Well, not personal, mind. I was in the crowd, and he blessed us all from the balcony."

"When did you leave?"

"Right after your cousin, Mary, had her baby."

Dree hadn't a clue which cousin had been pregnant. Nor did she care.

Franklin cleared his throat, and Gram Blake turned toward him and gave him a wave of her hand, one of her big composite diamond rings sparkling as the movement caused the stones to throw rainbow glitters. "Dree, honey, why'd you disappear? Nobody could find you, and," she nodded, "believe me, your Uncle Bill, he tried real hard. Your cousin, John, he put a whole half page ad in the paper, even—the Missoula one—paid for it himself to run it a full week trying to find you. This man...." She indicated Franklin. "Mr. Jarvis, here, it's his lawyer fellow who finally got a hold of me, tracked me down through Gerald to let me know you were fine. But I've been calling and calling around. Nobody knew where you'd gone. I thought you had some fancy phone that can reach anywhere, but that number's...well, it's just dead."

A little tick of irritation rose up in Dree. "You disappeared before I did, Gram."

Again, the woman waved her hand, silencing her. "Never you mind me. My business is my business, and I'm old enough and cussed enough to have earned that right, Dree Blake."

"Okay, Gram."

One of the lawyers sat forward. "Mrs. Blake."

"All right. Let's get to it, then. Small talk's done, I guess." Gram turned back to her. "Dree, my sons, they can't sell the ranch, honey. They don't own it. Your granddad put it in a land trust as soon as the law let him, and I'm the sole trustee, now."

Dree sat frozen in place, felt her breath catch. She waited for the rest.

"They all want to sell out. The whole family wants that. If you want that, too, then I'll agree and break the trust."

"I want my...Dad's ranch back."

Her gram patted her hand. The woman glanced over at the two men in suits. "Gerald, get out the paperwork."

The other lawyer shifted.

Franklin just sat, but he was leaned forward, now, elbows on his knees, hands clasped in front of him. Dree saw him give a nod to the other lawyer. "May I?" the other lawyer requested.

A black portfolio was passed over, one with gilt lettering similar to the one she'd been given to put the quarter-section into cultivation, but thicker. The lawyer took his time. Finally, the man looked up and gave a nod to Franklin.

Franklin sat back.

"We can go on, now?" Gram Blake asked, her eyes crinkling at the corner, one eyebrow doing its little quirky lift.

Dree began to relax.

"Dree, honey, if you really want your dad's part of the ranch back, and just that, then that's what we'll do. But what about if you could run the whole Blake ranch—all of it—the same as your granddad used to."

Dree's breath caught hard this time. She grabbed the couch arm, her hand gripping the fine wood there. "What's the whole ranch, Gram?" she whispered.

"There are a thirty-seven sections, total, Dree, fourteen of them not connected to the original ranch. My house is the center of the twenty-three connected sections."

Her Gram was talking about her dad's and both her uncle's places, not just home. Was that what her grandmother meant?

"It's not a lot of land, but it's good land, and your Grandfather Adrian, God Bless, he ran almost a thousand head on those twenty-three sections before he got the Parkinson's. We made enough to pay cash to buy out a family down on the Bitterroot which land he turned to hay for winter feeding. That's why the big barns around the house that you see. That's where we wintered the cows and stored in the hay to feed them through winter and calving, the calving in the big barns, the hay in the pole barns. You think you could handle that, Dree?"

Dree's hands were over her mouth.

"Of all my children and grandchildren, Adienne Annabelle Blake, namesake of my late husband, namesake to me, you alone show the spirit that holds this land. Say the word, and I'll grant you management rights over the whole land patent and purchase. And if you *prove* your worth, then, once proved, I'll name you sole heir and trustee."

Dree couldn't find breath to respond.

"What's your answer, Dree, honey?"

She couldn't believe what her Gram spread before her. Was this real? A whole, huge ranch—her granddad's ranch, the way it used to be, the way he used to talk about. She tried to speak, to ask the questions that whirled around in her. All she managed to breathe out was "Yes."

The old woman laughed, her cackle rattling loud through the silent room. Then, she turned to look at the man she called Gerald and nodded.

His face quiet and still, Franklin rose, nodded once to her, then left the room.

Finally, finally, Dree found her voice. "What's Uncle Bill and Uncle Pete going to say?"

Her gram looked over at her, a sad look coming into her eyes. "They dug their graves, Dree. Your Uncle Bill and Cousin John, they're in a lot of trouble. You haven't been back past your uncles' or over to your dad's place since you left, have you?"

That should have warned her; it should have prepared her. It didn't.

39

Razed, Gutted, & Sold

FRANKLIN THOUGHT he was letting him down easy, thought he was done. But Franklin didn't know. He hadn't kissed her, hadn't looked deep into her eyes, hadn't felt her respond. Jake didn't care that Dree Blake had decided to take control of her grandfather's legacy. He didn't care that it meant she'd chosen to run her own little ranch. He was bound to have the girl, anyway. They could do it all. Together they could. They'd find a way.

Dree was happy. That's what counted. He saw it in her eyes when, coming in for lunch with the crew after a morning of setting new posts, her eyes seemed at peace, her face radiant as her grandmother and his great-grandfather traded stories of life in 'the olden days'.

Jake was determined. If she wanted to do this, then he'd do what it took to help her. He told her so. And she smiled, thanking him. She told him she needed to think, to figure things out. She said no. She had to do this herself. Then, leaving him standing there, avoiding his eyes, she climbed in her truck and left.

As her truck rounded the curve, he turned to find Franklin standing there watching him, his face, his eyes holding a look that said everything. Turning back to look down the empty drive, Jake shook his head. "No."

"Where are you going?" Franklin demanded, as he got in his truck.

"I'm going after her."

"Jake—"

"Grandpa. Don't try to stop me. I'm going."

And Franklin stepped back...let him go.

D REE TOOK THE LONG WAY IN, following the old range road that led past Uncle Pete's place instead of going around on the highway. It would take her an hour longer to reach home, but her grandmother's words kept echoing through her—*you haven't been back, have you?*

When she got to Uncle Pete's place, or where it had been, she wasn't prepared. There was nothing except the skeletal ridge of the house's foundation—no barns, no fences, no house. Just the foundation sticking up out of the ground.

Scared, she drove on, coming up on her grandmother's house. Here, nothing had changed. Turning up the road cut in a quarter mile past it, she drove up to the trees that surrounded her Uncle Bill's place. The house—a prefab—was raised off its foundation. It had a sign on the door, and, here, again, the barns were gone, piles of boards, and stacks of corral rails bundled on pallets.

She got out, read the sign on the house, which was some sort of permit, then walked over to the pallets. The tags had a series of numbers written on them.

Scared, now, she headed for home. Cresting the hill, she breathed a sigh of relief as the barns, corrals, and house came into view. But, as she got closer, she saw that, here, too, was destruction. She stopped dead on the road and just stared.

The siding was stripped, the house down to tar paper. The windows were gone. So was the porch and the back stairs. The doors were open...or had been removed. She couldn't tell which. "Omigod."

Easing forward, she got closer, her eyes burning, her breath stopped in her throat. "Omigod."

Pulling in, she got out and, closing her eyes, steadied herself for the worst.

She couldn't get in—the sills were too high without stairs—but she looked, first through the back door, then through the front. In the kitchen and laundry room, they'd ripped out the sinks, hot water tank, the built-in range, the dishwasher, the washer and dryer, the fridge. They'd pulled up the living room carpet. The windows, frames and all, were just gone completely, marks where they'd been plain by the line of old paint. But the stairs were still there, and so were the walls and the floors. They hadn't gutted it. Yet.

Going out to the barn, she saw that pretty much everything was just as had been. Out in the fields, though, little wood slats were stuck here and there in what seemed an arbitrary arrangement, plastic orange tape fluttering in the breeze where it was wrapped around each stick's top. As she looked around, she saw that there were dozens of them covering the winter pastures, the yards, all the land she could see, all the way to the fence lines.

She walked to her hay field. More sticks with orange tape right up to it…. But the field was untouched. She dug fingers down in the ground. It needed water. Soon. Very soon, or she'd lose it and have to replant.

Turning around, she went back to the barn, and, finding a couple of cinder blocks, hauled them over to the house and stacked them up. Then she got more. When she had a rudimentary set of stair steps, she climbed up.

She was standing in what had been the living room when she saw Jake's truck pull in and park beside hers. He came to the front door, looked in at her, said, "Hi."

Dree shook her head. "They–they—" She closed her eyes, felt the red-black rise up. Swallowed and fought it.

THROUGH THE GAPING FRONT DOOR, he saw her sway, pushed himself up, then pulled himself in. He had the little envelope of powder. In his wallet. He hoped he remembered how much water to mix it in.

He reached her and put his hands on her arms, steadying her. "Dree, it's fixable. We can repair it. Make it better than it was."

She leaned into him, eyes shut tight, and groaned. He wrapped his arms around her, and she let him. That made him feel better...brought his confidence back that, yes, Franklin was wrong. He could still win her. "It's fixable, Dree. The siding's stacked around on the orchard side. I saw it when I rolled in."

"I didn't think they could do this. I thought—"

"Shhhh. It's okay. We can fix it. Have you checked the stock?"

She pushed away, standing free, her eyes snapping open, wide...scared. "No. I–I...didn't even think!"

She headed through the kitchen, Jake following her. "Let's take my truck," he said.

"No. Yours is too good. We take mine. ...Would you drive?"

"Happy to," he said, and he meant it. She wasn't shutting him out. She was including him.

She ran around to the passenger side and jumped in.

"We need to get the center pivot set back up," he said as they passed her hay fields.

"I know. And quick. The ground moisture is way, way down. The fourth cutting's just about worthless, now. It's still got to be cut, though."

"The center-pivot—that's a tomorrow job, then."

"Fran and I—"

"Dree. Fran's handled the Heron spread on her own for decades. Right now, it's first things first, second things second. We'll get it worked out."

He sounded sure. But he wasn't. He was used to Franklin figuring things out. *That* had to change. He should have paid more attention to how, why, and when the right things got done, not just wait for Franklin to tell him his job for the day.

They drove the tractor lane all the way to the end, saw no cows, not even when they crisscrossed the pastures.

"Probably on the other side of the creek," Jake said, though he already doubted it. He'd seen no sign. "Let's drive around to the bridge."

Getting over to the other side of the creek, still no cows.

Dree had gone quiet.

"You think they're up in the woods?" Jake asked her.

"There's no water up there."

"Yeah, but do you think they could be? It's hot. When it's hot, they like shade." He didn't add that they liked shade down by the creek. She would know that. But the woods, the hill country, was the only thing left to check.

"They could be," she agreed, but he heard heavy doubt in her voice. He doubted it, too, but he wanted to look to be sure. Even if what he suspected was right, there'd still probably be stragglers—cows missed.

Driving over close to where the hills began to get steeper, he ran to the high ground, drove till the first bench cut him off. "Let's walk," he said. "Let's check where the shade's heaviest."

There were no cows, though. An hour of hoofing it showed no fresh cow pies and the brush and grass hadn't been eaten down.

"They took them," Dree said. "Uncle Bill already sold them."

"Yeah. Or moved them, anyway."

She turned to look at him. "We need to go see Gram Blake."

Jake buried a grin in his arm, pretending to wipe away sweat. He wanted to shout. She'd said 'we'.

♦

"I SAW YOU DRIVE PAST a few hours ago. I wondered how long it'd take you to show," Dree's Gram Blake said.

The elderly lady sat them down in her parlor, as she called it, a small, formal living room. The décor was at odds with the heavy, dark-hued log walls, delicate, spindly-legged end tables set next to small, curl-armed chairs upholstered in needle-point. There were throw rugs on the floor. Jake almost fell when one of them skated across the floor under him as he stepped in.

"Adrian hated them, too," Gram Blake said with a chuckle. "He was always landing slam on his butt when he took the corner too fast like you just did. You have to walk like a gentleman in *this* house, young man."

"Where are the cattle, Gram?" Dree asked, getting right to the point. "And who tore down Uncle Pete's and Uncle Bill's places. Who tore off the siding and gutted Dad's place?"

"A development company. I've got them served papers already, but we're just getting started."

"They took the cows?"

The old woman chuckled at that. "No, Dree. That was your Uncle Bill. And he used his share of that money to buy him a house over in Adams—brand new and fancy."

"Where's Uncle Pete living?"

"In Adams, too. He's renting a small place just shy of the city limits."

"And Dad's share?"

"I'm not sure. It's supposed to pay his hospital bills and his stay at the nursing home, but when Gerald— my lawyer, you know—when he checked, none of the bills have yet been paid. We're working on that, too."

"Dad was running around two-hundred head of bred back cow-calf pairs. That would have grossed at least six-hundred-thousand," Dree said. "Are his hospital bills that much?"

"No, Dree. He's got insurance to pay most of it."

"Okay, so...."

"So, where's all the money? Like I said, we're working on that, trying to figure out exactly what happened, because your uncles were running a good five-hundred cow-calf pairs between them, Pete working for Bill, Bill running the show."

Jake did the arithmetic.

"What? Did Uncle Bill buy a McMansion, or something?" Dree asked, and Jake heard scorn. He wanted to laugh. Dree was country, through and through, just like him.

"No. Just a brand spankin' new, gabled two-story with a three-car garage, the house all fancied up with what's known as faux columns, not that he's gonna be able to keep it, I don't think. Development company's after him, now." She frowned, her eyebrows pinching together. "Has one of those funny-patterned, dyed, brick-laid driveways, too. And a sidewalk done up the same way. It was his money, those cows. Just like your Dad's were his, not yours."

There. She'd said it. Jake watched Dree's face tighten up.

"But I kept that place running," Dree said. "Surely some of Dad's share comes to me."

Gram Blake shook her head. "Not unless you can prove you loaned him that money, Dree, and expected a payback. Law's funny that way. Can you?"

Dree shook her head. "No."

Gram Blake was quiet for a time. "You still got your hay money, right?"

"Some. What I didn't use to keep Dad afloat and pay Franklin for moving my stuff out. Now, I'm going to have to pay for moving back, too." Dree shook her head. "So, not enough to buy back even a small herd, after that."

Gram Blake gave her an encouraging smile. "You'll get it worked out, Dree. I know you will."

◆

BACK IN THE TRUCK, Dree sat quiet all the way back to the house. Jake parked...waited. It was getting dark, and they had work to do starting early tomorrow. Finally, when Dree didn't say anything, he got out, went over and started his rig. Going to the passenger side of her truck, he pulled the door open.

"Come on, Dree. We need to go home. It's getting real late, and we've got a long drive."

"Home," she said, then looked at him. "You mean Franklin's ranch."

Jake shrugged. "Yeah, I mean where I live. I figure it's too far to drive to go all the way to Heron, tonight."

"Will Franklin be okay with that?"

He smiled, shaking his head. "Yeah. He'll be okay with it."

She got out...didn't walk around to the driver's side like he expected, but walked over and got in the passenger side of his rig. Surprised, he went around and got in, parked her truck in the machine shed, then locked it up. He found himself whistling softly, didn't even know that he'd started. Yeah, Franklin would be okay with it. *He* was real okay with it.

C. J. "Country" James

40

Pay Dirt

FTER DREE, WITH THE HELP of J.D., Jake, and Mike Guthrie, got the tools and equipment back to her Dad's place—her place, now, she corrected herself—then got the center-pivot set back up and doing its job, Franklin talked her into taking a few days to think about things. "Use that darned machine in my office," he said, pointing to his fancy computer. "It's got all that software on it that's *supposed* to figure things out. I'm guessing you, like Jake, know how to use it."

Dree laughed. A man who could run three money-making spreads who couldn't figure out how to handle a mouse. "Thanks. They sold Dad's cows, and, well, I've got to find my best way forward without them."

He nodded. "I'm here if you need me."

She did. She needed his knowledge about water and irrigation rights, especially. He was a gold mine when it came to understanding the hows and the wherefores of anything concerning the land. "What are you thinking, Dree?" he asked her.

"Of putting it all in alfalfa and timothy—all the bottom land."

"Irrigated, right?"

She nodded. "That's why all the questions. There are some good, deep wells, including the one I draw from now. I think they'll produce enough water to do it if I use pumping stations for the sections that are farthest away, so I won't *need* to pull from the creek or drill more wells."

"Doesn't hurt to stake out the irrigation claims to the creek water, though," he said.

"I know, but it already goes down pretty far by late August and on through till the rain starts. If I ever do decide to run cows on the high ground once I get my feet under me, then they'll need that water, and Gram's got the water rights to it. Just not for irrigation."

"Uh-huh. To stop folks upstream from pulling too much or reducing the flow with diversion or by damming it up. I've got the same. My lawyer says your water rights are locked in. So are your mineral rights—all critical."

Dree looked at him. "Thank you for helping me with this, Mr. Jarvis. I mean it."

He tipped his head, acknowledging. "Franklin."

Deciding, she turned his big monitor to face him. "What do you think?" Then, scared that he'd scoff or, worse, laugh, she wished she hadn't.

He actually took a step back, then stepped up close, his eyes running back and forth, up and down, pausing here, pausing there across the mapped plan she'd drawn up. He looked at the side, his eyes narrowing as he studied the figures she'd calculated. Then, she saw him shift to the column in a right-hand inset. Finally, he looked at her. "You did this all on that darned machine?"

She laughed. "Ag Ec," she said. "They teach you some useful things. I hadn't a clue when I started using this kind of software, either. But it comes in handy for some things. Just not for things like actually castrating the calves or mending the fences."

He frowned, and she held her breath. He shook his head. "Well, from what I think I'm seeing on this, it looks pretty solid. You're running it narrow, and that's smart. Nice conservative numbers for income and liberal with your costs, and it still comes out running in black."

"Thanks."

"So, why the worry, then?"

Dree looked up at him. Did her concerns really show that much in her face? She'd have to work on not being so damned transparent. "It's Gram," she answered him honestly. "I think she expects I'm going to run cattle like Granddad did. I think she's going to be disappointed when I tell her what I'm planning."

Franklin stepped over to a big black, high-backed leather chair that sat beside a small, stone-laid fireplace, one similar but smaller than the one in the great room. He settled in below the brand inlaid there. "Dree, I think you underestimate your Gram Blake." He paused, then, after a moment, said, "When my lawyer finally tracked down *her* lawyer back when this whole thing blew up, Gerald Weisinger only figured out who I was talking about when I mentioned you were the grandkid who worked the irrigated quarter-section on Jim Blake's place. A light bulb went on in his voice. Called you 'the hay girl.' Then, when I faxed him over your General Ledger at your grandmother's request, your grandmother called me. That's when I finally told them I knew where you were. Wouldn't tell them where, not with the way your uncles and cousin had been beating the bushes to find you since right after we pulled you out of there. I think she already knows that you know what you're about, so I wouldn't worry so much."

It was, Dree thought, the longest string of words she'd ever heard come out of him. She sat blinking at all that his words implied—that her uncles and her cousins had been chasing her, that Franklin protected her, that Franklin had gone out of his way to contact her missing grandmother. "Franklin?"

He tipped his head forward. "Go ahead."

"Were my uncles trying to... pull a fast one over on Gram?"

He chuckled. "Yes, Dree. They *were* trying. They were the ones who bought her the trip over on a luxury liner to England. From there, she maybe just went hog-wild all on her own, though I don't know that for certain. But they influenced her, encouraged her...knew where she was the whole time, I think. I know for a fact they hired the house-sitter. Got that from your grandmother's lawyer."

When Dree frowned question at him, he added, "Jake told me about the house-sitter."

She nodded. She remembered telling Jake about how irritating the woman was, claiming not to know anything at all about her Gram's whereabouts, and that wasn't like Gram.

"But, if the land was in trust, how could they arrange to sell it if Gram didn't know?"

"Your Uncle Bill forged her signature, with the help of a local notary, which is how the development company got into the deal. Got that from your gram's lawyer, too, before I'd even consider letting you all meet up here. It's not an uncommon thing, that kind of forgery. Actually happens a lot."

The memory of how her uncles had acted at the hospital—avoiding her, leaving the room, turning away from her—she'd never known either of them to act that way her whole growing up. It made sense of all the meetings her dad had down at the bar with Uncle

Bill and Counsin John, too. "It's all is beginning to make sense, then."

"What?"

"All the hedging, my uncles' cowardice at the hospital. Did you know Jake battled them down when they were...." She paused, remembering feeling so cornered that there was no escape, like one of her cats caught out in the equipment shed just before her father would shoot at it. Lucky for Dree and her cats, her dad had always been way too proud to wear his glasses. That night, her uncles had her caught up at close range, though. There'd been no escaping their bullets, not until Jake stopped them.

"He told me they had you run up a tree pretty bad, yes."

"Jake's brave, kind...thoughtful." Purposely, she smiled at him, then. "He's a whole lot like you, I think."

Predictably, the man ducked his head, got up from the chair. "Got work to do, Dree. If you need something else, somebody here will know where to find me."

Knowing she'd hit pay dirt, she grinned as she watched him escape.

41

Messing with Money

"**W**HAT DO YOU THINK?" Dree asked.

Jake took the papers she held, glanced at them, then looked harder. He blew air through his teeth, not meaning to, but because the terms were outrageous. "This one's even worse than the last."

"Yeah. I know. It's because I don't own the land. They keep mentioning that it's a non-secured loan."

"The equipment's technically what they've got for security, were things the way they're supposed to be."

"They aren't."

Jake knew that real well. The whole country, whole world, had gone stupid.

"This guy told me that, if I incorporated, the terms would be better, but, because I'm doing this as myself, that puts it in a category that they usually won't touch. He said the only reason they even considered it is because of my credit rating and my last name."

"Good thing you paid off your student loan early."

"And Gram. And kept my credit cards going, not canceled them out like I thought to."

"Yeah. …You're sure you don't want to ask your grandmother?"

Dree shook her head. "I will *not* ask Gram to do this. No. She's already pissed off the rest of the family more than enough."

"Can I hang onto this?"

"No. You're not going to Franklin. I won't have it, Jake Jarvis. I do this my way, or I don't do it at all."

"Okay." He handed her back her paperwork.

She'd said Franklin. She hadn't said anything about anyone else, though. He whistled his way through traffic, talked her into having lunch at The Pearl, then headed them toward home. Tomorrow they'd start laying the tractor lanes and measuring out and marking the quarter sections using the stakes left behind by the development company's surveyors. Tomorrow they'd start the work of building her dream.

"**H**OW YOU GOING TO GET THE MONEY into her account without her knowing who put it there," J.D. asked.

Jake pulled out a deposit slip. "She left her checkbook in the truck, so I appropriated this from the back."

"She still writes checks?"

"Yeah. Just like Franklin does."

J.D. frowned. "Maybe I ought to rethink giving 'em up. She's a smart little lady according to what I hear."

"From who?"

"Wa-aal, Jake-boy, who d'ya think?" His uncle smacked him lightly across the top of his head, knocking his hat off.

Jake grabbed it up, pretended to inspect it for damage, then jammed it back on his head. "Franklin."

"You *know* it," his uncle laughed. "So, okay. I'll go get a cashier's check down at the bank. I'll have it for you sometime this afternoon."

"Okay if I get it tomorrow morning?"

"If you come early. I'm pickin' up a load of good Jarvis beef goin' to Ne-eew Yo-ooke Ci-iity, where the girls think thar pritty and the boys are all sissies," he purposely drawled, feigning dumber-than-stupid.

"Four early enough?"

"I'll swing by around five. You be down at the underpass."

"'K.' Thanks, J.D."

"Hey. Thank *you*. I'll be makin' good money on this, and I don't have to risk getting clipped by some dumb, hurry-up four-wheeler to do it. Dumb suicide maniacs!"

"YOU LIKE RANCHING?"

Dree glanced over at him. "Of course I like ranching, Jake."

"Cattle, I mean."

Confused, she just kept watching him. She was bound and determined to master the skill.

Finally—finally—he caught her watching him. "...You seem to want to be a dirt scratcher."

Dree couldn't help herself. She broke out in a fit, her giggles embarrassing her. She clamped a hand over her mouth, but just wound up sounding like she was blowing raspberries as the concussive air from her laughter burst through, anyway. "Gawd, Jake. What a dumb thing to say! The only reason I want to grow hay is because it's the only thing I've done that seems to make any money. I tried hogs, poultry, even rabbits as a kid. The chickens were the worst with the cluckerplucker, as Dad nicknamed that stupid machine that's *supposed* to clean the feathers off."

"So you like cattle? Running them, I mean?"

"I love the whole life, Jake. But, honestly, the way we did it, it was way too big to call a hobby, but too small to make a living from. You have to run thousands of—" She shut up.

He glanced over at her. "You're not telling me anything I don't know. The margins are real slim. You run big, or you don't run, at all, mostly. Franklin's operation is a fluke, and, today, if he tried to start up, he wouldn't be able to do it. It's why we keep expanding. We have to keep up with demand or wind up losing out to someone who can. Franklin's in negotiations right now to buy up five ranches connected to ours. We're going to have to get bigger, again."

Dree blinked, fondled both dogs' ears, their noses laid one on each knee. "Franklin's expanding his herd to even bigger?"

"Yeah. He's going to double, maybe triple the herd. We're keeping a lot of the heifer calves back this year. Will next year, too, and probably the year after that. Demand is going up fast. I think people are giving up this idea that cow meat is bad."

Dree smiled. "You mean they figured out that it's sitting in front of the boob tube, sucking down sodas and chips, not beef that's giving them heart and sugar disease."

"Sugar disease?"

"Diabetes."

"Oh. Never heard it called that."

"It's Dad's."

"How *is* your dad?"

Dree smiled. "He's doing pretty well, actually, according to Gram."

"He still won't see you?"

"No. Gram says she thinks he feels guilty. I think he's embarrassed and mad."

Jake gave a short, quick, hard nod. Moments later, he eased the truck over till he was almost clipping the reflector markers on her side of the road. A car roared past, squeezing between him and the oncoming traffic. He hit the brakes hard as it nearly clipped their front end, and, hanging on to the dash, Dree braced herself. The ditch was right there, right under the running board, steep and nasty. She prayed.

They made it.

He pulled in on the next wide spot. "Gotta check Coal and Cougar," he said. His face was sheet white. She scrambled out, too.

"What kept us so stable?" Dree asked, when, animals fine, they started going, again.

"This is a fifth-wheel. It's what I traded my old trailer for last month. They're way more stable than bumper pulls."

"I've never driven one."

"You want to try it?"

She shook her head. "That was some feat of driving back there. Threading a camel through the eye of a needle," she said.

"And what they did was exactly what I did to you back in March, except I beat the oncoming traffic by at least the width of a whisker. I've never had anybody do that to me, though, not pulling a trailer." He glanced her way. "I'm glad you didn't wreck back then, and I'm never, *have* never, done it to anybody since then. And won't. Dree, I'm telling you I'm sorry, all over again."

She smiled. Mean as it felt, she was glad somebody had done to him what he'd done to her. "It's okay. You have to realize by now that I hate towing anything, except on the tractor in a nice, safe field somewhere."

He grinned.

S HE CAME LOOKING FOR HIM when she found it. He got less than forty-eight hours.

"Jake?"

He put on his poker face. "Yeah?"

"What do you know about this?"

She held out a sheet of paper with a print-out of a deposit slip, but wouldn't let him have it, jerking it back when he reached for it.

He shrugged. "Your loan came through?" It wasn't a lie. Not really. Her loan *had* gone through. Just not quite the way she'd planned on doing it.

She stared at him, her slate eyes gone dark. "I'm waiting."

He wanted to kiss her. He wanted to lay her down under him. He shrugged. "It's your deposit slip."

"It's your handwriting!"

"Huh?" He was having a devil's time keeping his face straight.

She slipped another piece of paper under his nose, this one a copy, and held them side by side—his note from the three-hundred dollars. "It's. Your. Handwriting." Then, "I told you no Franklin!"

She was really getting mad, now. "It wasn't Franklin."

"Then who?"

He grinned, then. "I *knew* I shoulda had J.D. make out that deposit slip. *Dang.*"

"The trucker?"

Jake nodded.

"Well, I'm sending his money back to him today." She turned and stomped off toward Franklin's office.

He trotted after, grabbed her arm.

She spun and jerked her arm loose. "Quit."

"J.D.'s got the money, and— ...Here. Hang on."

He dug out his smart phone. Dialed. Got his uncle on the line, grabbing back hold of Dree's arm when she began to walk off, again. "Here, Dree. J.D."

He watched as she listened, heard his uncle bark through the phone when she started to argue. Watched her listen some more. By the time she hit 'end', her eyes had changed from stormy to normal. He wasn't off the hook by a long shot, but she accepted the loan, J.D. telling him later that he just bulled his way through her arguments. "Told her the truth, Jake, and I think she listened. ...That this makes me good money without dodging four-wheelers. You sure you got your heart set on this gal? Seems to me she's wicked stubborn and mouthy, too."

"Granddad told you?"

"We talked, some, yes. But it weren't no secret. It's written plain on your face."

C. J. "Country" James

42

Cougar Rock

DREE WOULDN'T TALK TO HIM for a full week and a half, except for necessity. She bought her center-pivots, though, along with another used tractor, another baler, a moldboard, harrow, and disc, plus fertilizer and the seed that she needed. "She always buys used," Jake told Franklin.

"She bought her stock trailer new," was his answer. "And the center pivots are all brand new, too."

That, Jake had to concede. "Still, she lost a lot of tax write-offs."

"It's her operation, Jake. Not yours. You keep out of it."

"I am. Haven't said nothin'—not one word. It's her place." He grinned, then. "At least, right now it's just hers," and he watched Franklin eye him a minute, grunt, then go back to reading the paper.

HE'D SENT HER TO GET LUNCH. She'd objected, wanted to help finish the nasty job of coiling up the barbed wire. "Just go get us lunch, would you? I'm starving."

So she did, leaving him after she hobbled up Coal to stop him following Cougar back. "Pretty bad when a prize-winning Quarter Horse stud winds up mooning over a too big, rabbit-eared gelding," Jake said. "Must be cuz Coug's platinum blond."

Dree ignored his jibe. He was just getting even a little bit, blowing off some of the sting he always suffered.

It was a constant sore spot, the hands' teasing of him when Coal went nuts if she took Cougar out alone. Jake had to raise the height of Coal's run, sistering on higher posts and adding three more rails to stop him from jumping out and following when Franklin asked her to ride along with him out to check cows. There were some odd 'told-you-so's from Wil Strakes that actually got Jake red in the face, though Dree didn't really understand why Wil's jibes hit Jake worse than the sexual innuendos from the rest of the crew. Just like she kept out of it at the ranch, she kept her mouth shut about it here...now that she understood that it really did bother him that Coal wouldn't stay put, breaking ground-tie, breaking his halter, and getting hung up trying to scale the fence when he couldn't jump it.

Driving into town and back for burgers, fries, and milk shakes, Dree was only gone, maybe, an hour, but, when she got back to where she'd left him, their food in her saddle bags, their drinks now in thermos bottles, Jake was nowhere around. Neither was Coal. The last run of wire Jake had been rolling up lay splayed and sprung out all over the ground, like he'd just run off somewhere on the spur of the moment.

She got down and recoiled it, anchoring it down with a looped half twist, so a passing deer didn't tangle in it. Then, she cursed herself for locking her dogs in a stall to keep them from getting tangled, too, while Jake and she loosed the old fence line between what had been her dad's and her Uncle Bill's place. Mounting up, again, she headed Cougar up toward the top of the section they were working. When she got there, though, there was no sign of Jake.

She started following fence, but there was absolutely no sign of him or his black horse. She got to the start of the high ground, and, leaning to it, let Cougar climb. Finally, up on the first bench, she spied Coal trotting toward her from where he'd been grazing on brush. There was no Jake.

Calling out, she listened for an answer. There was none. Getting concerned, she looked for some sort of sign—tracks of where he might have been, but the ground wasn't showing her much. She called out again, but nothing answered except crows. Dismounting, she looked over Coal. He seemed fine and was cool to the touch. "Where's Jake, Coal?"

The horse went on grazing.

Cougar blew a few grunts, his ears going what she called 'crooked.' She let him loose, hoping maybe he'd lead her where she wanted to go like he had when the neighbor kids had been lost. "Where's Jake, Cougar? Find Jake."

The mule looked at her, blinked, then just stood.

"JAAAKE!" she hollered.

Nothing.

She left Cougar with Coal, and, her eyes on the ground, began working her way outward from the animals, her circle getting wider each circuit. When she got to the top of the next bench, she looked down and whistled. Cougar started up toward her, Coal following.

At a loss of where to look or where to go, she just followed the old cow trail that meandered along through a natural meadow. Fifteen minutes later, and she was at Cougar Rock, the odd outcropping where Cougar had earned his name because he could climb it where no horse could. "He wouldn't have come this far on foot," she reasoned, but, still, she walked on, Cougar and Coal trailing along behind her.

On the other side of the outcropping, she slid down the bank, still following the cow trail. A small herd of cows stood in the trees, all pointed one direction watching something. Cows! It struck her. Carrying her dad's brand, too. Maybe that was it. But why wasn't he still on Coal.

Dree hurried on, heading in the direction the cows were looking. Rounding the backside of Cougar Rock, she spied what held their attention—Jake hovered over something, his back working rhythmically. "Jake!"

He looked up. "Go for help. Her heart's stopped!"

"Omigod."

"Go for help!"

Dree whistled Cougar, and he trotted up. So did Coal. She hobbled the horse. "Whoa here," she commanded, then, mounting up, took off, spurring Cougar into a run. Sure-footed, he clambered up the bank, then lit out down the cow trail the way they'd come up.

Dree didn't slow down as they hit the top bench, just plunged over, Cougar not even hesitating. It was dangerous, but she trusted her mule. She cursed the fact that cell phone reception here was nil.

Down over the second bench, then finally making the flats, she pushed Cougar faster, got to the northeast corner and pulled out her phone. One bar. One *bar*. She dialed 9-1-1 and blessed the fact that that solitary one bar held. "There's a lady in cardiac arrest on the second bench, behind Cougar Rock. Jake Jarvis is doing CPR. We need help fast."

The woman wanted her name, and she told her.

The woman wanted her location, and she gave it.

The woman wanted her birthdate, and she gave her that, too, even though she knew the lady probably already had it up on her read-out.

"I've got an ambulance and deputies on their way," the woman assured her when she came back on the line. "Stay on the line with me. I'm getting your GPS coordinates from your phone."

"I'm a section east and some bit north of their actual position," Dree told her.

"Yes, Ma'am, but you're the only one who knows exactly where they're at. Stay with me and stay put. Help is on the way. You'll need to lead them in."

"Oh, God. You can't get rigs up there. They need ATVs."

"Sheriff deputy's in a four-wheel drive," she responded.

"A rig can't get up there. Believe me."

There was a pause…jargon that Dree only caught part of. Then, "I've relayed the message," the woman said. "Stay with me."

Twenty minutes later, a helicopter descended from overhead. Minutes after that, as the paramedics got gear out, two ATVs rolled into the pasture. She mounted up when they picked up the paramedics, then lit out, urging Cougar into a run back up the bench.

The four-wheelers closed in, following the track. Dree let Cougar take his own path, which wasn't something any all-terrain could climb. As the machines took the wider route, she waited for them, letting Cougar blow. When they came on, she again urged him into a run, and her wonderful mule didn't hesitate. Somehow, he seemed to know this was critical, sliding on his butt down the last bank into the trees, the ATVs almost on his tail. They had to slow down. He didn't.

The cow herd scattered, racing off into the trees, tails up and cranking. Coal spooked, almost going down in his hobbles, then settled, again.

Dree pulled up and pointed, letting the ATV's go on ahead. Then she got off and hugged her mule, walking the rest of the way to keep him moving while he caught his breath and cooled down.

The men on the ATVs made it to Jake's side. Heads went together, then a sort of coordinated pass off. Jake stood up, staggered, and, abruptly, sat down. Then he rolled over on his knees and vomited. All that came up was bile.

Getting a towel from her saddle bags, Dree went up to him. "Here. Are you going to be okay?"

He took the towel, wiped his mouth, dry wretched, again, then, after a few breaths, sat back on his butt and nodded. Said nothing. He looked like he'd had the life beaten out of him. Finally, he said, "I don't think I did enough. I don't think I did it right."

She sat down and, braving it, put her arms around him. "You did your best. That's all anyone can ask, and its more than most would do, Jake Jarvis."

She felt him shake his head, then go still, again. "She was just a kid, Dree. A kid."

Dree heard the 'was', and hugged him harder.

The deputy came up and began quizzing Jake about how he'd found the girl.

"I was working the fence-line down across the creek. I heard a scream, got on Coal and started going in the direction I thought I heard it come from.

"I saw someone running down the rocks—a guy in a white t-shirt, headed toward him, but he disappeared, even after I yelled.

"Then I got to thinking that the scream I heard wasn't a guy's yell, but a girl's, so I went up on the rocks. That's when I saw her down the backside.

"I rode down around and found her all broken up, but she wasn't breathing that I could tell, so I tried her neck and thought I felt a flutter there. I talked to her, but she was out cold. She was bleeding, her legs all—"

He choked up, squeezed Dree's hand hard and took a breath...swallowed. "So I checked her neck again, then took a chance and rolled her over as careful as I could.

"I took CPR in high school and, again, in college, but I've never done it for real. I just tried to do it right."

"What time was this do you think when you heard the scream."

I don't know. I don't know, at all. Sun was, maybe, noon.

He stopped, pulled his cell phone out of his pocket and checked something. "I tried dialing 9-1-1 at 12:11 it says. I got no signal, though, and I couldn't leave her. Smacked Coal on the ass and hoped he'd head for the barn. I guess he didn't.

The deputy put a hand on his shoulder. "It's okay. You did what you could, and you did right."

Dree thought those were the best words the man could have said.

"Can you tell me what the guy's hair color was? His build? His height?"

Jake blinked. "Ah…he was wearing jeans. …He had a wide, light-brown belt showing where his shirt was still tucked in. He had cuffs on his jeans," he said.

"Hair?"

"He looked almost…but not really, I guess. Ah…bald. So maybe real light hair, because it wasn't dark. …He didn't have a beard or mustache, either when he shot a look my way before skedaddling. But he did have really white skin and really, really blue eyes.

It was like they glowed. I remember thinking his face and arms looked as white almost as his shirt. And he was kind of stocky...soft-looking, you know? Not really fat, but...well, soft. Couldn't even begin to tell you how tall, though."

As Jake talked, Dree felt chills start running down her back. The person he was describing was too familiar. The cuffed jeans, the almost bald-looking head, the white skin and blue, blue eyes—eyes she hated—terrifying eyes, worse than Cousin John's mean ones. She clamped a hand over her mouth in horror.

One of the paramedics came over. "I need to check you over, just to make sure you're okay," he said.

"I'm fine."

"I still have to do it."

Jake frowned. "Why?"

"Just regulation."

He took Jake's pulse and blood pressure, checked his hands, especially his fingers, then listened to his heart and lungs...palpated his body. "You're good to go," he said, getting up. He shook his head at the deputy.

"Okay. Ms. Blake. We're going to want to investigate up on the rocks and down here, so if you can avoid the area for a few days?" the deputy asked.

Dree nodded. "I can't keep the cows away, though, but they'll probably avoid it, anyway."

The man nodded. "You two can take off, then. Go on back to the house."

Dree glanced toward where the other paramedic was still working on the girl. "Is she going to be all right?"

The paramedic who'd checked Jake out said, "I can't answer that, Miss. I'm not a doctor."

Dree stood, Jake pushing himself up with effort. She grabbed his hand and pulled him along, heading over to where Cougar was munching brush next to Coal.

"They're being cagey," Jake said. "She dead, but they don't want me to know that. I do, though. There wasn't any life in her under my hands after awhile. I could tell."

"You don't know that, Jake. She's probably in a coma."

"No. I *do* know that. I felt her soul leave."

C. J. "Country" James

43

Proposal

J AKE WAS RIGHT. It was on TV, then an obituary in the paper a couple days later. The girl had been seventeen years old—a senior in high school. Jake was tense and quiet. At night, he began sucking down whiskey like water, then woke up with a hangover the next morning. Three days later, he disappeared before dinner. Franklin was frantic. Oddly, Loretta, his mom, wasn't.

He came rolling in two days later looking like he hadn't slept, bathed, or eaten. He smelled like he'd rolled in a sewer.

"You need a bath," Dree heard Loretta tell him, then point up the stairs. "I'll bring you up a tray. You're going to bathe, eat, then get some sleep. Don't come down till tomorrow morning, unless it's because you want more food."

Dree helped Franklin lock up the whiskey along with everything else alcoholic in the house.

The deputy who had quizzed Jake at the scene showed up at Franklin's door a few days later and sat down in the great room with them. "I wanted you to know," he said, his eyes on Jake's. "There was nothing you did wrong that killed her. She died of a bad blow to the head. That's private information, but I know you've been blaming yourself. We all do."

Jake seemed better after that—acting almost normal, again...except that he kept up his drinking, heading out to town every night after dinner, then getting in sometime after Dree'd gone to bed. Every night, Dree watched Franklin and Old Man Jarvis wait up.

What the deputy hadn't told them was that the girl had been murdered. That came out in the news three weeks later with the arrest of an eighteen-year-old. But Dree already knew who it was. When Franklin heard it on TV, his eyes—hooded and dark—turned to look at her. The eighteen-year-old was Andrew Blake, one of Dree's cousins...Uncle Bill's youngest son.

◆

DESPITE STARTING EACH DAY with an obvious hangover, Jake continued to drive them over every day, then drive them back. Dree didn't say anything about the drinking. Experience with her dad told her it just made things worse.

They beat brush, tracking down the remnant cows that carried her Dad's or her uncles' brands, calling the neighboring ranches when they found a pair carrying somebody else's. Dree got to know all of the local ranch brands by the time they were done rounding up strays on her dad's and her uncles' spreads. When it was all said and done, she had over fifty cow-calf pairs penned at the barn.

She called Gram.

"You want them?" her grandmother asked.

"Sure."

"I'll twist me some arms, then. You call the brand inspector once I'm done twisting."

"The start of your new herd, Dree," Jake said, grinning.

"Pretty poor start," she said. But some of the cows—a handful—were some that she'd selected for Chocolate. She wondered if they'd taken by him, or were bred by one of her dad's poorer bulls.

◆

BY OCTOBER, THEY WERE FINISHED. The ground was ready for spring seeding, the center pivots due for delivery mid-April. The manufacturer would send a crew out to help set them up. Dree was exhausted, but happy.

The new thermal pane windows were in, better insulation blown into the exterior walls and under the house, and Jake started putting the clapboard back on. That was after Dree and he checked and repaired fence line on what had been the horse pastures, then on the rolling ground west of the creek, which was where she decided she was going to run her small herd next summer.

Jake never interfered, just went along like he agreed with what she was doing. It was a strange feeling, not to be over-lorded. She liked the fact that he let her make her own way, but she felt like she was in free fall with no parachute, too.

Finally, she asked him what he thought as they sipped coffee made on her new, used range. "Well, I think the ground is tired," he told her. "Your dad let this place slip pretty bad. Cows are hard on ground when it gets no relief."

"So what would you do?"

"I don't know. Your uncles did worse than your dad, so there you have it." Then, "What about the fourteen sections over by the Bitterroots your gram spoke of?"

"I'm leaving that under lease like she had it. The people are good, and they're happy and settled. ...Established. The income is good, so I don't see any reason to fix what's not broken."

"Smart."

"So what, then?"

He thought about it. "How about selling them next spring, once their calves hit the ground? You won't get as good a price as you get for bred heifers, but these cows are mostly 2's, maybe 3's, so it's not like you're selling old cows."

"I think they're all 2's. I checked their tag numbers against what I got out of Dad's records, and there are only a few that are on their third and fourth calves.

The ones that came from Bill's and Pete's herds, well, there it's anybody's guess."

"You don't have to decide, yet, do you?"

His words made her stop. That was *it*. She could have reached out and hugged him. He was right. She didn't have to decide. She was used to planning, but, too much planning was as bad as her dad's method of none. "You're right. I don't. Thanks, Jake."

He finished his coffee, rinsed out his cup, then set it in the drain rack, ready for morning. "We should get going. It's already two-thirty."

She nodded, getting up to toss the rest of her coffee down the drain. She set her cup in the sink and ran water in it, then stuck it in the rack next to his.

She braved it when they were on the final leg home. "This running back and forth to the ranch takes a whole half out of our work day."

"Yeah."

"The house is almost livable."

She saw him nod, but his face didn't give her any clues. *Darned Jarvis genes.* "You should have all been poker players," she snapped.

He glanced her way. "What? Where'd that come from? What'd I do?"

She laughed. "It's not you. It's the whole male side of your clan. I'm trying to feel you out, and you're not helping, as usual."

He shifted his eyes sideways for half a second, then he put his attention back on the road.

So she'd just say it: "Can I hire you? I'll pay you a good salary."

He was silent to that all the way up the climb to the house. He pulled into the garage, then shut the truck off and, finally, turned his face to her. "Nope."

Stunned, she couldn't believe he'd just done exactly what her dad used to do, just said 'no'.

"You can marry me."

H E COULD HAVE SHOT HIMSELF. The look on her face—maybe what people called 'dismay'. He hadn't meant to. His mouth had just blurted it out—stupid.

She turned away from him, sat a moment, then abruptly opened the cab door, her hands fumbling.

"Dree!" He reached to grab her, but she was out of the cab that fast, slipped from his fingers to disappear around the corner of Franklin's new truck, her head bowed, her footsteps quick, almost running.

Damn it! He knew better. He knew better with *her*, anyway. You had to really work things out ahead of time—prepare. You had to 'court' and 'woo' like the olden days—lull her into relaxing her guard, into smiles and laughter, into liking you over and over, again, because she stopped liking you, or, maybe, went back to guarding against you, not trusting your motives or your meaning right afterward.

He'd never worked so hard in his life for a woman, and he'd never had so little to show for it. And, now, he'd gone and ruined it all. But, damn it, he loved her. He loved the way she smelled, the way she laughed, the way she cared for things...*about* things, the way her eyes shone when she saw the sunrise or the stars, the way she got joy out of little things, and, yes, the way, when she finally got mad or hurt, she fought back—like a horse pushed too hard, like a mother cow who got fed up with you messing with her calf. Dree was tame as a nanny horse and fierce as an angry cougar.

"*Damn* it."

C. J. "Country" James

44

Damaged Goods

DREE MOVED BACK to her dad's house—her house, now—the next day. Jake showed up around ten, but she avoided him, concentrating on painting the upstairs. She made him lunch. As soon as he came in to eat, she went back upstairs and, locking the door and putting on headphones, her player running an audio book, she got back to painting.

He took the hint and left her alone. When he finally put the last clapboard in place, she told him to please not come back. "Franklin needs you. You've wasted enough time on this place. I'll never be able to pay you back for all your help."

"Dree—"

She closed the door on him, locking it, watched him hook up his fifth wheel, load Coal, the stallion whinnying for Cougar and Cougar brinnying back, the two of them calling, calling, back and forth, till Jake took the corner where the road turned toward town. Then she sat down and just stared at the wall for a very long time. She was finally alone. She was finally lonely, too, a new feeling. She missed him, already.

One of her cats came up, and, rubbing himself on her, started purring. He reached up a paw, patting her hand, and she picked him up, setting him on her lap.

Chip and Laddie came over, begging for strokes, too, and, with a sigh, she gave them her other hand, the one that wasn't stroking the cat. This was her new life. "Better get used to it, Dree," she told herself. "It's what you wanted—a ranch all your own to call home, no man dictating."

◆

IMMEDIATELY, THE FLOWERS started again. So did the candy and invitations to dinner. She didn't even try to send them back. She didn't respond, not to the invitations, not to his phone calls.

He didn't show up. She was thankful for *that* mercy. She couldn't have handled it.

Within a week, the dreams started, his eyes, his grin, his slow-talking manner…the feel of his kiss—both of them, the hard and the tender—his hands gentle, on her face, stroking her body. She buried herself in projects, but, even exhausted, the dreams woke her up.

When the dreams turned so real that she thought he was actually there laying beside her, holding her, his breath on her face, she decided to take the bull by the horns. "I'm going nuts," she told her friend, Caroline. "You're a shrink. *Help* me!"

"I'm not a 'shrink', Dree. I'm a marriage counselor."

"Well, this qualifies, I think. Enough, anyway."

"You ever think that maybe you're really in love?"

"No. I don't *feel* that way for him. Sure, I get, I don't know, maybe desire." She'd be damned if she'd say the word 'lust'. "And I like him as a friend...like I do you—"

"What do you think a good marriage is, Dree?"

Caroline had her there. She hadn't a clue.

"Look. I think I know somebody qualified. Dr. Carl is one of the best, in my opinion, and he *is* a real 'shrink'. Don't call him that, though," she said laughing. "He'd probably kick you out of his office."

"Why not you? I trust you."

"Because, Dree, we're friends. "I can't be as objective as I need to be."

"I hate those...pro*fe*s*s*ionals who just sit there and expect you to pour out your life. ...I can't afford it, anyway." Dree got up. "Thanks, though."

"Dr. Carl is a...bit more pro-active than that. In fact, a lot more pro-active. He charges two-hundred an hour, which is cheap for his level of education and experience. This is Montana, of course.... But, I will warn you, he's unorthodox and, well, tough. He doesn't soft pedal anything. Calls it enabling. ...And it is."

Dree shook her head, thinking 'wow' at the price. Tough she could deal with. The cost, no. She couldn't substantiate it...told Caroline so.

"Consider this, Dree. Is the rest of your life worth the cost of a couple of beef cows?"

Dree frowned.

Caroline pressed on. "In other words, I'd say a couple of thousand dollars to help you figure out some very life-critical answers isn't too much. Dr. Carl is in Missoula. Here's his card. Make an appointment. Please. Use my name. Say I referred you, if it helps. I'll even go with you, if you want. Let me drive."

◆

THAT FIRST APPOINTMENT WOUND UP being two solid hours of anger. All Caroline said when Dree finally came out was, "Wow. That was a lo-ong session. You okay?"

Dree nodded.

"Let's go have lunch. Food really helps."

Dree wanted a whiskey straight...like she'd had on her 21st birthday.

◆

A WEEK LATER, she made another appointment. She wasn't sure why, except maybe the dreams had gone away for a time. Then, they started up, again.

She went alone—no Caroline there holding her hand before she went in or when she came out. She went alone the next time, too. And the time after that.

By the week of Thanksgiving, she loved going—looked forward to it.

That's when he cut her off. He did it after presenting her with what he called his 'evaluation', and, just like her dad had said, in essence, he told her she was broken—damaged goods—not in those words, but that's what it boiled down to. She repressed...or was it 'suppressed'? She couldn't remember, exactly. The red-darkness, the roaring, the screams he called 'flashbacks'.

"You've got some real damage, Dree, and that damage could be there for life without some long, painful therapy because nobody bothered to get you what you needed when you most needed it, when the original trauma happened—not victim therapy, not grief therapy. You were eleven years old with a prior history of related incidents, related trauma—years of psychological...punishment, then the physical battering and deaths, never mind the attempted rape.

"The death of your ranch foreman—you give me hearsay; not your own memories, but how your father explained it to you. Your twin brother was shot, the killer then turning the gun on you. Then, the man you considered a friend and a mentor died protecting you. Your twin brother died; Rodrigo died; you didn't. There's a lot of guilt there.

"What I think happened—your 'red-darkness' and feelings of suffocation—you almost drowned in Rodrigo's blood, had the breath crushed out of you because he shielded you with his body. The facts are that someone you loved died for you, killed by someone you trusted, and you processed it as your fault. That's not something that's going to go away, Dree. With age regression therapy, maybe we can get you to accept and resolve it, maybe we can get you to touch your feelings about it.

"Now, for the question you walked in with—your love for Jake, and, yes, I said 'love'. You don't *feel* it because you've suppressed feeling anything. Love/fear, joy/sorrow, grief/ecstasy, they're all mixed together inside you, and, anytime you start to feel, you lock down. You're suspicious of anyone who shows you *real* love. So, in my opinion, marriage and motherhood are both ill-advised at this time."

He shifted some papers, pulled one out, scribbled something on two others, then handed them to her.

She expected the notation, outlining session begin and end times, but, usually, there was also an order to give to the receptionist for her next scheduled appointment. She frowned. One was an order to see a Dr. Willa Reasoner. The other was a prescription. "When do I next come here?"

"You don't."

Dree grasped the chair arm…leaned forward. Finally she blurted out, "But I *like* coming. I like *seeing* you. I look *forward* to it."

The man nodded, his cold face unmoved as ever. "Exactly. You feel safe here. So, I've become 'dad' or, in your case, 'grandpa', maybe elderly friend…those very few people you won't completely trust, but trust more than most. The relationship you have established with me is unhealthy for you, so we're done. I've referred you to a colleague of mine—a woman who's a specialist with childhood trauma."

The red-darkness rose up inside her. She battled it down. "S–So I can't ever come back?"

He blinked, then, his eyes steady on hers, said. "My colleague will see you. I've also made a note in your medical file should you ever become pregnant. Your Ob/Gyn will refer you to a specialist if ever the time comes, not for your sake, but for the child's."

He stood, nodded to her, and left the room.

Stunned, Dree stared at the door he'd vanished through. Then, suddenly, all at once, she found herself sobbing, tears streaming down her face to drip off her chin, her nose drooling snot.

She grabbed tissues from the box next to her chair—the first time she'd ever had need of them.

Finally done, finally rung out, she got up and went out to pay her bill at the receptionist's desk. She threw both the referral and the prescription into the trash. She'd fight her own battles, without drugs or doctors.

45

Gone

"JAKE. THERE'S A SHEILA GOLDSMITH asking for you?"

He shook his head. "I don't know a—" He stopped. The lady who'd taken Dree's chickens....

He took the phone from Franklin. "Hello?"

"I haven't seen Dree's truck since Monday. She didn't come home that night like she usually does, and she's still not back this afternoon. I'm worried. It's not like her.

"I went over, but the house is locked up. I threw some hay to the cow and the mule, gave them water, but there are dogs barking in the house and cats in the window. Do you know where she is? Is she in the hospital? I don't know who to call. The sheriff won't do anything. Not yet, anyway."

"I'll take care of it, Miss Goldsmith. I'll be down," he assured her, and, when she finally stopped talking, when she finally hung up, he went to find Franklin. "Dree's missing. Do you have her Gram Blake's number?"

But Gram Blake hadn't seen Dree, not since Jake and she'd last visited. "I'll call around. I know some of her friends. I'll get a hold of her uncles, too. And you call me if you find out anything. Promise me."

"I promise."

"I don't care what time of day or night, you call me."

"Yes, Ma'am. And if someone notifies you because she's been hurt, would *you* call *me*?"

"You bet I will, Jake."

"I'm heading down," he said, when he hung up the phone a second time.

Franklin had his hat on, his keys in his hand. "I'm right with you."

◆

JAKE PUSHED IT, RUNNING EIGHTY-FIVE, almost ninety, on the interstate, then on the four-lane, Franklin right on his tail. He took the old highway till he got to the range road, then, on the CB, told Franklin to keep to the highway. He'd meet him there. "You'll get there before me. She hides a spare key to the house under the back stairs, tucked in what feels like any old rock under the lowest step. It's hollowed out, though, so it's lighter."

"I'll find it."

◆

HER TRUCK WASN'T ANYWHERE—not wrecked on the range road, not crashed on the highway somewhere. It wasn't in town, either, both him and Franklin having run down every street and up every alley.

It wasn't to be seen on the land. Jake started at one end, Franklin the other, then they swapped after crossing the creek. It was dark by the time they got back to her house.

Jake fried up bacon using the microwave while Franklin scrambled up eggs on the range. They were both famished. And worried.

"These laws that won't take an adult missing person report seriously for days," Franklin growled. "And it's too late to call Powell. Nothing he can do till morning to push it."

"I'm staying."

"I know. I'll head on home. Call if you need me. I'll see you tomorrow. I'll be here by ten."

"Thanks for cleaning up the dog shit."

Franklin laughed. "I left the kitty pans for you."

"You're all heart." It was nine—a night with no moon.

He tried watching TV. He watched the clock, instead, his eyes going from the screen to the hands on the old wind-up grandfather clock—ten, ten-o-four.... He got himself some whiskey from the truck and went outside in the cold to drink it. Five weeks till Christmas, and they still hadn't had snow even in the higher elevations that would stick over night. The weather scared him. He knew it bothered the hell out of Franklin, too. "Dree, babe, come home," Jake pleaded, his eyes on the stars she so loved.

He went back inside and planted himself back in front of the TV, but left it off. He picked up a book, instead. It was bookmarked at a page on alfalfa yields. Down to the last of his whiskey, he nursed it. He should have brought two bottles. He knew he drank too much. Franklin punished him for it, giving him the worst jobs. He didn't care. He had no reason to care. She didn't want him. He'd screwed himself.

Something woke him around midnight, and pulling himself out of the overstuffed, he went to the back door, then flung it open as she climbed the steps. "Thank God you're all right."

She looked up at him, her hair wild, her clothes trashed, her eyes ringed with deep circles. "Yes," she said. "I'll marry you. One year from today if you cut your drinking down to a dull roar."

She brushed past him to disappear through the kitchen doorway. She stunk of bad liquor and vomit. He heard her boot treads on the stairs. He closed the door and reached to grab hold of the back of a kitchen chair. Then, he sat down—hard.

DREE HEARD THE 'YEEEE-HAW!' It was loud enough that she swore anyone within a mile of the house should have, too. She heard the phone blip, then Jake talking to someone downstairs. Carefully, she picked up the extension. Holding the little lever down, she let it up very carefully.

"You find her yet?" Dree heard her grandmother say.

"She's here. She's safe. She *just* got home."

"Where was she?"

"I don't know. Didn't ask." A pause. Then, "She came home and said she'd marry me."

Dree heard her grandmother cackle. "Go-ood. You're a good man, and she's a good woman. I can bless this union. And will. Congratulations. Goodnight."

"'Night."

Dree waited for the disconnect before lowering the extension. She nodded, then let herself smile. Yes, he *was* a good man—a very good man. She wanted to sing out to the world. Jake Jarvis loved her…and she loved him…as much as she could love anyone. Maybe the *most* that she could love anyone. And it hit her as if for the very first time. Jake Jarvis! She was going to marry Jake Jarvis, one of the most eligible of the eligibles west of the Missouri…at least as far as she was concerned. She was marrying a cattle man—a real live cowboy—something she'd only thought of as a make-believe, fairy-tale dream. "Ho-ly wow!"

And she knew she was drunk—*very* drunk—the first real 'bender' she'd ever been on in her life.

46

Between Full Moon & Sunrise

TRUE TO HIS WORD, Jake cut out drinking altogether for a month. Then he presented her with the fact.

Dree acknowledged that he had.

He told her he was going to limit himself to four fingers of whiskey as an end of the day let-me-down-easy. "For the rest of my life. No more than that. That suit you as a dull enough roar?" he asked.

Dree laughed, agreeing it was.

"So about this year...."

"Let's talk about this after New Year's," she told him.

♦

DREE'S GRANDMOTHER CAME OVER— actually drove over. Jake drove in right behind her. "Let's have us all a little sit-down, shall we, Dree, honey?"

Dree poured Gram Blake a snifter of brandy from the special bottle bought just for her occasional visits, then settled in, tense. It was about her insistence to wait a full year.

"I want to see you married," Gram said. "And I'm not getting any younger, Dree. Plus, I want to see my great-grandchildren, so hurry it on up."

Dree didn't break it to her that she wasn't planning on having kids. She'd told Jake, and he hadn't balked...hadn't said anything much, just shrugged with a kind of hazy "whatever you want."

"It's tradition, you know," Gram Blake pressed.

Dree frowned. "What's tradition, Gram?"

"The Jarvises," she said. "Look it up on that Internet thing you use. It's part of Montana history."

"Why don't you just tell me?"

"I think I'll let your Jake do that," she said, eyeing him.

He shook his head. "It's not important."

Gram Blake smacked the table with her palm. "Of course it is! You know it, and I know it. Franklin himself has called me twice already."

"Tell me," Dree said, watching him.

Jake looked uncomfortable, so Dree guessed this was going to be a hard pill to swallow. She just hoped what was expected wasn't embarrassing like a shivaree or something, the western tradition of family and friends banging pots and pans outside the window on the wedding night. She knew it was still done...because she herself had participated in one as a kid. Of course, she hadn't understood what it was about, then, like she did, now.

"It's traditional for Jarvises to be married on horseback up on Black Badger Mountain The first full moon in May. With a judge or a clergy pronouncing us man and wife at exactly sunrise." He blurted it, pouring it out so fast she could hardly keep up, his face turning five shades of red.

Dree just blinked. She waited for the rest. When he said nothing more, she said, "And?"

"And nothing. Just that.... Well, Franklin was married that way and so was Old Man Jarvis, my great granddad. All Franklin's brothers, too. My dad and uncles.... He expects me...." Jake's voice trailed off to silence.

"He expects his number one heir to get married the traditional way," Gram Blake snapped, "and I want you to honor that, Adrienne Annabelle Blake!" Her hand popped the table, again.

"Okay, Gram."

Jake's eyes snapped to hers. "You'll do it?"

"Sure. That gives me, what? A whole half a year longer to figure out what to wear?" She said it, making sure to keep her face serious and her voice normal. But, at the crestfallen look that descended Jake's face when her meaning came clear, she lost all control, her laughter breaking through every iron hold she thought she had on it. He didn't get it, though. Troubled eyes and crinkled brows just watched her in incredulity.

"I don't mean it, Jake," she gasped between spasms. "Really. I'll marry you this very next May, just like a good, biddable bride should who's marrying the catch of the territory."

Gram Blake barked a guffaw at that, but patted Dree's hand, then gathered Jake's and put it over Dree's. "That's settled, then."

Finally—finally—Jake caught on, a grin followed by a chuckle breaking open his face to chase away the clouds. "I love you," he said, then bolted out of his chair to grab her up into his arms and kiss her. When he let her up for air, he grabbed his phone up. "I've got to call Granddad."

Gram Blake's eyes were sparkling. She nodded at Dree. "You just made your to-be and your gram very happy."

47

Green & Hot

PREPARATIONS FOR THE WEDDING were huge. Dree had hoped that, since it was going to be up on a mountain, requiring them to start out way before sunrise, it would be small, private, and lacking formality. Instead, it was just the opposite. She was given a wedding guest list from Jake's family that was over three hundred names. Her grandmother presented her with a list of a hundred-and-fifty-six. Most wouldn't be at the ceremony—almost none from her side of the family, except Gram Blake. The ceremony was private—very. But everyone would be there for the reception. That would be held at the ranch, she was told.

"Where are we going to fit everybody? What are we going to do if it rains?"

Jake just grinned. "Franklin and your grandmother decided on one of the big barns, and I don't care if it rains, hails, or even snows."

"Can we just elope?"

Jake rolled an eye at her.

"Yeah, yeah, I know. Tradition."

"Franklin's picked out some horses to choose from. Want to drive up and look?"

"Horses?"

"For the ceremony."

"I thought I was riding Cougar."

"Ah...well, I'm supposed to ride black and you're supposed to ride white."

"Cougar's a silver-dun," Dree offered.

"Horse."

"I hope she's tame and sure-footed," Dree muttered.

◆

FRANKLIN BROUGHT OUT TWO HORSES, one a buttermilk buckskin—white body with black points and a black mane and tail—and a long-maned, long-tailed, almost lackluster gray who was old enough to almost be pure white except for some faint dappling on her shoulders and quarters. Both were nice animals, but Dree's heart went with the buckskin. "She's beautiful."

"Yep," Franklin said. "That's the one I thought you'd choose. She's a little green still, but okay. Hang tight while we saddle her, then give her a try."

They brought her out with a silver-mounted side-saddle on her. Dree stood staring. "Ah...I've never ridden a side-saddle in my life."

"Well, they say they're a surer seat than a regular rig, so you should be safe enough."

Dree thought about her knee. Dree thought about her dignity, then shrugged. "Okay. Let me figure this out."

She put a left foot in the stirrup like usual.

"Mount with your right foot," Wil Strakes said.

Dree tried it, grabbing one of the hook-like things, and heaved herself up to stand looking at the problem. The mare shifted a bit, bracing her legs at the one-sided load, then stilled as Wil, who was holding her, scratched her around the ear.

Dree got it, twisted, and, once settled, butt in the seat, she adjusted her legs, lifting the right one over to lay into the top hook, then picked up the stirrup with her left, which automatically snugged her left thigh against the down-curled hook. "Okay. I can see why they say it's a very sure seat," she said, picking up the reins.

As Dree arranged her weight distribution better, the mare relaxed her bracing. The animal blew a soft snort, ducking her head a couple of times, then rubbed it against Wil's shoulder. He scratched her ear, again, and she settled.

"Okay?" Franklin asked as Dree adjusted the reins.

Dree nodded. "Okay."

Wil walked the mare forward…let the mare go in the round pen, and shut the gate. Dree nudged the mare with her heel. The horse stopped and wouldn't budge. Dree nudged her again, and the mare took a step, pulled her head for more slack, then took off at a hesitant walk.

It was an odd feeling to have nothing but air to the offside, no nice sense of security that she was used to straddling Cougar, but, as she got used to it, she found her body compensating, the mare relaxing more and more as Dree got her balance and weight positioned correctly.

She tried a jog, and that gave her more clues. The leg hooks were key. Dree found she had to think herself forward over her hips rather than down into her stirrups, the single stirrup more to brace her left leg against the bottom hook. Gravity snugged her right leg into the upper hook, and she felt quite secure.

The mare's jog was comfortable, but she started to crow-hop a bit when Dree nudged her into a canter. Freezing her fingers to set the bit, she gave the mare a hard kick with her heel, reinforcing it with a flick of the end of the romal—the long quirt-like piece of braided leather attached to the fancy California reins. The mare's bucking stopped as she straightened out with the demand for more speed. Dree felt her relax and asked her to slow into the nice rocking horse canter that Quarter Horses were so good at. Twice around the big round pen, and Dree dropped her down to a jog, again. The crow-hopping had given her a true feel for the security of the saddle. Her legs had automatically clamped themselves into the hooks, and the saddle's fit had her butt firmly anchored into the soft, padded seat.

"You're a natural," Franklin observed. "And I think the mare might work out. Didn't think so, at first, because, like I said, she's pretty green and pretty hot, but it looks like you can handle her. The gray is steadier, though, so you think on that."

He always said that—*you think on that*—when he meant he thought she should choose wiser. Dree settled the mare to a stop. "Can I try her, too?"

"You bet. Hop down."

Figuring out how to dismount took Dree a bit of doing. Jake came over and offered his arms, but Dree shook her head. "I want to be able to dismount on my own if I need to."

In the end, she got down exactly backwards of the way she got up, same as any saddle, except clumsier using her right leg.

"Mount up again, and try getting off with Jake there to catch you," Franklin suggested. At Dree's look, he said, "Just try it."

She did as bid, unhooking her leg to sit sideways on the saddle, then slipping down into Jake's arms. It was…warming. It still didn't solve the problem of getting comfortable dismounting if she had, though.

They pulled the saddle from the buttermilk buckskin and put it on the older mare. The wrangler brought out a bozal, put it on mare's head, then took a fancy spade bit carried on a silver-laden bridle off from where he had it slung over his shoulder. Dree had seen these get-ups, but had never used one. It looked like a torture device.

The wrangler saw her look. "You'll see," he said. "And I'm setting it so you can't hurt her with it if you make a mistake and tighten up."

Dree was dubious as she watched him slip the huge thing into the mare's mouth. Oddly, the mare opened her mouth and practically grabbed the thing. Then, surprisingly, she started to suck on it, her pink tongue just peeking out from between her lips. Her eyes went sleepy. "She likes it! What did you do? Smear it with treacle?"

"Nope. It's her bit. Bridle isn't her usual one, but the bit's hers. Mount up," Wil said as he buckled a strap from the bit's shank hobble to the front of the noseband, then wrapped another through the cheek rings, completely immobilizing the bit. The mare champed and shook her head. Wil stroked her. "I know, but she ain't used to you, Cassie. Or it," he murmured. He looked at Dree. "You can't hurt her, now. Mount up and just use the reins on the bozal."

Dree did as bid, settling herself relatively easy this time, then picked up the bozal's reins, leaving the bit's reins where Wil anchored them with a snap he hooked to the saddle.

Immediately, the mare alerted, her ears snapping forward as she arched her neck and tucked her head. Dree felt her quarters bunch under her.

Startled, Dree grabbed the pommel with her right hand.

"Relax," Wil said, and Dree saw Franklin and Jake both grin, though they were trying their level best not to.

She gripped the hooks with her legs, prepared for the worst.

This time, they didn't lead the mare into the round pen. This time, they just stepped back and waited. Dree eyed them, then, taking a breath, just tucked her left heel against the mare's side.

The animal came up, arching her neck even further and literally stepped into a canter. Dree's mouth dropped open as the mare practically floated, her long mane swinging in rhythm. Touching the reins to ask her to circle, Dree found herself in a spin. "Whoa!"

The mare stopped dead, and Dree was very glad she still was grabbing leather, her right hand clenched tight.

"Relax," said the wrangler. "If you relax, she'll relax for you."

Doing her best, Dree tried again, just tensed and quickly released the muscles of her left calf. The mare tucked up, but this time stepped out in a slow jog. "She's smooth...quick," Dree said.

"She's a California reining horse," the wrangler said. "Trained old style. You shift your weight, and she goes that way. Need to turn, basically, if you use the spade, all you need to do is think. Your body and hands telegraph subtle signals to her through the reins. She sucks the bit, so she feels your hands thinking. Now, sit back and relax, and she should walk down for you."

Easing her weight back and relaxing her legs' grip, Dree was pleased when the mare settled into a nice, pleasant walk. Dree blew a breath of relief and just let the mare walk at will. "Whoa," she whispered, afraid to even touch the bozal's reins. The mare immediately stopped.

"Well?" Franklin asked.

"Um...she seems even hotter than the buckskin."

He chuckled. "Well, you think on it, and then come back and try 'em both again next week."

"I'll put some more miles on the buckskin," Wil said.

48

Stuffed Sausage

THE DRESS WAS A *HUGE* PROBLEM. Dree thought she looked pretty good in an empire waist, but that wouldn't do riding a horse—too billowy and absolutely shapeless draped over a saddle. She'd really look like a blimp, no matter how skinny she got, and she was dropping five pounds a week on her crash diet coupled with a trick she knew from treating horses and cows.

She looked through dozens of pictures she found on the Internet, mostly turn of the 19th to 20th century images—tin plates, black-and-white photos, or etchings. There were also modern horse show pictures. All of them featured a tailored suit on top, something she looked absolutely horrible in, akin to a stuffed sausage. She was too short-waisted for them. She did find several engravings of her favored empire style. One in particular of a woman riding a high-stepping, dock-tailed horse really nixed the idea of the empire style as an option.

She called a college friend who had always been big into showing her Arabs and asked her for advice. "Ah...wow. You're getting married on horseback?! I am soooo jealous."

"That helps a lot," Dree replied.

"Okay. Let me think. I'll call you back."

Jeanette called her back about two hours later. "Meet me in town at Humphrey's tomorrow around one. We're going to Missoula."

"Why?"

"There's a shop there I use, and the seamstress is great. I just talked with her about your problem, and she wants to measure you."

"How expensive is she?"

"Not bad, really. No more than the wedding dress shops."

Jeanette couldn't see Dree's rolling eyes. More money to spend.

At breakfast, she told Jake, who was staying to help with planting, that she had to go to Missoula. He didn't ask her why, just did his usual grin and nod. "I'm going to rototill the garden, then shower and go," she told him.

"I can rototill."

"No. I've got time."

"'K."

Still not used to his easy-going manner, Dree watched him soak up yolk with his toast. "Aren't you even curious why?"

He glanced up at her, toast paused halfway to mouth. "Sure, but I figure you'll tell me if you want."

"I've got to find a wedding dress, and nothing I had in mind works riding a horse."

He nodded and bit into his toast.

Disgruntled, Dree finished her OJ, then began stacking the pans and her breakfast dishes into the dishwasher.

"You could always just use the one my mom wore."

Dree turned to look at him. "Your mom got married on horseback?"

"She married my dad, remember? He's a Jarvis, so, yeah, up on the ranch the same way we are. I told you. It's tradition. Give her a call."

Dree shook her head, immediately embarrassed.

"Okay. *I'll* call her."

"Oh, gawd, *no!*" Dree fled.

She was halfway done with rototilling when a brand new suburban showed up. Covered in mud, Dree cringed at the thought of what she must look like, but went over to the car anyway. It was Jake's mom, Loretta, a Hispanic lady with her. "Jake must have called you."

Loretta smiled. "He did. I brought along Isobel. She my tailor, and she's great. Can you spare time from that machine, right now, or should we go grab a bite and come back."

"No. I mean, yes, I can spare the time, and, no, don't go. I *will* need to take a quick shower, though."

"We're in no hurry."

Dree called Jeanette and postponed, then settled Loretta and Isobel with coffee and some slices of pound cake before running upstairs to scrape off the garden dirt. Tying up her wet hair, she went downstairs. Stopping dead at the bottom, she gasped. There, spread across the couch was an ocean of satin brocade and lace with what must have been dozens of ruffled petticoats peeking out from under the hem. It was as white as snow and shimmered where the sunlight touched it.

"What do you think?" Loretta asked.

It was beautiful, and Dree said so, but, yet again, it had that fitted waistline—a drop waistline, to boot.

"Try it on. You're as slim as I was, so it will probably fit just right."

Dree sincerely doubted that she was slimmer than Loretta had been. The woman was hard and trim, and she was long-waisted.

As it was, the dress fit pretty well, except that Dree felt and, when she checked the full length mirror in the hallway, also looked just exactly as she'd feared— stuffed sausage. She loved that the back dragged the ground behind her, though, the front raised just enough to show a bit of the fluffy layered petticoat beneath. But the top. Dree shook her head. She was going to look like a plump dumpling, no matter what, it seemed, despite her crash diet.

Isobel clucked and, rifling through a bag she'd brought with her, took out a huge swath of white brocade satin. She untied the back of the dress, which was done up, not with a zipper, but lacing, pulled the gown's left shoulder down, tucking it inside the dress under Dree's arm, then laced the dress back up. Then she draped the satin over Dree's right shoulder, gathered it there, then pulled it diagonally across her body, pinning it at her left hip. She fussed and clucked a bit more, then tied a huge bow, doubling it back to create another, then yet another set of bow loops on top of the first.

Isobel said something in Spanish, spinning her finger. "Turn," Loretta said, and, when Dree did, the Latina adjusted something behind, then had her spin again.

Dree saw Loretta smile and nod. "See what you think, Dree."

Dree stepped back to the mirror and just stood. "Omigod. It's…it's—"

"*Perfectamente?*" Isobel asked.

Dree turned and, eyes stinging and her grinning like something stupid, nodded. "*Muchas perfectamente. Muchas, muchas gracias.*" The sash and bow masked her short-waistedness completely. She actually looked like a girl, not a short-bodied lump like she usually did in anything fitted.

They all heard the tread of boots on the back steps. Isobel stepped in front of Dree chattering in quick Spanish as Loretta flew into the kitchen. "Oh, no you don't, Jake Jarvis. Get yourself gone. You can't see the bride in her gown until the wedding ceremony."

Dree heard a mumbled, "Sorry," as the boots retreated back down the steps.

"How much?" Dree asked Loretta when she came back.

"For the gown?" She laughed. "Same price I paid for it—nothing. Isobel will need to be paid for her work and for the satin, but this gown and two others are Jarvis bride gowns, passed down from bride to bride. This one was originally made for Jake's great-grandfather's wife, the man you know as Old Man Jarvis, and I happened to be the lucky girl it fit when my turn came. Now, it's your turn, and I'm so happy, because, well, let's leave it as 'just because'."

Dree turned to Isobel. "How much for the work and the, well, for everything?" she asked.

The woman turned toward Loretta and shrugged.

"Eight hundred? More?" Dree asked.

Isobel looked at her. "Six," she said.

Dree gave her six one-hundred dollar bills and the woman grinned and folded the money into a wallet she pulled from a pocket in her dress.

"Next week," Isobel said, then spoke in Spanish to Loretta who answered back in the same language.

"Isobel will want to do a final fitting next week, okay?"

Dree nodded. "I can drive up."

"Good. I'll meet you at The Pearl in Missoula and lead you to Isobel's shop."

Loretta wrote down the address. "Just in case," she said. Then, after more coffee and a pleasant lunch of soup and some pre-cooked boxed pizza Dree popped in the oven, she and Isobel left.

Jake came up to the back door. "Can I come in, now?"

"Yes."

He opened the door, grinning at her. "Can't blame a guy for trying."

C. J. "Country" James

49

Sex, But No Get

"**G**RAM BLAKE CALLED," Franklin said. Then, "By the way, I think my old man and Gram Blake are stepping out in secret. He disappears every Saturday morning, regular as clockwork, and doesn't get in till late Sunday."

"That doesn't mean anything," Jake said.

"It does when I happen to drive by Gram Blake's place and see his truck parked in her drive."

"*Happen* to drive by? …You're spying on your own *dad*?"

"Yes. Like he did on me, and I do on you."

Jake grinned. "He's a lot older than she is."

"Twelve years doesn't mean much at their age, Jake. Anyway, like I was saying, Gram Blake called. She's been pestering Dree about the honeymoon. She finally got the girl mad enough to spill. Gram Blake was pushing for a Rome or Paris honeymoon. Seems Dree wants to camp in the mountains under the stars. And she wants to get there, get this, by horseback…or, in her case, on Cougar."

Jake couldn't think of an answer. When something finally came out, it was a cross between a laugh and a croak. He felt like he was going to swallow his tongue.

"What do you think about taking her up for two weeks at the hunting camp?"

Jake thought it was perfect. He just couldn't tell Franklin that. He couldn't get his mouth to make noise.

"I'll take that as 'yes'. I'll get Wil and Lane to pack in enough food and supplies, and chop up some firewood. There's still going to be snow up there. The cold ought to make things happen."

Jake dogged his head, his face burning.

Franklin chuckled. Then: "I want a great-grandson, a Franklin Jacob Jarvis, the Sixth. Within a year, mind."

Now, Jake's mouth decided to work…when he didn't want it to. This would crush Franklin. He spit it out. "She doesn't want kids."

Franklin looked at him. "That'll change."

Jake shook his head, the sadness he felt overwhelming him. "I don't think so, Grandpa."

"That'll *change*. Trust me."

IT COULDN'T BE WORSE THAN A PELVIC or a pap smear, Dree thought. Sex was something she'd never wanted to experience, not after what she'd suffered her prom night. And marriage meant sex.

Discomfited, she tried to find a book on the subject, but, except for one written for Jewish couples that didn't say anything pertinent at all, there wasn't anything that remotely seemed to provide a basic, genteel instruction guide on what to expect, what to do, and what not to do.

Animals were easy. The cow was in heat, and, if she didn't run off, the bull mounted, and that was that. Same with hogs and horses, though gilts and mares could and would violently object sometimes, and, if they objected enough, the boar or stallion usually backed off. Dree very much doubted that it was quite that simple with humans. There had to be rituals, expectations and, well, other things. Both in high school and at college, girlfriends had often made vague, sometimes, even vulgar references that suggested skills about which Dree didn't have a clue.

"Bull by the horns," her grandmother would say. Dree picked up the phone book, found a female doctor. There was one in Adams. She dialed and made an appointment.

♦

AFTER FILLING IN ALL THE FORMS, the receptionist smiled and told her it would be a few minutes. That, of course, meant at least fifteen, if not longer. Dree was surprised when, within ten, her name was called and she was led to a small exam room. The nurse took her blood pressure, pulse, and temperature, then ask her the typical list of questions. "Doctor Bremmer will be in shortly," she said. She never asked why Dree was there—a relief.

A short, strawberry blonde bundle of a forty-something poked her head in a few minutes later. "Dree Blake?"

"Yes."

The woman came in. "Hi. I'm Dr. Bremmer." She extended a hand, and, standing up, Dree shook it.

"And you're here today for…" She looked at the chart she was holding. "I have no idea. What are you here for, today?"

Dree felt her face flush, then, when the woman sat down on a rolling stool, blurted out, "I'm getting married, and…."

The doctor waited.

"…I need to know about sex."

Dree looked away out the small window, feeling totally humiliated.

Dr. Bremmer didn't reply for so long that Dree finally stole a glance at her.

The woman just sat there watching her until Dree finally faced her, again. "About birth control?" Bremmer asked.

That, too, Dree thought. *One thing at a time.* "The act." She felt her face flame hot.

Dr. Bremmer nodded. Looked down at the clipboard, then, after a pause, looked up, again. "Okay. So, you know about penises and vaginas, right?"

Dree rolled her eyes. "Yes. I had sex education in high school, and I run a ranch and know about...breeding."

"Well, it's not that much different for humans, except that there's shyness, expectations, surprise, and often pain for the woman the first time. I'm going to assume you're a virgin?"

Dree nodded, then shook her head. Then, "I don't know."

Bremmer waited.

"He tried...not Jake, a boy in high school. I got my arms free and punched him, then kicked him till he...."

She stopped. Looked away.

"Did he penetrate you?"

She shook her head. "I don't think so."

Silence. Then, "Have you had yearly pelvic exams?"

"Yes."

"Is your fiancé a virgin?"

Dree suddenly felt absolutely giddy...couldn't help herself. The laughter just boiled out of her. "No. He's...um...very well-educated."

"That will help."

Startled, Dree shot back, "Who? Him or me?"

"You."

Again, Dree turned away, the flush to her face now so hot she swore she'd burn up.

"You're afraid," Bremmer said.

Dree flared. "*Yes*, I'm afraid. I'm afraid of making a complete *fool* of myself!"

The doctor laughed, and Dree almost got up and left, but the woman waved a hand at her to sit. "Ms. Blake," she said, "First off, you're very brave after what happened to you. Second, men love innocence. You've got absolutely nothing to worry about. If it does come to talking, and it usually doesn't, just be honest with him and tell him you haven't a clue. Tell him you're scared. I promise it will be okay. And, believe me, you'll get this figured out in a very short time."

Dr. Bremmer stood up and went to a cabinet. "But I do have a something for you that's going to help you physically." She handed Dree a tube. "This is a very pleasant lubricating gel. Use it up to two hours before, and things will go...easy."

Dree took the tube, stuffing it in her bag.

"Now, remember, since you're a virgin, there may be a bit of discomfort—a feeling of stretching or even tearing. This is normal, and any soreness and discomfort will pass within a few days. If it doesn't, come back and see me, okay?"

Dree had no intention of ever seeing Dr. Bremmer again. Fleeing the clinic after paying her bill, Dree sat in her truck, just thinking, then, calling her regular doctor, made an appointment with him, this time for birth control, not the subject of sex.

♦

BIRTH CONTROL TURNED OUT to be yet another problem, though. The man who'd been her doctor since she'd been a little kid didn't believe in it and refused to prescribe. Shocked by his adamant refusal, she wound up going back to Dr. Bremmer the following week. After a blood draw and a pelvic, the woman spent some time at the computer, and, finally, Dree asked if something was wrong.

"No. I'm familiarizing myself with your medical history." The woman turned. "It's rather extensive." Her voice held a cautious sympathy.

She swiveled around on her rolling stool. "I want to see you next week. Meanwhile, you've got a couple of choices…well, close to a dozen, and I want you to read up on all the plusses and minuses for each" She handed Dree a folder of papers. "I'll go over the results of your tests with you next visit."

She paused, then got up and, pulling a slim, largish, gray, hardbound book from a shelf, she handed it to Dree. "This was my mother's and her mother's before that. I want it back, but you're welcome to make a copy of it if you think you need to."

The book had no printing on the outside. Dree opened it to a random page, stared, then checked the title page and copyright. It was a first edition, published in 1949. Her eyes burning like salt in a wound, she looked at the woman. "Thank you."

♦

DREE SPENT THE EVENING in her room going page-by-page through the antique book, looking at the pictures, reading the short descriptions under them. Then she went back and read the book, cover to cover. It was only fifty pages, including the foreword, most of them illustrated with simple drawings and short, but gently-worded explanations and direct instructions …about having sex with a man. It was written by a woman. Dree made a copy of it using her color laser's scanning feature, then put the sheets away in a folder. She wasn't sure why, but she wanted to keep a copy.

Deciding on which kind of birth control was relatively easy after reading through the details of effectiveness and possible side-effects. Returning the old book at her next visit, Dree told Dr. Bremmer that she wanted the implant, and the woman thought it a good choice. She did the procedure right then, after numbing Dree's arm.

C. J. "Country" James

50

Revelations

GETTING FITTED FOR THE SUIT just about drove Jake to break his promise to Dree of only one whiskey a day. Franklin ran him, Lane, who was Jake's choice for best man, Wil, and his great-granddad into Missoula over and over, never quite satisfied with the lay of their pants, the way the suits hung, the length of the sleeves, the fit of the shoulders. "How about if we all just wear black jeans and silk shirts," Jake begged as he got stuck one more time by a pin.

"Jake. Be quiet, and let the man work."

"Yes, sir."

"God, you're a bull. Where'd you get those big shoulders?!"

Jake stared at his granddad, then at his snickering great-granddad, smirking Lane, and Wil who was doing his best to keep a straight face. He didn't say it, not even one word.

He got his revenge when the tailor started working on fitting up Franklin.

"WHAT ARE YOU GOING TO WEAR on your wedding night," Caroline asked Dree over coffee after Isobel had done a last fitting adjusting Caroline's bridesmaid's dress. Of course, Caroline got to wear something fitted and looked great. When Dree just sat there, Caroline said, "Haven't thought about it, hmm?"

Dree hadn't. It was all she thought about after, though—her ugly body exposed to Jake. She wanted to call the whole thing off. She wanted to leave town. She buried herself under the covers. Even sat awhile in the closet...until Laddie scratched on the door over and over. "Quit. You're ruining the paint," she yelled. He kept scratching, forcing her to come out or face having to paint, again. "Bad dog." He wagged. She ruffled his ears. "I know. Bad Dree."

Facing reality, she pulled out the phone book after finishing chores the following morning. Surprised to find Adams had such a place, she drove up and found the address, parked, grabbed her purse, and, trying not to look furtive, slipped inside.

The shop was tiny. It was also discreetly set up. She looked skeptically at the collections of underthings on display.

"May I help you, Dree?"

Dree turned to see one of her high school classmates, Maddie Somner, smiling at her. "Ah...." Damn it all, she should have known better...should have gone to the city to do this. "I need new bras, panties, and some good nightgowns," Dree blurted out, then, as usual, felt her face turn to flame. This was getting old.

"Okay. What size are you, do you know?"

"Um…last I bought some at Walmart, I wore a size 5 underwear and a 34-B on top."

"Is this for a special occasion?"

Dree blew a breath. "Yes."

"Um…how special?"

Does everybody have to know my personal business to help me? "I'm getting married."

Maddie's nose wrinkled up strangely, then she grinned. She laughed, covering her mouth. Dree thought it an odd reaction, especially when, opening her eyes wide, Maddie grabbed Dree's hands, the suddenness and shock of the touch making Dree jump. "That's *wonderful*, Dree. I'm so *happy* for you. Who's the lucky guy?"

Dree hesitated, but it was going to be in the paper, anyway, and very, very soon. She'd held that off as long as possible, too. "Jake Jarvis."

Maggie's face went blank. Her mouth gaped. Then, "You mean *the* Jake Jarvis from up north?"

Dree frowned. "How do *you* know him?"

"I went *out* with him!"

♦

D REE DIDN'T BUY ANYTHING. She was too
embarrassed, too upset after Maddie gave her an
earful about Jake Jarvis.

Dree fled.

The next day, she drove to Missoula and did her
shopping there, in safe anonymity.

She knew Jake had been around, or, maybe better,
made the rounds. She didn't hold it against him. She
expected it. Her father, even though married, had
stepped out quite a few times. He didn't hide it. It was
a 'man thing', he'd told her when, having gone into
town with her mom, she saw his truck and moseyed
down to where it was parked. Wanting to see him, she
followed a man through the door. She found him at
the bar, a lady who wasn't her mother kissing him. He
took her home. Then her mom and her dad had a
fight.

She remembered her mother saying those same
words—a 'man thing'—to someone who came visiting.
She knew it was true of her Uncle Bill, too. Not Uncle
Pete, she didn't think, though she didn't know much
about that side of him, since he was pretty keep-to-
himself.

Jake was open about his experiences—no details,
just that he'd dated a lot of girls, "mostly one nighters,"
he called them. The few he'd "stepped out with"—that
quaint phrase Dree found delightful—had ever only
lasted a few months. "Except for Becky Turner," he

said, his brown eyes smiling, even though his mouth didn't. "I asked her to marry me."

"What happened?" Dree asked, cold fear and a strange sorrow rising to chill her inside and out. She tried, and probably failed, at nonchalance.

"She ran away screaming."

Dree frowned, the world suspended around her. …Waited.

"We were in first grade. I was six, and she was seven."

C. J. "Country" James

51

At Wits End

JAKE DIDN'T SHOW UP for two days. He didn't call, either. That wasn't like him. She kept dialing his cell phone, but it just went to voicemail. When Franklin's black dually pulled in, his dad with him, Dree felt the blood drain out of her body and run out her feet. Old Man Jarvis never came with…always drove his own rig. Never with Franklin.

Feeling like she was wading through sludge, she made it to the door. The world echoed, and she was barely able to keep her head clear of the rush of burn welling up in her to get to the door and invite them in. Their faces were stone—death walking. Something had happened—a tractor rolling, bales breaking loose of their stack, a bull crushing him—the day-to-day dangers of ranching.

"Dree," Franklin said. "We need to speak."

She eased herself down into a kitchen chair. Her diamond engagement ring flashed, catching sunlight. The red-black, the roar in her ears, reared up, flooded in, winning over her will to keep them at bay.

"I need Jake at the ranch," Franklin said, his voice echoing strangely, his face blurring.

Dree blinked, the roar dulling her ears, the red-black filling her up.

"I know you love this place—"

She pushed herself up, her legs tired, heavy. Her heart pounded. The red-black.... "Is he okay?" she whispered.

"Dree!"

♦

FRANKLIN WAS HOLDING a cold cloth to her head. She was laying on the couch.

Words, muffled and slurred, passed between him and someone nearby. His father had come with him, she remembered, now. She watched them, their blurred forms coming clearer each moment. She was trying to make sense of why she was here laying down, them silhouetted by sunshine coming through the living room windows.

"Dree? Can you hear me?"

She nodded, tried to sit up.

Hands—large, but gentle—helped her do it. "Easy. Sip this."

"What is it?"

"It's a tonic powder mixed up in some orange juice I got from your fridge. Sip."

It was awful, but, him urging her, she obeyed, swallowing a bit more.

He sat down on her coffee table, the wood protesting. He sat right in front of her, his knees practically touching hers, his eyes worried.

"I'm okay," she said. "This stuff's awful. You ruined good OJ."

He chuckled a bit, but the worry crowding his eyes didn't match it. "I got it from Doc Perkins after the last time you did this. Just sip it a little bit at a time."

"A sedative?"

"He called it something else."

"You carry it with you?" She was aghast at the thought.

"So does Jake," he said. "Why would you think something happened to Jake?"

She breathed in deep. "Your faces...he hasn't been by. He's not answering his phone."

Old Man Jarvis started chuckling. "I warned you, Franklin."

Franklin Jarvis rolled his eyes up and aside. "Yes, Dad." Then, "Okay, Dree. Jake's fine. He's out of cell range. He will be for another day and a night, till the morning of the ceremony. He's safe. Wil and Lane are with him. So are a bunch of others."

She got it. The notorious three-day Jarvis Bachelor's Party. Jake had told her about it way back, right after Gram Blake's visit about 'honoring tradition'. She just didn't put two-and-two together.

She wanted to hide. She was ashamed. Embarrassed, too. Thankfully, the two men weren't ones to resort to bawdy innuendo and crude comments. "Thanks for.... Thanks. At least he's okay."

Then, remembering, she said, "You said you wanted to talk to me."

"We'll save it for later, Dree."

"No. There's a reason why you came all this way, a reason you looked...why I thought.... You looked like death walking. You scared the life out of me. So, now, tell me what's so important that you and your dad are here? *Tell* me. Please."

Franklin cast a glance toward his father. His father hitched his shoulders, then pushed back his hat.

"Tell me," she repeated.

"I need you and Jake to live at the ranch."

He blurted it out—not like him. She frowned. "I thought that was understood," she said softly. She was confused.

He looked more so.

Her brain whirled, then, all of sudden, epiphany. "Jake didn't tell you," she said. *As usual.* She blew breath and saw Franklin's hands twitch.

She smiled. "I'm okay, Franklin."

She got up and went into her office. She came back out with two pieces of paper and handed them to him. "Read."

Old Man Jarvis sidled up, reading, too. Dree went to the kitchen to get them some coffee. Her head felt like it was glowing. She felt light as air. The drug, whatever it was, she realized.

♦

"Y OU'RE TURNING THE RANCH over to your Uncle Pete?!" Franklin demanded when she came back with their cups. His face was a close to livid as she'd ever seen.

Dree shook her head, handing off the cups. Franklin set his down and just kept hard eyes on her.

She sat down. "No. I'm turning this house over to him to live in. He'll get an hourly wage for any work that he does. Uncle Pete—he's the gentle one, Franklin. He's not hardened like you, Dad, or Uncle Bill. He's...weak-kneed. But he cares. He'll do a good job following orders."

Franklin was shaking his head. Old Man Jarvis looked crestfallen.

"Hold up and listen. Or read the next contract."

The men watched her, waiting. Dree wanted to groan. "I'm still going to run it, but I'm turning the day-to-day management over to a woman I met at MSU. We were roommates my last two semesters. She grew up on a hay operation over in Idaho. She really knows the business."

When Franklin just kept frowning, she went on. "She got aced out by her father, a lot like mine tried doing to me, had to find a job, move to the city. She's been working for a hay broker down in Boise, since, and she hates it. ...What would have happened to me, if you and Jake hadn't stepped in.

"She's a highly capable woman. She's got experience with cattle, too. Her father had a small herd of Angus."

"You're keeping the cattle." He said it like he disapproved, but, behind him, Old Man Jarvis grinned.

"I'm keeping the cattle, yes. For Gram Blake's sake. We'll slowly build up the herd as the land heals, but probably never run more than a few hundred head. Chocolate's calves hit the ground, and they're.... Well, come see for yourself."

She had Franklin drive them out to the fenced quarter-section and pointed. "That one, that one there, that one...." Franklin and Old Man Jarvis both nodded as she singled out particular pairs. "They're nowhere near the quality of yours, but, in time, with AI, I'll get them there."

Franklin slid his eyes sideways. "AI?"

Dree smiled. "Fran's coming down with straws from Chocolate to rebreed them when they cycle, and I'm keeping this year's heifers I know are by Chocolate from their calving dates and their mother's tag numbers. The rest of the calves, I'll sell like usual."

Old Man Jarvis twisted around in the passenger seat to grin at her. He winked.

She dared a touch to Franklin's arm. He turned his head.

"Franklin, when I was up at the ranch the end of March, Jake took me on a walk to his favorite 'thinking place'. We talked for a long, long time."

"I saw you two go off."

Dree felt her face flush. *Blast it!* She sighed, plowed on. "Originally, I wanted just to stay here. Jake knows you need him there. He knows he's got to learn, take a more active role and pay attention to how you handle things, not just wait for you to tell him what's next."

The man turned his face away. Looked out the side window. A cow-calf pair, the cow carrying heavy scars on her front legs, ambled by. Dree decided to just get to the point.

"I'd never jeopardize your operation, Franklin. Never. You're going to be stuck with me, my dogs *and* my cats, my Jersey and mule underfoot. Is that okay?"

She heard him sigh.

Breath catching, she waited. The cats were the biggest hurdle. "...I think I can train Bear not to eat them."

Old Man Jarvis chuckled.

Franklin turned to her…smiled. "Yes, Dree, I'm okay with that.

"Even the cats?'

"Even the cats."

"In the house?"

He laughed. She swore she saw more shine come to his eyes.

52

Montana Sapphires & Silk

THE WEATHER FORECAST said sunny. Three a.m. in a chilly room, the only heat a small fire burning in the room's fireplace. Caroline and Loretta kept fussing and primping—Dree wanted to scream.

"Hold still," Loretta scolded. "No. Don't sit. You'll wrinkle yourself. This isn't modern material, and it took Isobel hours to press it."

"I'm going to be sitting on Cassie for hours. What difference does it make?"

Loretta cast her a look, and Dree acquiesced. It was kind of Loretta to do this for her, since none of her cousins or aunts had offered. The whole family, save Pete, were still mad at her for shattering their dreams of quick riches, dreams snuffed with the failed sale to the development company. Her 'wedding party' consisted of two—Caroline, her maid of honor, and Gram who was being driven up by Old Man Jarvis in an 19th Century buggy.

Her relatives wouldn't be at the ceremony, but they weren't missing the reception, so not too mad to miss getting listed as registered guests at a Jarvis wedding.

Dree wasn't looking forward to drunk Blakes or drunk Carters, never mind the Turner clan.

"Okay. I think we're ready," Loretta said. "Dree, close your eyes."

Dree frowned. "Why?"

Again, the look.

"Okay. Closing them."

There was the sound of a box opening, a rustling. Dree squeezed her eyes. She'd never realized just how hard it was to keep her eyes closed on purpose. Her lids twitched with the effort.

"Okay. Your eyes still closed?"

Exasperation. "Yes."

Something was put on her head—a hat? Soft filmy fabric—a veil, Dree realized…attached to a hat. "Can I open them, now?"

"Not yet."

More rustling…something pressed onto the hat on her head. She braced her neck.

Clinking, and someone's hands slipped something heavy and cold around her neck, latching it.

"Okay. You can look."

Opening her eyes, she twisted to see herself in the mirror.

"It's silk, and it's very old," Loretta said. "And it fits, too. I had to tack in a padded band, then use hat pins, too, because it kept dropping down over my eyes." She laughed, then. "What do you think?"

Dree just stared. She glittered. "Wow."

"It's silk over beaver fur felt, and, yes, it's made by Stetson. The veil is original, too."

Dree turned to the woman, saw the questioning eyes. Loretta's hand reached to fluff out the veil. "It's…I love it, Loretta. Really." How could she not—a cowboy hat fit for a queen, a sparkling, dainty tiara running around it as a hatband, the Jarvis brand centered in front. The matching necklace, which was a more elaborate affair, troubled her. "Are they rhinestones?"

"They're Montana sapphires."

Dree's face froze. "Ah…no. I'm not going to be responsible for this. No. No…. *No.* Take it all off."

"Dree—"

"*Off.*"

"I guess we should have lied, right?" Caroline said.

Dree looked at her friend. Caroline's face was stern. Loretta looked crushed. "What if one falls *out*?"

"That's happened. It gets replaced," Loretta said. "Dree. This means the world to Franklin and Jake …and, to be truthful, to Old Man Jarvis. Please, honey."

Why did everyone insist on calling her 'honey'?

A knock at the door. Wil Strake's voice. "Fifteen minutes, and we've got to mount out."

"I've got to get my dress on," Loretta said.

Do this, Caroline mouthed.

Dree closed her eyes, but nodded.

F RANKLIN GRUMBLED and cursed, ripped the knot out, again.

"That was me, and he was you at *his* wedding," his great-grandfather whispered. "Go help him. I'll be outside."

Sobering his grin, Jake walked over to where his granddad was leaned into the mirror. "Here. Let me do it," Jake said, grabbing the silk.

He rewrapped the traditional neckerchief around Franklin's bull of a neck, setting the knot just the way Old Man Jarvis had showed him. He was calm, happy, completely at ease. His granddad was completely on edge.

"Where's Dad?" Franklin demanded.

"Hold still. Quit worrying. I think he just went out to the buggy. Gram Blake got here a few minutes ago. Everybody's ready to roll...ride."

"We're holding things up?!"

"No. We're ahead of schedule, Wil says."

And they were. The hands who were running as outriders, lighting the way with torches, were mounted up and had already traded out the one horse that had spooked and just wouldn't settle when the torches were lit.

"What about Fran?!"

"Fran's ready, too, along with the rest of the crew, the bulls waiting to run.

Someone tapped on the door, and Franklin jerked. "Yeah. We're coming."

"Ten minutes till we're ready to mount out," said Wil's voice. "Franklin? You got the blindfold?"

"Dammit!" He shoved his hands in his suit pockets, panicking until he finally located the strip of black, folded silk in his right front pants pocket. "Got it," he yelled. He relaxed, then. A bit.

"Should I get you a whiskey?" Jake asked.

"No. Go sit down."

"Yes, sir."

"READY, DREE?" Caroline asked.
        "No."

"What? The bathroom, again?"

"No. I'm trying to...here it is. I thought I'd lost it. Would you put this on me?"

Caroline took the necklace. "You want to wear this with the one you've already got on?!" She looked thunderstruck.

"No. I want this one only."

Loretta came over. "Why, honey?"

Dree wanted to groan. "Jake gave it to me. I want to wear it."

"Instead of the necklace? Really?"

Dree nodded. "Please. I know it's not the tradition, but please."

She saw Loretta look at Caroline, then nod. Dree could have wept.

They slipped off the sapphire necklace, replacing it with her amethyst, the single teardrop stone on its thin golden chain Jake had given her—his 'Sorry Stone'. *My wishing crystal.*

"Actually," Loretta said, smiling, "that's even better. Look, Dree."

And it was.

53

The Promise

"WIL? LANE?"

The door opened, and they stepped in.

"Okay, Jake.   Just like we practiced, now," Wil said.

Jake grinned. "No tricks."

"No tricks."

Jake stood up, Lane standing to one side, Wil to the other. Franklin walked up to him. "Ready?"

"Yes, sir." Jake closed his eyes.

He felt Lane pull his hat off, Franklin's fingers tying the blindfold on. Then Lane put his hat back on.

He heard Franklin mutter.   Fingers tapped the crown of his hat...adjusted the angle of the brim. "Good."

They led him to the door, Lane and Wil both with a hand on each of his arms. Then they waited. Jake heard Franklin go out, his footsteps steady and solid as they faded off down the hall. He'd calmed down. Now, Jake was the one feeling jumpy.

Dree was terrified that she'd stumble, trip, fall. The dress was heavier than she remembered.

Franklin walked up. "You look beautiful, Dree." He held out his arm.

She made it to Cassie. By the light of the flickering torches the men held, their horses ranged in a circle around the front of Jake's grandfather's grandfather's original log homestead, she made it. Her eyes caught on the bright, moonlit land far below where Franklin's house nestled at the foot of this mountain, all its lights snuffed.

Torchlight glittered off the silver-laid saddles and bridles of the horses nearby, drawing her sight, mesmerizing her. Pulling herself away from the dream state that threatened to swallow her, she gathered her skirts just as she'd practiced, Caroline and Loretta helping to shift and maneuver the train. She stepped to the mounting block and, without tripping in the high-heeled boots like she had earlier, she made it all the way up, Franklin supporting her arm.

Once seated and settled into the side-saddle, Cassie still as a statue, they arranged her gown all around her so it draped like it was designed to, the train caped over Cassie's rump and tail. Franklin mounted the block. "Ready, Dree?"

She nodded.

He kissed her on the cheek. "Keep breathing. Stay calm," he whispered, then pulled her veil up and over, draping it over her face to drift down to rest gently on Cassie's neck.

He stepped down off the mounting block, turned and went back to the front door. "Bring out the groom," he called.

Someone led Coal up, and Dree blinked. The stallion was saddled and bridled in shimmering gold.

Moments later, Dree saw Jake ushered out, all dressed in black from his boots to his hat, Lane and Wil to each side, guiding him.

He was blindfolded, but, despite not being able to see, she watched him swing up easy. Watching him, she wanted to cry. She couldn't believe he was real, that she was actually marrying him.

Her chest ached; her breath caught. She felt terrified; she felt happy. They should have eloped, but she wouldn't have missed this for anything. She wished she was just a bystander, watching it all from afar, but she was glad that she was the bride. *Is this love?* she wondered, and decided it must be.

Franklin rode up beside her on Monty, Mike Guthrie handing him the silver-wrapped lead that was clipped to Cassie's bozal. Monty's hide glittered gold in the torchlight; so did his saddle and bridle, matches for those on Coal. And Dree wondered.

Lane and Wil mounted up, Wil riding her Cougar to keep Coal from constantly jigging and whinnying. Dree smiled at her mule all decked out in his finery, his dun coat shimmering silver under the torchlight, almost as bright as the saddle cinched on him.

Then, suddenly, finally, it hit her. She finally grasped the tradition—the colors, the brand—the white and the black, the gold and silver, the line running through…. The Jarvis ranch colors and brand, symbolic of the day and the night, the sun and the moon, the line…. The circle was life; the vow, their bond with the land. *That's why the ceremony has to be on the top of this mountain between the night and the morning of the full moon and sunrise.*

Omigod. Jake and I, we're symbolic, our troth, not just to each other, but to the life and the land, too—to the tradition and culture. And one part of her celebrated, feeling the pride and the glory of it. It brought tears up. But another part of her cringed, quivering in fear at the idea of yet another overlord—the responsibility of carrying the torch onto the next and the next generation. *What have I gotten myself into?!*

And now she knew why this wedding, this ceremony, was so important to Franklin and to Old Man Jarvis. They were passing that burning torch on. It was…it was almost pagan. "Oh…my…God!"

But, suddenly, it was okay. She looked over at Jake, sitting so tall on Coal. She looked up.

The stars were twinkling. To the west, the full moon was sinking down toward the Big Sky horizon. She twisted, and, there, over the crest of the mountain above her, the faint sign of morning—her childhood dream coming real.

THE WHISTLE—IT FINALLY CAME. Gunshots.... The crack of a bull whip creasing the air. He twitched the reins to keep Coal's attention. He braced.

He wanted to see it, again, to watch like he had as a kid. He wanted to jerk off the blindfold.

The ground shook as the thunder of hooves came toward him. A horse whinnied. He felt the wind of them, smelled them as they passed—his grandfather's herd sires.

Horses galloped by, Coal jigging a little, and he twitched the reins once more. "Whoa, Coal. It's okay."

A body bumped his right leg—the mule—and his big horse settled, pulled a rib-spreading breath that made the saddle squeak. Jake reached out a hand and patted the stallion up on the neck. "Go easy, big guy."

"Here we go," Lane said.

Jake grinned, grabbing leather as Coal launched himself off his big quarters, leaping to follow the bulls, Lane to his left and Wil on the mule to his right, them keeping him centered on track as they made the run for the summit. *Yeah. Here we go, renewing our brand, renewing our vow to the life and the land, to each other, ever faithful, we swear, through better and worse.*

THE BEGINNING

AUTHOR'S NOTE

There are good folks and bad folks in every micro-culture of the world. This story contains both. While it's fiction, the characters drawn here are composites of people I have known, with whom I've lived and worked, and from whom I've learned. My hope is that this gives you a glimpse into their characters, their culture, their traditions.

Franklin is characteristic of more than several ranch owners I know and love—his speech and mannerisms, his attitudes, his humor, and his natural authority.

Jake, also, is very characteristic of the young men who grow up to become the Franklins later in their lives. They mature late, tend toward the wild, yet innocent, and, yes, a bit dumb, side in their late teens through twenties, then begin to hit their stride in their thirties if they don't wind up ruined by bad choices.

Dree is, likewise, very characteristic in many ways. She's the product of a family with typical problems—drink, passion, violence. But girls who stick to the decent side often survive the trauma of childhood to become the smart, savvy women who maintain home, hearth, and ranch, the bedrock of their families and communities.

The bond with the life and the land in these people is strong, passed down generation upon generation, their faith in it and themselves unshakable. And, when the greedy and the nefarious, even if their own kin, violate that bond and that trust, blood often flows.

www.CountryJames.com